rer

THE LEGATUS MYSTERY

THE LEGATUS MYSTERY

Rosemary Rowe

WINDSOR
PARAGON

THORNDIKE

This Large Print edition is published by BBC Audiobooks Ltd, Bath, England and by Thorndike Press, Waterville, Maine, USA.

Published in 2004 in the U.K. by arrangement with Headline Book Publishing, Ltd.

Published in 2004 in the U.S. by arrangement with Headline Book Publishing, Ltd.

U.K. Hardcover ISBN 0–7540–8695–X (Windsor Series)
U.K. Softcover ISBN 0–7540–9360–3 (Paragon Series)
U.S. Softcover ISBN 0–7862–5953–1 (General)

The text of this Large Print edition is unabridged.
Other aspects of the book may vary from the original edition.

Set in 16 pt. New Times Roman.

Printed in Great Britain on acid-free paper.

British Library Cataloguing in Publication Data available

Rowe, Rosemary.
      The Legatus mystery / Rosemary Rowe.
          p.   cm.
      ISBN 0–7862–5953–1 (lg. print : sc : alk. paper)
      1. Great Britain—History—Roman period, 55 B.C.–
449 A.D.—Fiction. 2. Libertus (Fictitious character : Rowe)—
Fiction. 3. Romans—Great Britain—Fiction. 4. Large type
books. I. Title.
PR6118.O97L44 2004
823'.92—dc22   2003060746

For Keava and Vonnie
with love from Granny Rose.

FOREWORD

The Legatus Mystery is set late in AD 187, at a time when Britain had been for almost two hundred years the northernmost province of the hugely successful Roman Empire: occupied by Roman legions, criss-crossed by Roman roads, subject to Roman laws and taxed and ruled over by a provincial governor answerable directly to Rome, where the increasingly unbalanced Emperor Commodus still wore the imperial purple and ruled the Empire with an autocratic and capricious hand.

The visit of an official imperial ambassador was therefore a considerable event for any city-state within the Empire, and Glevum (modern Gloucester), founded as a *colonia* for retired legionaries, and by now a republic in its own right within the province, would have been no exception. There is no such historical character as the Marcellus Fabius in this narrative, but the story of his rise from legionary officer to imperial legate overseas is not untypical. A legate would travel with a retinue, protected by an imperial warrant and seal—interference with which was a capital offence—generally carried a seal-ring so that he could issue official documents, and could expect civic entertainment at any town he visited en route. A visit to an outlying province like Britannia would presuppose a tour of several weeks, even given the excellent state of the military roads and the provision of official transport.

In the Britannia that he visited Latin was the language of the educated, and most people aspired to emulate Roman ways, although native dialects still existed and Celtic ways were not altogether lost. The conquerors had brought with them not only laws and customs, but their religion too—a whole pantheon of gods, ranging from the familiar names like Jupiter and Mars, and the household *lares et penates*, to a whole host of minor deities responsible for every aspect of daily life, such as Pales, goddess of the herds, or Consus, protector of the granaries. Another import was the Imperial cult, in which dead emperors were worshipped—though Commodus had modified this tradition by declaring that he was the reincarnation of Hercules and therefore a god already. None the less Imperial worship was formally required (it was the refusal to accept this which led to the persecution of the Christians—the religion itself was not forbidden at this period) although conformity to the cult appears to have been more a matter of good citizenship and a profession of loyalty to Rome than one requiring any deep-held spiritual belief. The Romans were generally quite tolerant of other cults, provided that this condition was met. There is evidence of many foreign cults in Britain during this period, those of Mithras and Isis in particular, and most local gods and goddesses continued to be worshipped as alternative manifestations of the Roman deities. Only the Druids were at this time legally forbidden to practise their beliefs, perhaps because they called for human sacrifice.

State religious observance in the main was not as we might imagine it today. Roman temples were not, in general, designed for congregational worship. The priests, who often had other jobs as well, entered the temple and offered sacrifice to propitiate or bargain with the gods, and most temples had several shrines in the precinct, where sacrificial offering could be made. Imperial altars are known to have existed in some Capitoline shrines. There are even occasions where a small second temple was erected, or a sacred wood enclosed, as in this narrative—though there is no evidence that such a thing existed in Glevum.

Ritual and omens had a vital role to play— correct procedure had less to do with individual faith than with proper adherence to the rites, and any trivial mistake or omission was seen as an evil augury, requiring to be propitiated by a new round of ritual. Immense importance was accorded to signs and portents, charms and amulets were in great demand, and the whole calendar revolved around days which were judged auspicious or inauspicious. It seems that every major provincial temple at this period had its own local augurer, whose job it was to read the signs and report his conclusions to the high priest and the highest-ranking local magistrate. It was these men who decided what action was appropriate—a clear indication of the close relationship between religion and civic government.

Jupiter was particularly venerated, especially in legionary towns, since he was not only father of the gods, but also identified with the protection of the state, and every army unit worshipped him. The ritual 'burying of the altar' alluded to in the book is an attested fact, and it is known that there was substantial worship of Jupiter in Glevum at the period, and there was a huge statue of him in the forum. Some details of that cult (in particular those relating the exacting restrictions and strange costume required of the Flamen of Jupiter) are well attested, both in manuscript and monumental records. The precise rituals of the Imperial cult are not recorded, however, though it is known that the priesthood was reserved for freedmen, rather than those born free, and that it was—as the narrative suggests—an expensive honour, but a sought-after one, as it opened the way to advancement for its holders.

Accounts are somewhat ambiguous. It is

clear that there was a council of Augustales from which a new sevir was appointed every year, but one source appears to speak of 'two assistants' at a ritual, who may have been seviri-in-training, and that is the interpretation which is adopted here.

The distinction between freemen and slaves was an important one, though a man might move between these two conditions in a lifetime and it was much easier to get into slavery than out of it. A man, like Libertus, might be born free, captured and sold into slavery and later inherit both his freedom and the coveted rank of citizen from his master. Others might be driven into slavery by want or debt, some were sentenced to it for crimes against the state, and some gamblers staked their freedom on the fall of a die. Not all masters were harsh, and slaves might manage large estates, like Meritus, or be the indulged favourites of their owners, like others in the story. Many a poor free peasant, scratching out a precarious living on the land, must have lived a less enviable existence than the majority of slaves, who at least were certain of food and shelter.

Other slaves, however, lived pitiable lives: especially female slaves who were the explicit sexual property of their owners, and might be called upon to fulfil any whim. Children born of these liaisons were automatically slaves, and the owner had the power of life and death over such offspring, who had no rights until they were literally 'taken up' from the floor, and might be disposed of in any way their owner/father chose. (Even restrictions about burying corpses within the walls do not appear to have applied to such infants, and several mass graves have been discovered—though some commentators blame epidemics of childhood disease.) Slaves were not permitted to marry—'taking' another man's slave was tantamount to theft—and once a person became a slave any pre-existing marriage was legally annulled. Equally, a freeman or citizen marrying a slave automatically forfeited his status; although it was open to him to legally manumit his own servant and then marry her, and there are several attested incidents of that.

The Romano-British background in this book has been derived from exhibitions, excavations, interviews with experts and a wide variety of (sometimes contradictory) pictorial and written sources. This is, however, a work of fiction, and although I have done my best to create an accurate picture there is no claim to total academic authenticity. The existence of the Roman governor, Pertinax, and his promotion to Africa at about this date, is historical, although there is no reliable evidence to show the exact date of his departure, or, interestingly, the name of his successor.

All other characters are the product of my

imagination, as are the rituals of the Imperial cult.

Relata refero. Ne Iupiter quidem omnibus placet. I only tell you what I heard. Jove himself can't please everybody.

Roman Britain

CHAPTER ONE

'Marcus Aurelius Septimus is here?' I asked the attendant slave at Glevum baths, as I stripped off my cloak, sandals and tunic and stuffed them into one of the stone 'doveholes' provided for the purpose.

The boy eyed me doubtfully. I could not blame him. I had come here without an attendant slave, my clothes were travel-stained and dusty, and I had not even been wearing a belt around my tunic. I scarcely looked like a Roman citizen, let alone a fit bath companion for the most important man in Glevum.

'He is expecting me,' I assured him, as I wrapped a linen *toella* around my nether parts. It was not obligatory—indeed many men visit the baths without wrapping themselves in anything—but a humble pavement-maker like myself can hardly meet the personal representative of the provincial governor of all Britannia dressed only in his own drooping skin. Besides, if I knew Marcus, he would be at this moment sitting in the *caldarium*, the hot room where he sometimes came, like other influential Romans, to conduct business and meet acquaintances. To my thin, fifty-year-old Celtic posterior the stone seats in the caldarium soon seem uncomfortably hot, and I knew I might find myself very glad of the

1

protection of my towel.

In the absence of my own slave, I slipped the bath attendant a *quadrans* to watch my clothes.

The boy took the coin. It seemed to loosen his tongue. 'His Excellence is here all right, and his attendants with him. He's been here all the afternoon, with no end of important people coming to see him—I think something special is going on. That slave watching his clothes has been waiting there for hours.'

He gestured towards a servant boy in a bordered tunic who was sitting with patient boredom in a nearby niche, keeping guard over a pile of neatly folded garments on a bench. It was a necessary precaution. Many a fine citizen has left the baths—here as in every other city—with a poorer cloak than he arrived in. One or two unfortunates have even been known to lose the 'bath tunic' (which most people wear under their cloaks when travelling to and from the baths) with humorously embarrassing results which have been the topic of town gossip for weeks afterwards. But Marcus's garments were more than usually worth stealing—even from here I could see the wide purple border of his toga. Marcus was very conscious of his patrician status, and famously wore that cumbersome badge of citizenship even to the baths.

'You'll find His Excellence in the hot room,' the bath boy said.

I nodded, and began to make my way in the direction of the warm pools and the *tepidarium*. Little time for me to linger there—I should have to plunge almost immediately into the caldarium.

'I hope you're right about his wanting to see you,' the boy called after me. 'He doesn't take kindly to being unexpectedly interrupted at his ablutions.'

He hardly needed to tell me that. I had been extremely surprised by the messenger myself. Normally, when Marcus wants me—often at the most inconvenient hour—he summons me to come to his apartments or to his official rooms, where he can keep me waiting in comfort. But here? Marcus may regard a visit to the baths as an excellent opportunity to discuss affairs, but usually with patrician friends and town dignitaries, not a mere mosaic-maker like myself. Roman citizen I might be—indeed I was born a nobleman in my own tribe—but I was also an ex-slave and a tradesman, and the gulf between myself and Marcus was as great as that between me and the bath-house attendant himself. Without the most explicit instructions I would never have dared to come to seek my patron here. What was so critical that he had sent for me?

Perhaps he was irritated that I had not called on him at once, the night before, when I had returned from a journey to Londinium. That was a worrying possibility. Indeed, I should probably have done so, had we not come home to all the usual time-consuming problems created by prolonged absence—damp blankets, reluctant firewood and the discovery that a large rat had made his home in the bedding—and had consequently slept until long after sunup. At least—I comforted myself as I hurried through the tepidarium and entered the caldarium, where the hot steam gushed out to meet me—here in Britannia a rich man's protégés, his *clientes*, are not expected to attend him flatteringly at dawn every morning, as they are in Rome.

I need not have worried. Marcus greeted me cordially enough. 'Ah, Libertus! I have been waiting for you. Come in. Welcome.' He raised himself a little on one elbow and blinked at me benevolently through the steam. He was elegantly draped in a long swathe of blue linen towel, and wore a pair of thick-soled bath slippers against the heat of the floor. He was looking wonderfully bronzed and relaxed. Although his short blond curls were plastered to his head and his handsome young patrician face was slightly flushed, he seemed otherwise unmoved by the temperature. He held out a languid hand for me to kiss.

I was not altogether sure of the protocol. How does a mere ex-slave mosaic-maker—however much of a citizen he may finally come to be—greet his patron with dignity, draped only in a skimpy towel? I made a swift bow

4

over the hand, an equally swift grab for my wrappings and sat down gratefully on the lower bench he indicated, lifting my bare feet clear of the floor. Marcus's bath slippers were not merely for show. Glevum caldarium is not as hot as some, but the tiles still left my soles stinging.

I was ready with apologies, but Marcus waved them aside. 'Libertus my old friend, it is a long journey to Londinium, even for a younger man. Days of travelling are wearisome. Naturally I forgive you for any lapse of courtesy.'

I was on my guard. When Marcus calls me his old friend it is almost always because he wants my services and, since he was elegantly pointing out how magnanimous he was being, I had an uncomfortable feeling that this was no exception. On the other hand, perhaps he genuinely wanted my news. After all, I had been the guest of the Roman governor, Pertinax, who was Marcus's particular friend and advocate. (Even patrons may have patrons of their own.) 'You are gracious, Excellence,' I said.

'I hear you were of great service to the governor,' Marcus said approvingly.

I murmured something suitably deprecating. 'A mere matter of a dead corn officer . . .' but Marcus made an impatient gesture.

'Of course, of course—he has told me all that in his letter.'

On reflection, I should not have been surprised. The imperial post, carried at top speed by a single man on horseback, is obviously faster than a man in a carriage. Marcus would have heard the news from Londinium days ago. And he had 'forgiven me' for failing to call on him. So it was some other matter on which he wished to see me. Knowing that Marcus refused to 'insult me' by ever offering me money for my service and advice, I fervently hoped that the reason for this meeting was not the 'something important' which the bath slave had mentioned. I had been away from Glevum for almost a month, and the store chests and shelves in my humble workroom and garret were depressingly empty.

Marcus fixed me with a vague smile. An attendant, dripping perspiration in his tunic, brought him a dipper of cool water from the apse at the door, and Marcus buried his face in it.

I, however, did not merit this luxury, and in the circumstances it would be disastrously impolite of me to move. I squirmed a little on my bench. It was hot, even through the linen. I was already beginning to turn pink-faced and wilt like a limp leaf. Whatever Marcus wanted, I thought, I hoped it would be quick.

'And you have not only been helpful to the governor, Libertus,' Marcus said, wafting away the steam as he spoke. 'I have received a communication from Rome. The Emperor is minded to be pleased with you, for your part in uncovering that plot against his life.'

'I am honoured, Excellence,' I said faintly, feeling the sweat prickle down my back. But it was cold sweat now rather than a product of the heat. The Emperor Commodus is an erratic man—or god, I should say, as he regards himself as a reincarnation of Hercules and requires to be addressed accordingly. He is also fanatical about his safety, and sees plots everywhere: often with reason, as my investigations had proved. However, his favouritisms are notoriously as short-lived as they are violent, and any man who attracts imperial attention—for whatever reason—is sooner or later bound to wish that he had remained safely anonymous. I obviously dared not say so, however. Commodus is reputed to spend a fortune on his spies, and there were no doubt paid ears and eyes even in this provincial bath-house.

Marcus nodded, and looked thoughtfully at the slave with the water pot. He was as well aware of the dangers as I was. 'As a result of your actions,' he said, with every outward evidence of satisfaction, 'His Imperial Mightiness has deigned to honour our city. There is to be a special service of thanksgiving at the Imperial birthday celebrations.'

Since he was officially a god, of course, Commodus's birthday was a religious feast day, and on that date every citizen was

7

expected to attend and take part in a sacrifice in honour of the Emperor—as the army did every day of the year. The Imperial cult had been introduced in the time of Augustus—a kind of declaration of loyalty and a celebration of the power of Rome—and all the emperors since then had joined the pantheon after death, but Commodus had not even waited to die before declaring himself a deity.

I nodded, and Marcus went on. 'We are to be treated to a visit from the highest-ranking Imperial priest in all the province, who will conduct the sacrifices at the temple and lead the services. Naturally there will have to be commemorative games, and special celebrations.' He sighed.

I understood the reason for that sigh. Birthday celebrations for a god were likely to prove a very costly business.

'It is a great honour for the city—and for me personally of course,' Marcus added, glancing at the slave. 'There will even be an ambassadorial visitor from Rome—an imperial *legatus* to represent the Emperor. I think I know the man—a certain Fabius Marcellus Verus—used to be commander of a legion, when I lived in Rome.' There was a small annexe to one side of the hot-room, a sort of open-ended cubicle with a raised stone slab in the centre. Marcus got up suddenly, and occupied it, still talking to me over his shoulder as he went. 'Fabius's arrival in the city will coincide with the departure of the governor. You know of course that Governor Pertinax is leaving these islands? He has been appointed governor of the African provinces.'

'So he told me, Excellence,' I said, shifting on my seat and hoping that my buttocks were not cooking. Because Marcus was a close friend of the governor, he was obviously proud to give this sign of his association with him. I did not add that all Britannia must have heard the news by this time: I had been told the same thing—with embellishments—by an innkeeper, a night watchman and a beggar, among others, on the road back from Londinium.

'There are to be farewell rituals for that, too, of course,' Marcus said. He arranged himself on the slab as the slave stood by. It was probably cooler in the cubicle, I thought; it was further from the furnace. He raised his head again. 'I thought—a small commemorative piece perhaps? In honour of both these memorable occasions.'

I breathed again. So that was what Marcus wanted! A mosaic in a hurry—that explained this extraordinary summons. And it made financial sense for him, one memorial piece instead of two. It was just a month to the Emperor's birthday—I began to make calculations in my head. With the help of Junio, my servant-cum-assistant, I thought that I could manage. 'It would be a privilege, Excellence,' I said.

9

'What I had in mind,' Marcus said dreamily, allowing the slave to rub him with a little olive oil from a flask, 'was something a little different. A commemorative shrine—in one of the public spaces perhaps: a statue of Hercules of course, in honour of the Emperor, but mosaic on the wall and in the niche itself.' He gestured towards the flask invitingly, but I felt that adding oil to my flesh would only result in fried Libertus, and I shook my head in what I hoped was a suitably respectful manner.

Marcus waved the slave away and went on outlining his design. 'Blue and white and yellow, that would be the thing. Tiles rather than stone, I think, and a design of birds and dogs worked into the frieze? Pertinax is fond of hunting. I've seen the sort of thing I want, in Rome, though I've never seen one in Britannia. Could it be managed, do you think?'

I was asking myself the same question. A simple floor mosaic was one thing. I had developed many techniques to speed the work. But a curved niche? That was something new.

'Only the finest materials, of course,' Marcus went on. 'And fine workmanship. I can find somebody else, naturally, if you do not feel you can . . .'

Without undue arrogance, I doubted that. There are few men in Glevum with my skills. If Marcus wanted this mosaic, I should have to do it—as he knew. Besides, I needed the money, as he no doubt also knew.

'I should be honoured to attempt it, Excellence.' I mopped my dripping forehead and tried to look as eager as a man can when he is streaming with sweat and coming to a slow boil.

There was a pause. Marcus gestured to the slave, who busied himself with a strigil, scraping combined oil and sweat from Marcus's oiled body—and taking the dirt with it.

I waited—it would have been inexcusable to go—until Marcus wrapped himself back into his towel and came back into the main caldarium. In a moment, I knew, he would go next door and take a cold plunge before being massaged with perfumed oil and having his nose-hairs pulled. I only hoped that I had been dismissed by then.

He sat down upon his bench again, and looked at me. 'Well then, the commission is yours. Though, of course, I know you have additional responsibilities now. Pertinax tells me you found your Gwellia. I hope that has been satisfactory?'

Gwellia. The wife that I had lost for twenty years and who now had miraculously been restored to me. Junio had found her, in the hands of a slave-trader, and Pertinax had purchased her for me as a reward for my efforts. Even now it was almost more than I could comprehend. I glanced at Marcus. He was smiling indulgently.

11

I swallowed. Marcus wanted this mosaic badly. This was probably a good moment to ask a favour. 'There is something I would like to ask you, Excellence, in that regard.'

He inclined his head. 'Go on.'

Sweat was still streaming into my eyes. I outlined my request.

Marcus sat suddenly upright. 'Marry her, Libertus? I don't understand! You already own the woman. What more do you want?' He was tapping one bronzed thigh as he spoke, I noticed.

I recognised the gesture. My patron was impatient. I fidgeted uncomfortably on my own hot bench opposite.

'I simply don't see the difficulty,' Marcus persisted.

I sighed. Impossible to explain to a wealthy Roman. I flapped at the clouds of steam, miserably aware of how hot and pink I was, and tried to peer at Marcus. 'It is a difficult position, Excellence. Of course, our marriage was automatically dissolved when we were captured and sold as slaves.' I thought of that once lovely face, now so tired and strained and worn. 'She is no longer legally my wife.'

'Of course she isn't! Slaves are not permitted to be married to anyone.'

'Exactly, Excellence! That is why I am asking you to help me. I can't marry her again, without first arranging to have her freed.'

Marcus understood that, of course. As the

highest-ranking magistrate in the *colonia*, he knew the intricacies of the law better than I did. What he could not comprehend was why on earth it mattered. I owned the woman, as he said—and could therefore summon her to my bed as often as I pleased.

He said as much now, with a laugh. 'You Celts are too indulgent with your womenfolk. Too indulgent by half. If a woman won't come to your bed willingly, beat her till she does—that's what my father used to say.' He spoke with cheerful confidence. Marcus was young, handsome and powerful, and until his recent marriage the most beautiful women in Glevum had queued up to offer him favours. 'Though goodness knows what she expects in that department, Libertus—you're not young. Still, you're not bad-looking and you're in fair shape for your age.'

I smiled. It was certainly not a question of unwillingness. It was true, there had been some reticence at first—on both our parts—but reconciliation had been all the sweeter for the wait. But now . . . 'Excellence, it is more a matter—'

I was going to say 'of the dignity that she deserves', but the words were never uttered. A young man had burst into the steam room and flung himself to the tiled floor at Marcus's feet. He was—remarkably—still half dressed, in the distinctive tunic of a temple slave, and the steam was already dampening the cloth

13

and settling in little droplets on the metal of his clasp.

'What is the meaning of this intrusion!' Marcus was angry. He got to his feet and so—rather groggily—did I, to the anguish of my feet and the great relief of my posterior.

'Most honoured Excellence! A thousand thousand apologies. I bring important news.' The man had not moved from his position, and already the moisture was beginning to course down his face and drip from his nose and chin.

'Very well,' Marcus said, and the man struggled to his feet.

'I come from the senior Sevir Augustalis,' he blurted, 'Meritus, high priest of the Imperial cult in Glevum. He sends his humble greetings to your Excellence . . .'

'Never mind all that,' Marcus said testily. 'What's the news?'

'Citizen, there was dreadful moaning in the temple earlier—not even the High Priest of Jupiter knew what was causing it. Then Sevir Meritus went into the inner sanctum of the shrine at noon, to read the auguries.' The messenger looked at us wildly. Suddenly he blurted, as though he had forgotten his carefully prepared text, 'The long and short of it is, there was a body in there on the floor. A body in rich civilian clothing. And oh, Excellence . . .' he threw himself back on the floor as if by humbling himself he could

14

somehow undo the horror of his words, 'judging by the documents that the priest found in his belt, it seems to be the body of an imperial embassy.'

CHAPTER TWO

An imperial ambassador! I caught my breath. 'Dear Jupiter!' Marcus was visibly shocked. 'The last time anything happened to an imperial legate to Britannia . . .'

He did not finish, but we all knew what he meant. It was a story to frighten children with. The legate and his two bodyguards had been set upon and brutally murdered, apparently by marauding wayside thieves. All three had been hacked into pieces and left for the wolves—all for the sake of the bag of silver they were carrying. Parts of the bodies had never been recovered and there were terrible reprisals in the town concerned. So much so, legend said, that one tribal elder who witnessed the slaughter called down the vengeance of the gods on all things Roman—and instead brought a dreadful vengeance on himself. They'd half flayed him, bound him to a stake, and wheeled him in—still breathing—to the arena beasts, for daring to defy the word of Rome.

And all this was under the previous

emperor, Marcus Aurelius, who was famously just! What his unpredictable son might do to Glevum in the same circumstances was too horrible to contemplate.

I glanced at Marcus. He had turned pale. 'Of course, Excellence,' I said nervously, 'that earlier incident *was* further south, and put down to displaced Iceni. The Romans have never trusted the Iceni, ever since the revolt of Boudicca.' It was a forlorn attempt at comfort. Marcus knew the likely consequences as well as I did.

He shook his head, and then moved with a sudden alacrity which would have made a battle-charger look sluggish. 'Come on,' he said, jumping up from his bench, and leading the way out of the room. 'There is no time to be lost.'

I followed him—there was nothing else to do—and the temple slave trotted obediently after us.

Marcus was in a hurry. He ignored the tepid pools in the adjoining room and made his way directly to the *frigidarium*, where he launched himself instantly into the cold plunge. The temple slave glanced at me uncertainly.

Desperate times call for desperate measures, and I could hardly back out of this without looking foolish. I handed the slave my towel and, closing my eyes, followed Marcus into the pool as boldly as I could. The shock of that sudden immersion would have made a

16

statue squeal, but the temple slave was watching me and I controlled myself, only emitting the faintest of gasps.

The cold water was reviving, however, once I caught my breath again. Marcus was soon out of the pool, waving aside the proffered massage (to the chagrin of the massage-slave, who'd been hoping for a tip), and a moment later we were all striding back to the changing room. Marcus's attendant was still patiently sitting guard over my patron's clothes. There was no sign of the boy I had paid to look after mine.

'Quickly!' Marcus barked to his slave, and allowed himself to be swiftly dried and draped elegantly in his toga while I dabbed at myself ineffectively with my damp towel. I was still trying to come to terms with what I'd heard.

'An imperial legate,' I ventured at last, pulling my patched tunic over my head and wrapping myself in my cloak. 'Not . . .' I hardly dared to form the words, '. . . this Fabius Marcellus that you mentioned earlier?'

To my astonishment my patron shook his head. 'I thought of that at first, but on reflection I don't see how it can be,' he said thoughtfully, holding his hands out of the way while his slave twisted one end of the toga-cloth into a belt, in the latest fashion. 'In fact the whole thing is a puzzle. I received that communication from the Emperor only yesterday, and that was brought directly to me

17

by the fastest messengers. Even if Fabius had left Rome at the same instant, he would still be several days away—and according to the letter he was not due to leave until the Ides.'

I looked up from lacing my sandals. 'But if it isn't Fabius . . . ?'

Marcus's slave was fitting elegant red shoes to his master's feet. 'That is the problem, Libertus. Of course the Emperor has a thousand messengers, and he can send them anywhere he chooses—but I can't believe that there has been an imperial legation anywhere near Glevum without my hearing of it. If there was any formal embassy in Britannia I should have had word of his arrival as soon as he set foot on these shores.'

He was right, of course. The Emperor is not the only man with spies. If this corpse was only impersonating a *legatus*, that altered everything. That act in itself would have merited the death penalty, and there would be no danger to the city. I breathed again.

'So, Excellence,' I said. 'What do you propose?'

'I must see this Sevir Augustalis,' Marcus said. He turned to the temple slave. 'Remind me, who was the priest exactly, before he took the wreath?'

'He was a wealthy freedman, Excellence,' the slave recited dutifully.

Marcus snorted with impatience. 'Obviously—since members of the Board of

18

Augustales always are! I meant, how did this one come to be elected priest? Presumably the man had wealth, to join the Augustales in the first place. So where did the money come from? Always assuming he has any left, by this time.'

Now that the immediate danger seemed to have receded, I could not resist a grin. The expense of being a priest of the Imperial cult is legendary. The provision of games, festivals and votive offerings to mark the year of office have become obligatory, a kind of involuntary tax on the freedman chosen, so election to the post is a very dubious blessing. However, it is a certain route to civic distinction, and nomination—since the priest directly serves the Emperor—is not an honour that a man can easily refuse.

The temple slave was looking doubtful. 'I have heard that Meritus was formerly the estate-manager for a very wealthy man. He must have made a great success of it, too, because when his master died he bequeathed Meritus his freedom and a large part of the estate as a reward. Since then it has become an even bigger success. Or so they say. Charcoal, wool and timber apparently. Though I believe the real money came from metals, Excellence. Lead, iron and silver, and a little gold.'

'Metals? I thought that all the metals locally were in the hands of Rome?'

The temple slave shook his head. 'I only

know the rumours, Excellence. There was some disused mine on the land, it seems, but Meritus got a licence and started working it again—and has done very well out of it. There's a good market for all these things in Rome. He even trades in artefacts these days, I hear, provided that the metal's good enough. But of course that's only gossip, Excellence. I've never heard him talk about himself.'

I could believe that. Ex-slaves, especially those who have risen to a fortune, are not often anxious to talk about their humble origins.

Marcus nodded. 'I see.'

The temple slave paused in the act of wrapping himself in his outdoor cloak again. He had not had the benefit of a cold plunge and a towel: his face was still scarlet, and his hair and tunic were looking dismally damp. 'But surely you have met the sevir, Excellence.'

That was an unwise question. Marcus flushed with irritation. 'Certainly I have.'

Of course he had. As the highest-ranking local dignitary, Marcus had probably spent more time than he wished taking part in public sacrifice, and he could scarcely have avoided the senior local sevir. But I could see what was happening. One Imperial high priest is very like another, and the office is usually held only for a year. If I knew Marcus he would have paid no particular attention to the man. Yet he could hardly admit to that, in the light of this

20

dead ambassador. It might be interpreted as proof of a dangerous lack of seriousness in emperor worship, and anything of that kind would certainly be reported to Rome—the Seviri Augustales tend to have a very high opinion of their own importance. Marcus was sensibly trying to find out what he could, so as not to create a social embarrassment.

I did my best to help him. 'An older man, I seem to remember, with greying hair?'

It was a reasonable guess. Few men came to be Seviri Augustales under the age of forty at least. But the temple slave shook his head. 'Perhaps you are thinking of the Sevir Praxus, citizen—he was last year's high priest. Meritus is a much younger man than that—a very big man, broadshouldered, with darkish skin and curly hair.'

'Ah, *that* sevir,' Marcus said knowledgeably, though I was privately convinced that he had no more memory of the man than I had. He held out his hand, so that his slave could slide the heavy seal-rings onto his finger. 'Where was this estate of his, exactly?'

The temple slave looked surprised at the enquiry. 'On the western borders, Excellence. Near Ariconium.'

'The western borders?' Marcus looked at me and raised his eyebrows. That part of the province is notoriously wild. The thick forests there are rumoured to be stalked by wolves, bandits and worse—the rebel red-headed tribesmen of the Silures, who have never really accepted Roman rule. There are still occasionally skirmishes there, and even the Roman army rarely moves in the remoter areas without a cavalry escort. An ex-slave from that area was likely to have dangerous antecedents.

'So he was not from Glevum? But I presume this is where he took the wreath of office?'

'He has contributed a great deal to the Augustales here. Of course he came here often—exporting wood to Greece and Rome, and selling wool and animals in the local markets. And the metals, too, have always been brought to Glevum to be shipped down the river. He is quite a figure in the city.'

'Ah, of course,' Marcus said briskly. 'Now I recall. Very well. Go back and tell this Meritus we are coming. Libertus and I will follow shortly.' He took it for granted that I was going to the temple with him, I noticed.

'As you command, Excellence!' the temple slave said, and bowed himself out of the changing room at once, almost backing into a couple of incoming bathers as he did so.

'When you are ready, Libertus my old friend,' Marcus said heartily, as if I were the one who had been taking a long time to get dressed, and I found myself following him through the outer courtyard. Young men stopped their ballplay to watch us pass, and a party of gamblers, whom I had seen earlier under the colonnades, hid away their dice at our approach and became suddenly fascinated by the wares of a passing food-vendor. Gaming is still officially prohibited in public places and Marcus's impressive toga was having its usual effect.

We passed through the entrance lobby and out into the street, and at once we were enveloped by the commerce of the town.

'Live eels, citizens? Fresh caught in the Sabrina this morning . . .'

'Household images, best household images . . .'

'This way to the *lupinarium*, gentlemen. Nice girls—all with specialities . . . all clean. A special price for you . . .'

Marcus brushed them all aside, and stepping over the piles of leather belts, turnips, tombstones and ivory brooches set out for sale at the pavement edge, he made his way to the corner of the little street. There his servant was already summoning some carrying chairs, and I soon found myself lurching along beside my patron in a litter. The litter-carriers were skilled and practised, evading the crowds and taking us along at a near-run—so quickly that Marcus's slave was panting after us, and we were likely to arrive at the temple long before our messenger.

We turned the corner and into the forum. There were traders here too, of course, as well as the civic offices and council buildings—but mostly the central area was alive, as it always was, with dignified citizens in togas, and self-important weights and measures officers weighing both goods and money on official scales. We came to a stop outside the Capitoline shrine. It is a huge temple complex glittering with wealth, as befits the central shrine of Jupiter in a city originally built as a retirement settlement for veterans: the army has always held Jupiter in especial reverence.

The temple and its attendant shrines stand in a large courtyard area at one corner of the forum. We got down, leaving the slave to pay the carriers, and as we made our way towards it I felt a little shiver down my spine.

No doubt it is designed to that effect. The entire complex is enclosed by walls, with a great colonnaded entranceway reached by two shallow steps from the street and protected from the idle public gaze by a verandaed ambulatory on either side. Once through the massive gate—and only then—one can see the central temple. It is a lofty building, made more impressive still by being set towards the back of the courtyard on a *podium*, up an imposing flight of marble steps, its entrance screened by a further arrangement of towering columns. The mixture of soaring architecture and shadowed secretness is intended to impress the superstitious.

I have to say that it impresses me.

To the right-hand side of this edifice, towards the rear, there is an unpretentious building housing stores and slaves where the priests themselves retire to robe and rest. Priests do not sleep at the temple on the whole: most of them have other occupations, too, and keep up houses elsewhere in the town. The store block seems especially insignificant, however, since to the left, set back with mock-discretion in a grove, is the second temple. The temple of the emperors, where our business lay: much smaller than the Capitoline shrine, but no less elaborate—even from where I stood the columns were aglint with gold.

One of the problems of having a living emperor as a deity is the possibility that the god may one day choose to visit his shrine in person. In Glevum the city fathers had solved the difficulty by building a small Imperial shrine within the courtyard complex of the temple of Jupiter.

There is an elegance in this solution which amuses me. Jove is generally worshipped together with Minerva and Juno—the so-called Capitoline Triad—so he is presumably accustomed to sharing temple space, while even Commodus can scarcely take offence at finding himself worshipped in such distinguished company. And, should the Divine Commodus ever deign to visit, an effective revelation of his godhead is ensured. There is apparently a private entrance at the back of the complex from the town house of the High Priest of Jupiter, so that any visiting deity could enter the precinct unseen and emerge dramatically onto the front steps of the great temple at a suitably theatrical moment— thereby dazzling the credulous. The chief priest does the same thing at every festival.

Even the irony of all this, however, did not make me smile today. There was something eerily amiss.

I looked around the courtyard. Gigantic statues of the gods stood in their accustomed places, gazing down from mighty plinths upon the open altars at their feet. The many-times-life-size faces of the immortals still looked thunderously down upon us from the pediment. But there was something missing. And suddenly I realised what it was.

The temple courtyard was empty. There was nobody in sight.

CHAPTER THREE

Usually, of course, the place is thronged with people. But not today. Today there was not a priest, not a temple slave, not a worshipper— not even a money-changer or a seller of sacrificial birds. Only the stone gods and silent colonnades. I am not a superstitious man—I

26

have more respect for the ancient gods of wood and stone than for the carved deities of Rome—but standing under the verandaed entranceway, alone with Marcus in that silent place, I felt the hairs on the back of my neck prickle. A hundred basalt eyes seemed to be upon me.

Even Marcus seemed momentarily uncertain, and his slave (who had finished paying the litter-carriers and just now arrived) looked around the courtyard and shivered visibly.

'Dear Mercury!' he muttered, and when he thought Marcus wasn't looking he shifted the towel and bath slippers he was carrying and fished in his tunic for a coin. I heard the splash as he dropped a propitiatory *as* into one of the great stone water bowls at the door. It must have represented his tip for the entire afternoon.

As if in answer to the gesture a priest suddenly appeared from the temple. Not a sevir, by his robes, but one of the junior Priests of Jupiter, resplendent in a white *toga praetexta* banded in purple and gold, with a narrow circlet of silver around his head. He moved out of the shadow of the columns and came busily down the steps towards us. 'I regret . . .' he began, holding up his hands as if to ward us off, but Marcus cut off his explanations.

'I am Marcus Aurelius Septimus.'

The young man turned an embarrassed

shade of puce. At the name, probably. Aurelius has become the commonest surname in the Empire, but Marcus is widely rumoured to be related to the imperial family itself and (given that patrician toga) the young priest hardly knew how to conduct himself.

'Most honoured Excellence, of course—in normal circumstances . . . But I have been instructed, Mightiness, that no one is permitted in the temple court today, for religious reasons.'

Marcus regarded him frostily. 'The Sevir Meritus is expecting me. Would you be good enough to let him know I'm here?'

'Ah! Then you know about the . . .' the young priest hesitated, 'the unpleasant incident?'

'Indeed! And who are you, and what's your function here?'

'I'm the sub-Sacerdos Trinunculus,' the young man said. 'The newest neophyte. The senior priests are busy with the rites—there has been a desecration of the shrine, and there will have to be a day of ritual cleansing. I am afraid, Excellence, I shall have to ask you, too . . .' he gestured apologetically towards the great urn and basin by the door, 'if you would bathe your hands and face? This is such a dreadful omen, Excellence.'

'Not least for the imperial ambassador,' Marcus said dryly, but he made the ritual cleansing as requested.

Trinunculus—the very word means

'beginner' so whether that was his name or his official rank I could not tell—seemed oblivious of any irony. 'I will tell the sevir you are here. If you would be good enough to wait . . .' He bowed himself away and, without finishing the sentence, scuttled off across the courtyard in a most unpriestly fashion.

We waited, under the painted roof of the arcade, looking out over the great courtyard. It was eerily quiet, with its dancing shadows and bloodstained altars and the smoke of sacrifice still hanging in the air.

There is a smell about temples which is unmistakable: part perfumed oils, part charring meat, part fragrant herbs, part abattoir. And hanging over the whole place like a pall, stronger than burning feathers and the smell of blood, there is something else: a scent of human sweat, and greed and fear. It is a potent mixture. I do not know that I have ever experienced it more strongly than that afternoon, standing in slanting sunlight in the colonnade and—ironic after an hour in the baths—rinsing my face in the cold water from the urn. Perhaps it was my imagination, but the water seemed unnaturally cold.

We waited for what seemed a long time, but at last Trinunculus came hurrying back. He was more apologetic than ever. 'The Sevir Meritus regrets, Excellence, but he cannot come to greet you in person for the moment. He is engaged in a sacrifice of purification.

29

However, if you would care to follow me . . .?'
He began to lead the way towards the inner
shrine.

I hesitated. This was as far into the temple
as I had ever been. I had come here, of course,
on days of festival as every citizen is expected
to do, to attend the major public rituals—but
only to the outer courtyard. The place is very
different on those occasions, with half the
populace cramming the steps and entranceway
to see the processions—pipes, priests, pigeons,
sheep and bulls—and standing on tiptoe to see
the spectacle that followed—prayers, incense,
invocations and the final dramatic moment
when the High Priest of Jupiter gives the
signal, and the knife is plunged into the
creature's throat so that the hot blood pours
out on the altar-front. I have roared with the
rest as the heart of the beast is cut out and
burned with herbs and incense on the sacred
hearth and cheered as the remainder of the
carcass is dragged away—sometimes to be
roasted and ritually eaten by the priests,
sometimes even distributed to us.

But all this always took place in the safety of
the outer courtyard, with the people watching
from the ambulatory: only the great and
mighty dared to approach the altars or mount
the steps beyond. And there were always
crowds of people then. Today there was only
silence, and the smell of death, and I could
feel the hairs on the back of my neck standing

30

up at the thought of crossing the inner courtyard between those mighty shrines. Suppose this priest led us right up onto the podium and under the colonnade? That would take us to the real centre of the temple, its most sacred place, the *cella* of the divinity, which is not usually entered except by the most devout of worshippers. This was a Roman temple, not a Celtic one, and—on all but the rarest of occasions—for ordinary mortals the inner sanctum was a forbidden place. Only the priests and temple slaves could enter there.

Of course, I told myself, this *was* a rare occasion. And I was accompanying Marcus, who was a dignitary, with the religious honour due to rank. All the same, as the assembled gods scowled stonily down on me, I hesitated. The temple had already been desecrated. By trespassing into the inner shrine I was likely to desecrate it further. Marcus's slave was obviously of the same opinion, and he hung back with me under the veranda.

'Libertus?' Marcus had stopped and was gazing back towards me. He sounded exasperated.

The possible irritation of the gods seemed suddenly preferable to the certainty of my patron's wrath. I thrust my damp towel towards the slave and followed Marcus and Trinunculus. Somewhat to my relief, our guide did not lead us into the inner temple, but round the side of the complex towards the

Imperial shrine.

Through the little grove of trees which fronted it, we could see it clearly now: elegant marble pillars forming an outer passageway around the tiny shrine. The outer walls were decorated with magnificent wall paintings in vibrant colours, depicting the Emperor in heroic guise. There was a mosaic, too (of intricate design but indifferent workmanship), forming a path in the space created by the pillars. The entrance was a heavy wooden door flanked by life-sized marble statues in niches, and edged by carved posts in richly gilded wood. Lead curse and blessing tablets were nailed to the posts—only a few petitions, compared to other temples I had seen, but even the Imperial gods, it seemed, are worth a try in an emergency. One supplicant, 'Lucianus the wretched', had left a whole cluster of petitions, and there was the glint of gold among the coin offerings in the water basin, perhaps offered as additional inducement for the gods' attention.

The door of the sanctuary was closed, and in front of it a priest in mauve and reddish-purple robes was burning something on an outdoor altar while two—clearly lesser—priests stood by. Clouds of aromatic smoke arose, and there was the chanted rhythm of a prayer. The priest raised his hands and wafted the smoke towards the temple, then towards himself, and finally towards his attendants.

Then he scattered something onto the altar from a silver flask, and all three prostrated themselves upon the ground. I could not help noticing, as they revealed their feet, that all three were wearing exquisite shoes of costly soft purple leather. Of course, I thought, all Augustales were wealthy men!

There was a short pause, and then the chief scvir rose, pushed back the part of his robe with which he had covered his head—as required for the ceremony—and came striding towards us. He walked slowly and impressively, and I had to resist a temptation to fling myself to my knees in his presence.

Tall, broad-shouldered, swarthy-skinned, with the bronze diadem of an Imperial priest pressed down upon a riot of dark curly hair—this could only be the sevir Meritus who had been described to us. He was, certainly, a commanding figure. There are tall men in Glevum, but this man was one of the tallest that I have ever seen. He might have been as much as six feet tall—perhaps even a little more—and he was commensurately broad. The hands which he was extending to us in welcome were the size of dinner bowls, and the muscles in the brawny arms were evident even under the heavy folds of the draped robe he wore.

His voice, too, made the columns ring.

'In the name of the Immortal Commodus Britannicus, Emperor of these islands and of the provinces across the sea, I welcome you to this unhappy temple.'

Marcus's voice seemed muted in comparison. 'This is where the ambassador was killed?'

'Where he was found,' the sevir said, in a more normal tone. 'As for killed, I cannot say. There was no weapon, no sign of any struggle, simply the body lying on the floor. I found him, myself, this morning when I went in to read the noontime auguries.'

I saw Marcus stiffen. There is an official *auspex*, of course, in any major town, to warn of evil omens and auspicious days—but reading auguries is a particular calling. Men are especially trained to it, and decisions on what should be done as a result are usually made in conjunction with a senior magistrate. No doubt this fellow was a skilled *hirospex*, entitled to read the entrails of sacrificed animals to judge the pleasure of the gods, but even so the idea of a Sevir Augustalis presuming to read other omens at the temple was something clearly not to Marcus's taste.

'And what did the omens tell you?' Marcus said.

Meritus refused to be snubbed. 'I could not read the signs with that ill portent there, Excellence. I covered the body with a cloth, and then came out at once and locked the door. I called for my assistant priests and we began the purification rites immediately. And

I sent for you—it was not clear to me what we should do with the body.'

'You are sure the man was dead?'

Meritus looked at him pityingly. 'I am quite certain, Excellence. He was not breathing and he was quite, quite cold.'

'And you are convinced it was an ambassador?'

The sevir frowned. 'I believe so, Excellence. He had a sealed warrant at his belt, and an imperial ring on his finger. I did not touch the document, of course. I felt that—with respect, Excellence—that was your affair.'

I could understand his decision—tampering with an imperial seal is in itself a capital offence. 'An imperial warrant?' I enquired.

'I am no expert, citizen, but it looked like one to me.' He turned to Marcus. 'I am sure, Excellence, that you would be a better judge of that than I am. The document is still hanging at his belt. Come and examine it for yourself.'

Marcus nodded. 'Very well,' he said with a sigh. 'We had better see this body, I suppose. Libertus, come with me. You too, Meritus. I shall want a witness if I break the seal.'

The sevir selected a key from his belt and offered it to Marcus. Together we skirted the still-smoking altar and approached the door. One of the assistant priests scraped a little warm ash from the fire and spread it reverently on our foreheads as we passed.

Marcus fitted the key to the lock and the

door swung open. The shrine was a tiny building, no more than a few feet square. There was a small silver statuette of Augustus in a niche, a life-size bronze statue of Commodus in an alcove at the back, and a small marble altar in the centre. Nothing else.

Of the body of a *legatus* there was no sign whatever.

CHAPTER FOUR

There was a stunned silence.

Marcus whirled around. 'What is the meaning of this disgrace,' he demanded, but Meritus was staring at the altar and shaking his head in disbelief. Astonishment seemed actually to have diminished him in stature.

'Excellence,' he stammered, 'this is impossible. I left him here and locked the door myself. I spoke to you, Trinunculus, as soon as I came out.'

Trinunculus nodded. 'That is so, Excellence. I was attending at the door.' He turned to Marcus. 'The sevir sent me off to find a temple slave, while he went to find the Priest of Jupiter.'

'So for a few moments there was no one at the shrine?' my patron said, looking at me with the triumphant air of a viper-tamer producing an unexpected snake from his sleeve.

36

Trinunculus looked as though his face would crumple. 'On the contrary, Excellence, Hirsus and Scribonius were outside all the time. Oh, by all the deities . . .'

The sevir quelled him with a look.

'Hirsus and Scribonius . . . ?' Marcus asked.

'My two assistant Imperial priests,' Meritus explained, with some return to his previous confident manner. 'They were already standing by, preparing the noontime sacrifice. It is the custom to offer a small bird, or something similar, but today there was to be a bigger sacrifice, because the auguries were to be read.'

'Ah yes, of course, the auguries!' Marcus let his disapproval show.

'Permit me, Excellence,' the older of the other priests piped up. He was a small, thin man with a rim of greying hair—he seemed half the size and twice the age of Meritus. 'The senior sevir is permitted to read the entrails in the temple, under certain circumstances laid down in the laws. And certainly I felt that it was justified today. Because of that dreadful sound we heard this morning—I see now it was an omen of this death. But of course, we didn't know that at the time.' His Latin had the prim precision of a scholar.

Marcus glared him. 'And who are you?'

'I am Scribonius, Mightiness. Auxiliary sevir at this shrine. And I assure you there was no impropriety. We are shortly expecting the visit of a very senior priest and it was . . .'

Marcus brushed all this aside. 'So you were in the courtyard all the time?'

Scribonius nodded. 'Naturally, Excellence. There is much to do before a sacrifice. It is all laid down strictly in the ritual. All of the implements to be cleaned and blessed. Dry herbs and kindling for the offering—it would be terribly inauspicious if anything was out of order.' In the circumstances that sounded unfortunate, and he tailed off helplessly.

Marcus was still frowning. 'And is there no other entrance to the shrine?' It was an obvious question. Almost every temple has a discreet door at the back, for the use of the priests. Once through that, of course, the body might be smuggled out though the 'Emperor's Entrance'. It would be very risky—there were people in the courtyard and in the high priest's house—but it was at least an explanation.

Meritus's face cleared. 'Of course. There is a small door there, behind the statue of the Emperor, though it has never been used in my experience. That is why the image I donated was placed in front of it.' He crossed to the life-size statue as he spoke, and then stopped, frowning. 'But the door is still fastened from the inner side—see for yourself, Excellence.'

My patron signalled for me to confirm his words, but of course the priest was right. The little door was fastened by a heavy wooden bolt, and it was clearly drawn across. I tried to open it, but the bolt was stiff. 'I don't think anyone went this way, Excellence,' I said. 'It couldn't have been bolted from outside, anyway.'

'In that case . . .' Meritus stopped, and shook his head. 'I still cannot believe it. It is impossible—simply impossible—that anyone could have moved that body out of here. I locked the other door myself, in full sight of everyone, and there has been somcone at the outer altar ever since.' He raised his huge hands helplessly.

I looked around the little shrine, but I found no inspiration therc either. There was no othcr way out that I could see. There were window spaces, of course, but windows in Roman temples are designed to let out sacrificial smoke rather than admit thc light—mysterious semi-darkness is part of the atmosphere—and these windows were no exception. They were narrow slits, high up under the eaves and very small. A committed young acrobat might just have manoeuvred himself through those apertures, but I could not imagine anyone else doing it—especially not someone carrying a corpse with him.

The other priest, who had not spoken yet— a nervous-looking man with a pale face and a shock of reddish hair—suddenly let out an anguished wail. 'It is a judgement, a judgement from the gods. First that appalling moaning sound this morning, and now this. We are all

39

cursed, all of us. Oh, blest divinities, have mercy on us all!' He moved past us to the altar, flung himself to his knees and began sobbing hysterically.

'Be quiet, Hirsus!' Meritus was sharp. 'If we have angered the gods we must make a proper propitiation. Whatever has happened, it is clearly no ordinary matter. You are unlikely to help by making an exhibition of yourself—and now see. You have sullied your sacrificial robes.'

Hirsus glanced down at himself in distress. It was true—in flinging himself to his knees in that fashion, he had knelt in something that I should have seen before, a dark stain in the shadows at the altar's foot. He touched the place with an exploring hand, and the fingers came away dark with a red and sticky substance.

Hirsus gave a helpless sob. 'Now I will have to purify myself again.' He staggered back towards the entrance, drunk with terror, and I heard him splashing himself with the water from the basin I had seen.

Marcus looked at me uneasily. Disappearing bodies were one thing, but that blood was real enough.

Meritus was clearly thinking the same thing. 'So there was a body here,' he said slowly. We must have all looked startled, because he hurried on. 'A real body, not merely the illusion of one. I was beginning to wonder, for

40

a moment, if I had been afforded a vision. But the corpse *was* here, just as I thought it was.' He seemed slightly relieved by this conclusion.

The balding priest, the one they called Scribonius, piped up again. 'This is the result of taking short-cuts with the rites—I told Hirsus we should have started the prayers again after he fumbled and dropped the sacrificial knife. But he wouldn't pay attention. And now see what has happened. The next thing we know there will be comets in the sky—it's all attested in the manuscripts.' He had few teeth, but his thin lips smiled with a kind of ghoulish satisfaction at his predictions having proved correct.

'This can't be all Hirsus's fault,' Trinunculus put in, with unexpected decisiveness. 'There was that dreadful noise as well. Perhaps he couldn't help dropping the knife—that is a kind of omen in itself. Oh, Great Jupiter preserve us. This must all be some kind of portent. Something serious. And at this shrine, too, among all the others. The priestly college warned of this sort of thing. Do you think it is a threat of some kind to the Emperor?' He hesitated. 'Should we send a warning to His Imperial Mightiness?'

There was a terrible pause. All of us, I imagine, were thinking the same thing. If this really was a dreadful warning from the gods— and even I could think of no other rational explanation—then clearly Commodus should

41

be told. But warned of what? That his fears of conspiracy were justified? Or that his lifestyle —cruelty, opulence, lechery and debauchery— had attracted the anger of his fellow gods? Whatever the message, it would be a brave man who carried it to Rome. And a very dead one, shortly afterwards. Commodus has a reputation for dealing briskly with bringers of unwelcome messages.

It was Meritus who broke the silence. 'Surely, the chief priest told me only this morning that there was an ambassador visiting Britainnia? Perhaps he could . . .'

Marcus's face cleared. 'Of course! Fabius Marcellus! The very man. We should send word to him at once. Indeed, he is on his way here at this moment.'

Meritus frowned. 'The body that I saw was an imperial legate,' he said slowly. 'That was clear from his seals and documents. If this was an omen . . .'

'Then he must be stopped,' Trinunculus finished. 'That's the meaning of the portent, surely! If the ambassador comes here, he will die. You are right, sevir, he must be warned at once.'

There was an almost audible sigh of relief from everyone at this more convenient interpretation. Marcus said, 'Of course!' Meritus looked as if a load had lifted from his head, and even Scribonius almost managed a smile. Hirsus, who had rejoined us, dripping

42

from his ablutions, cried 'Thank Hercules!' in a dramatic tone and threw himself to his knees before the altar again, promising offerings to the deity if the Emperor was spared. (Ironic, I thought, to offer a god sacrifices for preserving himself.)

After a moment Hirsus got to his feet. He had sullied his robe again, I noticed. I looked at Marcus. He was discussing with the sevir ways of sending a warning message to Ambassador Fabius, and seemed at ease again, but I could not share his evident relief. Interpretation of the 'sign' did not make the disappearing body any less a mystery. I bent to look more closely at that sticky stain—and as I did so my hand knocked something shiny at the base of the altar. I picked it up. It was a ring, a heavy seal-ring with the imperial insignia blazoned on it. A little lopsided, but a handsome thing. The sort of ring an ambassador might wear.

I got slowly to my feet, and held my find out for everyone to see.

There was a little pause. Then Meritus took the ring from me. 'I think, Excellence, with your permission, the high priest should see this.'

Marcus nodded. 'I will take it to him. And we can make arrangements for the message to be sent to Fabius, from both of us.'

'I should be grateful,' Meritus returned. 'I should attend to purifying the shrine. Finding a dead man here was bad enough, but then to touch his blood and then his ring! The omens for the shrine are terrible. We must cleanse ourselves, and it, at once. The four elements, you think, Scribonius?'

The thin priest nodded. 'The four elements at least, sevir.'

'Very well. Salt, Hirsus, and herbs—at once. And purify yourself again before you go. You, Scribonius, fetch a temple slave, since this floor must be scrubbed and cleansed by fire. Then you can purify the place with incense smoke. And you, Excellence, will you join us for the sacrifice?'

To my relief my patron shook his head. 'I think,' he said, 'that the high priest should hear of this at once. He should have finished the noonday sacrifice by now. We will leave you to your ablutions. Trinunculus here will show me where to go.'

The sevir nodded. 'As you please, Excellence. Though, I think, a little more ash upon your forehead as you leave?' He led the way to the outer altar, and supervised Trinunculus as he scooped up a handful of the still-warm dust and rubbed it reverently on our hair and faces. 'I would anoint you myself, only I have touched the ring, you know, and Scribonius would declare my hands unclean.' As we left him he was plunging the offending hand into the water jar.

Trinunculus led the way, back across the

courtyard to the central temple. 'I still don't understand,' he said, as we approached the podium and climbed the steps towards the inner cell, 'what can have happened to the body.'

I nodded. I had been thinking much the same thing. 'Always supposing,' I said suddenly, 'that it was a corpse at all.'

The others were looking at me in astonishment.

I was thinking aloud. 'Because a man is lying in blood, it does not follow that the blood is his—especially in a place like this, where sacrificial animals are offered every day. And I noticed myself how extraordinarily chill the water was. If a man wanted to make himself seem cold . . .'

'Is there,' Marcus said, 'anywhere in there a man could hide?'

Trinunculus looked baffled for a moment. Then he smiled. 'That statue of the Emperor, perhaps. I believe it's hollow. Meritus would know—he gave it to the temple when he was appointed. But even if it were, how could a man possibly get into it? It would have to come apart somehow.'

'Perhaps it does,' Marcus said. 'Libertus, go and have a look.'

I gulped. Walking into the priests' section of the temple was one thing. Manhandling a statue of a god—even a god I did not personally believe in—was quite another.

45

Especially when someone was already dead. I considered begging to be spared the honour, but then I looked at my patron's face. I swallowed hard and took a reluctant step towards the grove.

And as I did so there emerged—it seemed from the very columns around us—a high, unearthly, throbbing wail. A terrible inhuman sound that made my blood run cold.

I thought of men in torment, and was suddenly reminded—for no reason that I could explain—of the legend of that defiant old Icenian in the arena, screaming his last among the ravening dogs, and of his curse on all things sent from Rome. All things sent from Rome . . .

The sound faded, quivered, rose to a climax and died again.

Marcus or no Marcus, I turned tail and fled back towards the entrance gates. Even then, when I arrived at the safety of the veranda, my patron was there before me, with Trinunculus hard at his heels. The poor little slave boy, whom we had left there waiting our return, had thrown himself to his knees with my towel over his head, and was gibbering with fright.

And so, I must admit, was I.

CHAPTER FIVE

Trinunculus was the first to recover his composure. He took a long slow breath, settled his novice's wreath more firmly on his head (it had fallen sideways in his hurry), and said with as much priestly dignity as he could muster, 'That was the peculiar sound we told you about, Excellence. I wonder what trouble it foretells this time.'

'Whatever was it, in the name of Mars?' Marcus was looking decidedly shaken. His words confirmed how very shocked he was. It is not like Marcus to make meaningless enquiries. If the young priest had been able to tell us anything, he would surely have done so instead of bolting for the veranda with us like a startled rat.

He said as much, with patient courtesy. 'I regret, Excellence, that I don't know the answer to that question. Everyone in the temple has been asking themselves the same thing ever since this morning. There have been some wild rumours—animals, demons, spirits of the dead—but no one seems to have the slightest real idea. It is impossible even to say exactly where the sound is coming from.'

I nodded. I had thought myself that it had seemed to echo from the very walls. But though supernatural voices are the very stuff

47

of every religion, they are uncomfortable things to come across in person. I was as anxious as anyone to find some earthly explanation.

'Could it have been some kind of instrument?' I suggested. 'Some peculiar trumpet, possibly?' As soon as the words were uttered I regretted them. Of course it hadn't been a trumpet. It didn't sound remotely like any trumpet I'd ever heard, but I had felt the need to make some kind of down-to-earth suggestion—if only for the benefit of Marcus's slave, who was still visibly trembling.

Trinunculus extended his long-suffering courtesy to me. 'Certainly not one of the temple instruments, citizen. We have long-horns, certainly, and pipes and drums, but none of them could possibly make a noise like that. And it didn't seem to be a human sound. But here comes the person you should ask. If this *is* a portent, he's the one who'd know.'

He nodded across the courtyard. An aged priest in a toga and white robes was making doggedly towards us, supported down the temple steps by a pair of temple slaves.

'Ah!' Marcus said, without enthusiasm. 'The Chief Priest of Jupiter!'

I knew the man—and so, I imagine, did everyone in town. The *pontifex*, he liked to be called—the title they used to give to high-ranking priests in Rome. I am not sure that he was strictly entitled to the rank, though of

48

course the label is now much more loosely used. But even that distinction did not please the man. He had hoped, at one time, to be appointed to the highest priestly rank of all, the 'Flamen Dialis'—the Flamen of Jupiter. There is only one *flamen* for each deity—originally there were only three in all of Rome—but his failure to achieve the post had come to dominate his life. He was the next thing to a Flamen Dialis in the province, he insisted, and he voluntarily imposed upon himself many of the tiresome restrictions which attended that office.

There is some justification for his view, I suppose, since the Chief Priest of Jupiter in any city is the guardian of the sacred temple 'flame', and as such has the exclusive privilege of using it to light the altar-fire for public offerings. Certainly he was a most important dignitary and often the honoured celebrant at any civic festival. But this tall, cadaverous old man had held the post in Glevum for a decade, and his insistence on the flamanic rituals was the source of many jokes at his expense, especially since—like many priests—he had a much younger wife. His personal fire had dwindled with the years, the town wags said, until now there was very little 'flame' about him. Embers at best, they whispered, if not actually ashes.

His appearance, as he tottered towards us in his pale robes, certainly merited the description. He could not avoid the purple border on his toga, of course, since all Capitoline priests must wear that patrician stripe as a sign of their position, but apart from that he was entirely robed in white. His under-tunic was of purest wool, with only a suggestion of decoration at the hem, and that stitched in the palest gold and silver thread. Under his diadem of office he wore a white embroidered cap, very like the one the flamen must wear out of doors on all occasions. It even had the characteristic little strap beneath the chin, though he had not gone as far as having a copy of the flamen's famous little metal rod sticking up at the back. His hair— such as could be seen of it—was the merest straggling wisp of dusty white. So was his beard. His face was the colour of chalky ash, and he was generally so thin and frail that it seemed as if—like cinders—he would disintegrate to dust if stirred too enthusiastically with a stick.

His voice, too, was as fragile, dry and brittle as a fragment of burned parchment. He was hard of hearing, and notoriously chose to compensate by speaking in the merest murmur so that everyone else, also, had to strain their ears to hear. Today was no exception.

'Excellence!' he breathed, in that rustling ghost of a voice. 'I am sorry I was not here to greet you. But there were rituals . . . you understand.' He had reached us now, but we

50

all found ourselves bending forward a little to catch his words, Marcus included.

The pontifex chose to misinterpret this. He extended the sacerdotal staff of office in his ringless hand (another ostentatious choice, since *flamines* cannot of course tolerate the constriction of rings on their fingers, any more than they can permit knots anywhere on their person) and Marcus, for once, was forced to bend forward and kiss it reverently. It was not unheard of—even the mighty often choose to pay homage to the Rod of Jupiter—but I was sure that Marcus had not intended it. But it was an adroit way of establishing religious precedence. The old man was not as foolish as he looked, I thought. Meanwhile I dropped hastily to one knee. It would never do for me to remain standing while my patron bowed.

'All homage be to Jupiter, Greatest and Best, and to his priests who serve his temples.' Marcus muttered the formula dutifully, and straightened up again as quickly as protocol allowed. I followed suit, and grinned inwardly to see the forced smile on my patron's lips. But Marcus was not easily subdued. 'I was hoping to speak to you, most revered one,' he went on, speaking to the old priest firmly, but deliberately slowly and loudly, as though in deference to infirmity. I knew my patron; he was reasserting his authority. Sure enough . . . 'As representative of the governor, I have to make a decision. I felt I should at least ask

51

your opinion. About these unfortunate events this morning.'

The pontifex nodded slowly, but it was some moments before he spoke. The deliberation, and his frail appearance, gave him an air of thoughtful dignity. The dice were back in his cup. No wonder he was widely half revered as well as affectionately mocked. The old priest might need a discreet nudge from his acolytes at public festivals when it was his turn to speak, and mutter the rituals so that nobody could hear, but he knew how to impose himself when the occasion demanded it. I found myself wondering how much of his deafness and apparent dithering was a conscious choice.

'The body?' He did not avoid the ill-omened word, as Marcus had so carefully done. 'Alas, unfortunate events indeed. It is as well I did not go into the shrine myself. It is not permitted for a pontifex to set eyes on such a thing—but I heard that one had been found. A dreadful portent.'

'You heard that now it has disappeared?'

'*What* did you say?' No careful pauses now. The question seemed startled out of him, and the creaking voice was clearly audible.

'Dis-ap-peared, Mightiness,' Trinunculus repeated helpfully, stressing each syllable. 'Gone. Not there.' He outlined briefly what had happened since we arrived at the temple.

'But that's not possible,' the old priest said.

'Not *humanly* possible,' Trinunculus supplied.

The pontifex looked startled. 'Indeed.' The pale eyes flickered with sudden animation. It might have been anxiety, or amusement. 'Dear me. A sign from the gods right here in my own temple. We haven't had a proper sign for years.' He clasped his hands solemnly and raised his eyes to the symbol of the sun god on the pediment. 'Great and Immortal Jove, I am honoured,' he intoned. 'I vow a thank-offering to you this afternoon.' He unclasped his hands and refocused his attention on the assembled mortals. 'Well, this is very unexpected. A sign! Dear me.'

Marcus looked at me and raised an eyebrow, but when he turned back to the priest he was still resolutely smiling. 'And then there was that sound . . .'

'Sound? And when was this?'

'That appalling moaning. Only a few minutes ago. And I believe it happened once before, earlier this morning.'

The old man frowned. 'I think I was aware of something, now you mention it. Dear me. Another sign perhaps. Most odd.'

'But,' Marcus said, with increasing irritation, 'the question is, revered one, what it was a sign *of*. What was the meaning of it? Trinunculus here thinks these things are warnings.'

The pontifex nodded, the little cap dancing in sympathy. 'Oh, a warning, certainly. Clearly a warning.' He regarded us benevolently. 'They almost always are, you know. Warnings. I remember, when I was a young priest—'

This time Marcus cut him off. 'A warning, perhaps, to Fabius Marcellus? The ambassador from Rome? Trinunculus suggests that we should warn him not to come. After all, it was a legate's body that was found.'

The thin voice was no more than a rustle. 'Are we sure of that?'

'The sevir Meritus swears that the man was dressed in ambassadorial dress, and this was found beside the altar.' Marcus passed the ring to Trinunculus, to hand on to the old man. 'A seal-ring with an imperial eagle's head. That looks like a legate's ring to me.'

The old priest did not take it. He looked at it a moment, standing well back as though too close a contact with a ring might contaminate him, and gestured to Trinunculus to put it out of sight. 'Who was it who found the ring?' he said at last.

'The Citizen Libertus.' Marcus indicated me, and as the pale eyes flicked towards me in surprise I became uncomfortably aware of my disreputable attire. I had come dressed for an informal visit to the baths, not for an interview with the chief priest in his own temple. Marcus was obviously following a similar train of thought. 'I am his patron,' he said with dignity. 'He has assisted me many times with solving mysteries. He was at the baths when I was summoned here, and I asked him to accompany me, hoping he could help. And he has already done so, as you see.'

The pontifex produced another of his silences. I felt myself colour, and wondered again at the force of the personality disguised in that frail frame. Until a moment ago, I had not given a thought to the fact that I was inappropriately dressed. Of course, until Marcus identified my rank, the old priest must have mentally dismissed me as some kind of slave, and I had been effectively invisible.

'A citizen,' the old man murmured at last. 'I see. Well, citizen, what is your opinion? What is your explanation of events?' The tone was ironic, but he was admitting my existence by addressing me directly.

I felt that something concrete was expected. 'I do not have an explanation, Mightiness, but I do have a proposal. It has already been suggested that a message should be sent to Fabius Marcellus, warning him against visiting the city. In the circumstances, I think that would be wise—at least until we have cleared up this mystery.' That sounded unfortunate, in a temple, and I hastened to add, 'If there *is* a mystery. If this is a warning from the gods, that is all the more reason to prevent him coming.'

The pontifex held my eyes with his own pale ones. If there was fire within him there was no flicker of it in his gaze. His eyes were as cold and dispassionate as stone. 'But you do not believe in omens?'

That was dangerous. The succession of the Emperor had been partly based on omens. I found myself babbling. Of course I believed in omens, I declared—why, only the year before there had been a cloud over Glevum in the shape of a bird, and everyone now knew that meant a change of governor. 'If this had simply been a vision,' I finished breathlessly, 'I would have had no doubts. But the blood was real enough, and the ring was found by accident. Of course the gods could organise such things' (did I believe that? I wondered) 'but surely then these signs would have been immediately clear to everyone, and not discovered partially by chance.'

'But citizen,' Trinunculus had been following my words, 'if the gods intend us to have a sign, there is no such thing as chance. Perhaps the gods decreed that Hirsus should kneel down where he did, and that you should find the ring. In any case the temple slaves would have discovered everything, when they came to cleanse the shrine—as they would have to do, after an event like this.'

He was right, of course. I had no better explanation for any of it. Perhaps there really had been some divine intervention, and I'd been the unwitting tool of the gods. I shook my head. I didn't want to believe that. Or else the impossible had happened. I wanted to believe that even less.

'And then there was that unearthly noise as well,' Trinunculus went on. 'I agree with the citizen, Mightiness: someone should write to Fabius Marcellus without delay. Otherwise who knows what disasters might befall.'

The chief priest looked at his young acolyte with disfavour, and the thin, dry voice was drier than ever. 'The imperial ambassador was to honour this temple. And a flamen of the Imperial cult was coming here to lead the sacrifice. Special ceremonies and processions —I was to assist him—it was all arranged. And there would no doubt have been donations to the shrine. Dear me! It is most unfortunate. The Emperor's legates can be generous. It would have meant a great deal to the city.'

'And if anything happens to the legate, it will mean a great deal more to the city—most of it unpleasant!' Marcus put in impatiently. 'I don't need to remind you what happened last time . . .'

The old priest sighed. 'Indeed! Indeed! Well, I've no doubt you're right. I can scarcely ignore an augury like this.' He looked up to the pediment once more. 'As you command, O Mightiest and Best.' Another sigh. 'It seems a pity, that is all. Nevertheless, I suppose that we must send to Fabius Marcellus at once. To tell him that he should not come, you think?'

That was addressed to Marcus, and deliberately. It is up to the priests to interpret omens, but it is technically the responsibility of

57

the state to decide what averting action should be taken. And—in the absence of the Senate or the governor—that meant Marcus, in this instance. It was clear what the pontifex was up to. By publicly appealing to Marcus, he had astutely ensured that my patron, rather than himself, would be the one responsible if the Emperor's direct orders were countermanded. Marcus looked at me.

'To advise him, rather?' I suggested. 'Inform him of what's happened, and suggest he doesn't come—but perhaps the final decision should be his?'

Marcus nodded and the pontiff said, 'As you suggest, citizen.' There was an audible stirring of relief.

'I will see to it, revered one,' Marcus said, all courtesy again now that a formal decision had been reached. 'And if you would add your messenger to mine . . . If the ambassador decides not to arrive, presumably we should let that Imperial flamen from Londinium know. I am aware that the Emperor has written asking him to come here, but if there are bad omens in the temple, perhaps he would prefer not to attend either.'

Was it my imagination, or did the eyes of the pontifex flicker with satisfaction? Of course, being a flamen to the Imperial cult was by no means the same thing as being the Flamen of Jupiter. Every emperor had his own flamen these days, and no doubt this visitor had

58

merely been the flamen of one of the earlier Aurelians, retired to the provinces when his reign was done. But I suspected that, despite his words, the old man had not relished the prospect of taking second place to a flamen of any kind, especially in his own temple.

'Very well, I'll send to him this very afternoon,' the pontifex replied, with the ghost of a smile. 'As soon as I've made that sacrifice I vowed. Or should I wait until you've heard from Fabius Marcellus? It is possible that he will take no notice of your warnings. Dear me. Always a headstrong fellow. I knew him once.'

'You did?' Marcus was surprised.

'Commanded a garrison over to the west. I was called upon to make some altar offerings —at the burial, you know.'

We nodded. Even I had heard of this. Of course a pontifex cannot look upon a corpse— as he had just told us himself—but it was not a body they were burying. Jupiter was a favourite with the army and every year there was a major festival in which their old altar was interred with great ceremony in an unmarked place at the edge of the parade-ground—presumably to save it from desecration if the garrison moved on—and a new one was set up close by.

'I am sure even Fabius Marcellus will heed the warnings of the gods,' Marcus said. 'Especially if both of us are urging it. I will send my swiftest messenger to you, as soon as I have composed a letter to the legate. If you would be gracious enough to compose another, pontifex, my rider can take both despatches together. Then when we have an answer from Fabius, you can send a message to Londinium. That should still arrive in time to save the Imperial flamen a wasted journey.'

'Of course, Excellence, anything you wish,' the old priest assented, though with obvious reluctance. I wondered why, since he had virtually suggested this solution himself. Was he suddenly regretting those lost donations to the temple? Or was he unwilling to forgo the honour of appearing on a public podium in company with an imperial legate? 'The temple and its servants are naturally at your command, in anything that does not touch directly on the gods.'

If this was a struggle for authority, Marcus seemed oblivious of it. 'Then I shall return home and write to Fabius Marcellus at once. I'll send to you about the eighth hour. My man is an expert on horseback; he can leave tonight. I can arrange fresh mounts for him along the way, and safe passage for him across the sea to Gaul if necessary. Given fine weather he should reach Fabius Marcellus before he sails. For now, revered one, hail and farewell.'

The old priest inclined his head, and with a gesture of benediction walked unsteadily back to his temple, presumably to start his sacrifice.

Marcus watched him for a moment and then turned to me. 'You are looking thoughtful, my old friend. I know that face. You've thought of something which might help to throw some light on this unnerving affair?'

I was as mystified as he was, and if this was supernatural I didn't want to get involved, but I made my suggestion all the same. 'Merely that it might be prudent, Excellence—since the high priest has put the temple slaves at your disposal—to organise a little search. Of the temple and precinct and perhaps the streets around—just to be quite sure that someone hasn't hidden this body somewhere obvious.'

Marcus frowned. 'It's hard to see how anyone could have managed that. But as usual, old friend, you're right. It would be reassuring to find a human hand in this.' He turned to the temple slave who was still standing by. 'See to it.'

'At once, Excellence,' the man replied, and hurried off.

I made to do the same, and Marcus himself turned to leave, followed with evident relief by his servant. But before I could make my escape my patron called after me. 'And you, Libertus, check up on that statue in the shrine. And call on me at home, about the same hour as I told the pontifex. Give the citizen his towel, slave!'

The servant thrust the damp cloth into my hands, and they were gone.

CHAPTER SIX

I glanced uncertainly at Trinunculus who was still standing beside me. Of all the things I did not wish to do that afternoon, going back into that chilling little shrine was close to the very top of the list—ranking only a little after being sentenced to hard labour in the mines or being obliged to face the dogs in the arena. However, Marcus had given his instructions, and I was more or less obliged to obey them—otherwise there was a distinct chance that I might be faced with one of those even more disagreeable alternatives.

I swallowed. 'I suppose I must,' I said, and added with as much aplomb as I could muster: 'You will accompany me, of course?' If I was obliged to go, I thought, I would be much more comfortable in the company of a priest. In the company of anyone, in fact, but of a temple priest in particular.

Trinunculus nodded cheerfully. 'Of course. Are you not here on the orders of His Excellence?' He led the way from the veranda and back across the court towards the altar precinct. If he saw my nervousness he gave no sign of it. 'This way.'

Once more I followed him unwillingly.

It was no better the second time. If anything, the stone-faced giants on their plinths seemed to frown down at me with even more displeasure than before.

'You have heard the story of the curse?' I said, a little apprehensively—this hardly seemed the place for such a question.

Trinunculus however, gave me a cheery smile. 'I have, of course. There's been gossip about it ever since that body was discovered. But I don't believe that there is anything to fear from that. Not with this lady looking on.' He gestured to a particularly disapproving statue of Minerva. As I looked towards it, I saw a form scurry out of one of the outer buildings and hasten ahead of us towards the Imperial shrine.

Trinunculus had seen him too. 'We should hurry, citizen, if you wish to look at that statue this afternoon. They will be cleansing the temple otherwise, and you can hardly interrupt the rituals again. There's Scribonius, now.'

Of course it was Scribonius. Once it was pointed out to me, there was no mistaking that small anxious figure, but for a moment I hadn't recognised the man. He had clearly been into the robing rooms to change. He had abandoned his priestly robes, and his expensive shoes, and he was now hobbling barefoot, dressed only in a wretched sackcloth tunic, with arms bare and his hair artistically dishevelled. It was a chilly afternoon, and I almost felt sorry for the fellow.

I quickened my pace. 'This will be the

second time the senior sevir has had to purify the shrine today.' I was still thinking about that curse.

Trinunculus grinned. 'Well, we can rely on Scribonius to help him do it right. He knows every syllable of the rituals. See him now, stopping at the outer altar. Probably wants to get himself some ashes. Never a man to do a thing by halves!' And indeed, the auxiliary sevir was scooping up handfuls of ashes from the shrine and applying them not only to his forehead, but to his arms and legs as well. He was beginning to look more like a defendant at the law court, making a public show of penitence, than a respectable Imperial priest on his way to officiate at a shrine.

'A bit inclined to overdo the symbols, some of these seviri.' Trinunculus was grinning more widely now. 'Of course, Scribonius probably feels that he has to prove himself, given his background. He's always finding fault with Hirsus, for example, claiming that he's overlooked some part of the ritual and is about to bring bad luck upon us all. But here we are. You'd better wash your hands again, but that should be enough—those ritual ashes are still on your forehead.'

We were at the grove entrance now and there was nothing for it but to do what I had come for, although I would have liked to hear a little more. Even if there was no human puzzle here—and on balance I was certain that there was—I was still anxious for all the information I could get. And it wasn't going to be easy. One cannot demand answers from a priest in the same way as one can from other men. Not only do they trade in mystery, but if they *do* have supernatural powers the consequences of a mistake could be disastrous. I have no wish to find myself turned to stone, or transfixed by a thunderbolt from an affronted Jove. Besides, there was the story of the curse.

'Here we are,' Trinunculus said again.

His nonchalant confidence emboldened me. I took a deep breath, but when I went inside there was nothing particular to see. It was almost a disappointment. A temple slave was scrubbing at the floor, Scribonius was fussing with a censer, and Hirsus and Meritus (who were not wearing penitential tunics, but had confined themselves to unfastening their belts and leaving their garments disarrayed) were standing by the altar discussing the relative merits of a sheep or a pig as an extra sacrifice.

'Scribonius is quite right, you know,' Meritus was saying. 'Since the first offering was so inauspicious, naturally it is not enough merely to repeat the same. We must expiate the fault. A pig is the traditional—' He broke off when he saw me. 'Citizen?'

'The statue,' I said, in some embarrassment. 'I am to look at it. Marcus Aurelius Septimus's orders.'

Hirsus looked dismayed. 'But we are preparing . . .' He fluttered nervous hands at me.

Meritus silenced him with a gesture.

'Only a formality,' I said, feeling extremely foolish and in the way. In that small space there was scarcely room for me as well. I stepped over the toiling slave, edged past Scribonius and his waving incense, and made my way towards the huge gilded image, while the others watched me in disbelief. It was a formality, of course. The image may have been hollow but it was extremely heavy, and though there were one or two small holes in the statue, at the base and at the eyes for instance, there was clearly no way anyone could enter it.

'My thanks,' I murmured, and I shuffled out.

'I'm sure he entered the temple with his left foot first,' I heard Scribonius complain, as soon as he thought I was out of earshot. 'Oh, Hercules! More evil omens. Now we'll have to do it all again.'

I looked back. Scribonius was plying his censer as though I had contaminated the air, Hirsus was fanning the statue half-heartedly with sacred herbs, and Meritus was clearly urging the temple slave to wash the floor again, before he could begin the sacrifice. I began to feel like an evil *genius* being driven from his haunt.

It was a relief to get out of the grove and

66

find Trinunculus. 'If you have finished here, I will see you to the gate,' he offered, with that cheerful smile. 'Did you discover anything, citizen?'

'Nothing of any consequence. I think Marcus had some notion that the body, or perhaps the killer, might have been hidden in that statue of theirs, but there was obviously no possibility of that.'

'I think I could have told you so, citizen, before you looked—though obviously you had to see it for yourself. It took half a dozen slaves to bring that statue in, and even then they were struggling to move it. It was Meritus's endowment to the temple, when he was elected to office. Mind you, it was cast in his own metal, with his own gold used to gild it—he only had to pay the craftsman for the job. Though no one knows exactly who that craftsman was.'

'Is that something that a donor must disclose?' I said, wondering if some temple custom had been breached. I had never heard of it, but I knew that a priest's life is full of little prohibitions: even the mention of a nanny-goat, for instance, will send a Priest of Jupiter into a frenzy of ritual cleansing. 'I suppose a statue fashioned by inappropriate hands might be a dreadful omen in itself?'

Trinunculus smiled. 'That kind of thing is not important, citizen. What matters is what happens to it here. There's a fellow called

Lucianus—one of Meritus's supplicants—brings boxes of gifts to the Imperial altar almost every month. Bells, silver, statuettes, all kinds of things. No one knows where he obtains them from.'

'Lucianus the wretched?' I enquired, remembering the plaque, though from this account of his wealth he didn't sound very wretched to me.

He grinned. 'The very same. The temple slaves say he must have tried at all the other shrines, without success, and now he's trying the Imperial Divinities. Meritus must be delighted—the sevir's year of office is largely judged on the value of that year's offerings. That's why they make such handsome gifts themselves. But all offerings are simply laid before the gods, with a ritual prayer and sacrifice, and purified with sacred fire and water. That's all that is required. So there's nothing wrong with what the sevir did. It's simply odd, that's all.'

'Odd?'

'Most of the seviri, when they are appointed, are very anxious to tell everyone how much their "dowry" cost, and what important artists they paid to do the work. But not Meritus. Of course, there's no reason why he should have told us, but it is almost as if he relishes secrecy.' Trinunculus looked at me a moment, as if considering, and then added in an undertone, 'It's like the story of his life—he

68

never gives a full account of that.'

We were under Minerva's disapproving stare again, but this blatant piece of temple gossip stopped me in my tracks. I braved the goddess's anger long enough to say, 'But surely . . .? I heard he was slave-manager of an estate?'

'Oh, certainly he was,' Trinunculus replied. 'He has his *pilleus*—the freeman's cap—and his certificate to prove it. But how did he become the manager? He is no ordinary slave. He can do more than read and write his name—he knows the orators: and it is rumoured that he can ride a horse, play an instrument, even quote the Greek philosophers. How did he learn to do all that? It's clear he wasn't born on that estate. So was he born a slave at all? That's what I want to know.'

I looked at him. 'I was captured into slavery myself,' I said, with some feeling. 'I can understand why any man would avoid talking about it—or about the life he had to leave behind. Or he may have been the pet slave of some wealthy man. He is good-looking enough, and some of them are taught all sorts of things to be companions to their masters. If you had risen to wealth and dignity wouldn't *you* avoid talking about your humble beginnings? And what other explanations are there? That he sold himself into slavery to clear a debt? Or was sentenced to it, to atone

69

for a crime? Neither seems likely, for a man who made his master's fortune, and rose so high in his esteem.'

I had not meant to speak so sharply. Even to me it sounded like a rebuke. 'What made you question it?' I asked more gently.

The young priest looked abashed. 'It is only that he has such skills. And once when we were talking, he mentioned Aquae Sulis. Not casually, but as if he knew the town. Then when Scribonius pressed him, he tried to change the subject—said that he had been there with his master once.' He glanced at me. 'And most of all, I've noticed when he dons his robes he does not seem to have a brand. Or ever to have had one, if you see what I mean.'

I did see. I have unhappy memories, not only of the branding on my back, but of the painful surgery when it was removed. There is a deep scar on my shoulder to this day. All the same, I shook my head.

'Not every master brands his slaves, Trinunculus. And as for Aquae Sulis, his story may be true. After all, as manager he was engaged in trade. He must have travelled to many towns.'

'You may be quite right, citizen. And as I say, it is not in Meritus's nature to confide. Not like Hirsus, for example, who will talk about his wretched childhood to anyone who will listen. Now, he *was* a pet slave, though never to a man. He was given to his owner's

70

grandmother—her lucky talisman, she said. She was a superstitious woman—always consulting oracles—and mean as a tax-collector, by all accounts. But she promised him his freedom when she died, and a handsome pension with it. Hirsus had hopes of settling down—there was an attractive slave he knew, apparently, whom he hoped to buy and free and set up a household with.'

'But his mistress broke her promise?'

Trinunculus laughed. 'Not at all. Her will set him free, with a substantial sum. But he had to wait a long time to collect it. The old woman lived to an astounding age—outlived all her sons and daughters—she must have been quite eighty-five when she died. Yet she would never part with Hirsus while she lived. And then, of course, it was too late. The slave he had fallen in love with had been sold on, and at forty-five Hirsus was getting to be an old man himself.'

'He must have inherited a goodly sum and used it well, to have been made sevir here.'

'His investments flourished, certainly. The gods were smiling on him, he believed.' Trinunculus grinned. 'Though it is my belief he was just extremely cautious. He's like a woman in his ways sometimes. The old lady had him from a child, and instilled in him such a fear of omens that he will hardly change his sandals without consulting the auguries.'

'I thought all you priests were much the

71

same in that?' I said. Foolish! I meant it lightly but I saw the young priest flush. He had seen my words as a rebuke, again. I tried to repair the damage. 'Scribonius, for example, is a stickler for the rules. Why is that, do you think? You said that he felt he had to prove himself.'

Too late. Trinunculus had put a halter on his tongue. 'I talk too much,' he said. 'It is a fault of mine. The pontifex has had occasion to rebuke me for it before now. I am sorry, citizen, I have already said too much. I was accompanying you to the gate, I think.' He drew his robes around him, and walked purposefully on.

I did my best. I walked beside him, cajoling, flattering, urging. I even found myself pleading that, as a Capitoline priest, it was his duty to assist the governor—and I was the representative of his representative. To no avail.

'My duty as a priest,' Trinunculus replied, in a sing-song voice, 'is to save my tongue for sacred purposes, and not to talk about my fellow priests.' The little speech was obviously a formula, and I guessed that the high priest had obliged him to repeat those words many times as part of a penance. And that was all I could get out of him, all the way across the courtyard to the gate.

At least, I thought, as I stepped out into the commercial hubbub of the forum, and began to make my way home through the busy streets, this time there had bccn no infernal wailing to speed me on my way.

CHAPTER SEVEN

So I was going home. And Gwellia would be waiting for me. I could still hardly believe it. After years of searching for the woman who had once been my bride, I had bccn reunited with her less than a month ago, and that was in Londinium. This was the first time I had left her alone in my little workshop-cum-apartment in Glevum, and I had been much longer than I intended. I found that I was worrying about her a little as I hurried back. Would shc be anxious because I was late?

Ridiculous of course, but my heart gave a littlc skip; never, sincc I had been granted my freedom, had anyone but my slave Junio worried about me—except my patron, when he needed me. As I had said to Marcus, Gwellia was no longer legally my wife, but I found myself hurrying home like a new bridegroom as I turned into the little alley where my workshop lies.

I found myself looking at it with new eyes.

I rent a building in part of that straggling western suburb which has sprung up outside the city walls over the last hundred years. No fine Roman pavements or towering columns here, only a collection of ramshackle buildings huddled together along haphazard lanes, the gutters often running with filth and slime and the stinking mud from the river margins. Perhaps it is not the most congenial of places. But it's my home, and I'm attached to it. The rooms are humble but adequate, the rent's affordable, and—despite the presence of a tannery on one side and a candlemaker's on the other—the place has never actually caught fire or collapsed, as other buildings in the area have been known to do. And my work had prospered. Some of the wealthiest men in Glevum had come here to order pavements— or at least sent their servants here on their behalf.

Why did I suddenly find myself needing to defend it to myself? Because it was not the situation I'd dreamed of for my wife. Ah, well! I picked my way down the alley, waved aside a turnip-seller and his donkey, and under the bold eyes of a woman hawking pies stepped over a large pile of dirt and rubbish in an entry, and came to the open shopfront which was mine. There was nobody about. I frowned.

I had expected my slave boy, Junio, to be attending customers.

'Junio?' I stepped over the piles of stone and tile which were my stock-in-trade, and went round the partition to the inner room.

And stopped. I would hardly have

74

recognised the place.

The inner workroom had been scrubbed and swept. The dusty piles of coloured *tesserae* which usually lay in heaps around the floor had been scooped up and placed in what looked like brand-new baskets and my tools were now ranged neatly along the wall. The shelves in the alcove had been dusted and arranged, and the meagre contents—oil, candles, cheese and bread—looked even more meagre now. Even the table had been washed and the fire—which we'd had such trouble to ignite—had been damped down, the hearth stones had been swept of ash and something was bubbling in a clean pot on the embers.

The place was sweet and clean, and like a home again, although I shuddered to think how much effort it had cost—and how much precious water must have been fetched to do all this. And there was still no sign of anyone.

'Junio?' I hardly trusted my voice.

But he did not answer. Instead it was Gwellia who scrambled down from the makeshift space above, her hair full of cobwebs and her arms full of the reeds and rags which formed my customary bedding.

'Is that you, Jun- Why, Libertus! Master!' She looked around for somewhere to put down her load and made a sort of modest bob in my direction. It wrenched my heart. I hated this—yet it was a kind of progress in itself. When she first came back to me, she'd had a tendency actually to abase herself in my presence, as her previous owners had demanded. I'd persuaded her out of that, at least, and we'd come to this uncomfortable compromise. It was not a sign of slavery, she argued; many Roman wives greet their husbands in that fashion, and—since it made her comfortable—I'd reluctantly agreed.

She bobbed again. 'Master, I was not expecting you so soon.'

That semi-curtsy still distressed me, when all I wanted was to take her in my arms. But I knew that would just embarrass her, so I said, 'Where's Junio?' Suppressed emotion made me sound quite brusque.

She misinterpreted it as a rebuke. I saw the look of horror on her face. I'd forgotten how vulnerable she had become. I tried to soothe the hurt. 'You have been very busy here,' I said, more gently.

'It was the rats, master. I found another nest of them down here. I thought . . .' She looked around helplessly. 'I'm sorry, master. I wanted to make myself useful. Of course, I realise I had no right to touch your possessions or do any of this without your instructions.'

I reached out a hand and touched her arm. 'But you have done exactly as I asked you to! I insisted that you were still effectively my wife, and you have attempted to behave like one. If I did not wish my habits to be disturbed, I should have instructed you to keep your place.'

She was still looking at me doubtfully. She looked so worn and timid standing there, and so proud of her handiwork, I didn't have the heart to tell her that the first time we cut *tesserae* again the dust would be as bad as ever.

'You have done well, Gwellia,' I said carefully. 'And I am glad you got rid of the rats. But where is Junio? I left him here cutting tiles for a pavement. He should have them ready for delivery by now. Where is he? Off buying honeycakes again?' I was getting too indulgent with that boy, I told myself. He knew that a scolding was the worst he could expect, though many masters would have had him flogged—the maximum legal punishment was death—for leaving the premises except on business for me.

My attempt at teasing only made things worse. 'Oh, master—husband.' I could see confusion brimming in her eyes. 'He has gone to the river for water.' She glanced down at herself and rubbed her hands hastily on her tunic. 'I am ashamed to greet you in this way. I had intended to clean myself when Junio came back . . .'

'And here he is, master,' Junio said, poking his curly head round the partition. I sensed a certain wariness in his manner, although outwardly he was his usual cheerful self. 'I have another water pail here.' He came into the room and set it down—a misshapen hammered copper affair with a handle, which I had found once abandoned on a heap, and usually reserved for mixing mortar in. Now most of it had been chiselled clean and it was brimful of water—though not from the river, clearly, since there was no trace of mud in it. This must have come from one of the public fountains, inside the city gates. Junio had had a lengthy walk.

Junio attempted to read my face. 'I am sorry, master,' he began at last. 'I didn't know . . .'

'I left you here to look after the shop,' I said patiently. 'I don't expect you to go off into the town without permission.'

Junio looked crestfallen, and gazed at the floor. It was Gwellia who spoke. 'Don't be angry with him, master. He thought to help me, that's all. I know fetching water is usually a woman's job. I was fetching it myself, at first, but he saw me struggling . . .'

'Are you telling me he volunteered? You must tell me what your secret is!' I smiled. Junio has carried water to the shop for years, but usually he complains at every step.

Junio looked at me uncertainly. 'Forgive me, master, what was I to do? I knew the lady was your wife, I saw she was having difficulties . . .'

'My back . . .' Gwellia said helplessly.

Of course. I regretted my teasing instantly. I had seen her naked shoulders, and I knew the scars of cruel whip marks they bore, where an

78

angry mistress had once had her flogged till bone and muscle had been laid bare. Gwellia still moved one arm with difficulty. I had a sudden vision of Junio, watching the woman I'd searched for all these years, seeing her struggling with the water pots—and my heart was filled with love for both of them.

For a moment I found myself deprived of speech: there seemed to be something in my throat.

'I am sorry, dear master, if I've done wrong,' Gwellia said earnestly. 'But the boy had finished his cutting. Besides, while he was working I couldn't clear the room . . .' She glanced at me, and added with a smile, 'I have tried to keep everything separate. All the colours in different baskets. And do not worry where I got those from. I found a denarius under all the dust. It had gone down between the floorboards. It paid for all the rushes and to spare.'

'No doubt a coin from the Phrygian steward, master?' Junio said. He glanced up at me slyly but swiftly returned to staring at the floor. He has a witty turn of mind, but I have strict rules about not mocking the customers.

But I had seen his lips twitch, and in spite of myself I was half laughing too. Of course I knew what he was alluding to. The Phrygian had been the particularly pompous and patronising household steward of a patrician customer of mine. He had visited us, with all the condescension of a god descending, and pulled out a purse to pay his master's bill—with such a flourish that he scattered the contents. That had punctured his dignity. He had sworn by all the furies that he had lost a coin, but we had never found it—though Junio and I had spent an entertaining half-hour watching him scrabble for it in the stone chippings.

'Then it seems he has donated these baskets for my tiles,' I said, knowing that I had capitulated. Somehow, with Junio, I find it hard to be strict for very long. Marcus is always mocking me about it. And now Gwellia had joined the household too! One look from her could always melt my heart. I would have to be doubly careful in future, I told myself. The Romans do not esteem any man who is not master in his own household. But I was still grinning like an idiot.

'Very well!' I went on, with a pretence at severity. 'We will say no more about it. This time! But in future, Junio, please don't leave the workshop unattended without my permission. Suppose a customer had called?'

'Pardon me, dear master, but a customer did call,' Gwellia said, with a shy smile. 'A wealthy gentleman. He wanted you to repair a pavement for him. He must have been in a hurry, because he came in person—offering fifty sesterces if you'd come at once.'

'And what did you tell him?'

'I told him you were otherwise engaged today—on important business with your patron.'

I turned to Junio. 'You see?' Fifty sesterces was not a princely sum, but it was something: and agreeing a job like that, where a price is fixed, is as good as a contract under law. 'I doubt if he will venture here again. So, while you were out, we lost an opportunity.'

That was unfair, and I knew it. Junio was often absent from the workshop, usually with me. I did not dare to think of all the similar opportunities that must have escaped us, over the years.

'But you have not lost it, citizen!' Gwellia was looking at me with something of the old sparkle in her eyes. 'I told him that, if he were to increase the fee a little, perhaps you could be induced to see him next.' She looked at me, smiling openly at my astonishment. 'I am sorry, dear citizen, if that was a mistake. It is something I used to hear one of my masters say. It always seemed to have the right effect. It did here, too. Now he's promising a hundred sesterces for the repair if you will call and look at it before tomorrow night.'

'A hundred sesterces?' That was a handsome increase. I would never have dared to ask for half as much. I found myself smiling broadly in return. I had forgotten that my ex-wife had such unexpected talents. I attempted to reassert my dignity by saying, judiciously,

81

'But it is doubtful I could do it very quickly. Marcus wants me to solve this problem at the temple.'

'It's not a very large repair, he says. Some of the outer border of the pattern was made of poor quality tile. He says you would remember the pavement—it is in his entranceway. You laid a mosaic for him once before, he tells me, in his dining room, and you warned him about this problem when you came.'

'I did?' For a moment I could not recall anything about it. 'Who was this customer? Did he leave a name?'

'Gaius Honorius Optimus. He seemed to think that it would mean something to you.'

It did. I looked at Junio and we both burst out laughing together. Honorius Optimus was the customer with the pompous Phrygian steward.

'Well, he can afford a hundred sesterces, master. He used to be a commander in the legions, and he made a fortune out of it. As you know—you've seen that great town house of his.' Junio grinned back at me, obviously delighted at this new turn of events. 'He must be in a hurry too, to offer double the fee. He always seemed to me a man who'd walk a mile to save a quadrans.'

'He is. That's why he had some idiot lay that cheap pavement at his door,' I said drily. 'A few more sesterces, and he could have had marble, or proper tiles at least. But these! I

82

could see they were lifting and splitting then—
they had not been laid for long, and that was
almost two years ago. I offered to replace
them at the time, but he refused. I wonder why
he's in such a hurry now?'

'He's hoping for an important guest, that's
why!' Gwellia said. 'Some imperial ambassador
who is visiting the town.'

I thought of the temple and that
disappearing corpse, and I felt a shiver run
down my spine. 'There is an imperial
ambassador? Here? Now?'

'Not now,' Gwellia said, with a smile. 'But
there's one expected in a little while.
Something about a special service for the
Emperor at the Imperial shrine.'

'Surely not Fabius Marcellus!' I exclaimed.

'I think that *was* the name.' Gwellia frowned
with concentration. 'Of course, it didn't mean
anything to me. But your Honorius Optimus
was terribly impressed. Apparently he knew
the man, because they were in the army
together. Not that they were especially friendly
then. They were officers in the same unit—
only this Fabius Marcellus person had wealthy
patronage, and he soon went on to higher
things. From the way your client talked about
it, I don't think he was very pleased at the
time—but of course now his old rival's an
imperial ambassador, he's very keen to claim
acquaintanceship.'

'Gwellia, you are a marvel. You gleaned all

this in a few moments' conversation. Optimus would never had said any of that to me.'

Gwellia smiled. 'Ah, but he wasn't really saying it to me. He was talking to some pompous steward he brought with him. I am a woman, and a slave—he hardly noticed I was standing there.' She looked at me. 'What are you frowning at, Libertus? Do you doubt the truth of what he said?'

'Something has just occurred to me. Oh, there's an imperial legate on his way all right. And his name is Fabius Marcellus. But how in the name of all the gods did Optimus know that? Only my patron and the high priests knew about it—and they only received the communication this morning.'

'Other people know about it now. He said his wife's slave heard it in the market-place,' Gwellia said. 'Taking back a length of woollen cloth.'

I nodded, impressed again by her talent for deriving information.

'Then there's your answer, master,' Junio put in. 'The pontifex knew: no doubt he told his wife—and she'll have sent into the town for cloth. Something very expensive too, I expect, which will have set the whole town's tongues wagging again.' He saw my quizzical look and added quickly, 'Well, you know what he's like, master, always trying to be as holy as a flamen. But insofar as he's the flamen, master, she is his flaminia. You know how strict the regulations are, and yet she manages to find a way around them. She has quite a reputation for fashion. He will not let her comb her hair, but last year when the style was for long blond hairpieces, she had a fair-haired slave girl sent in specially from the Rhinelands. She had *that* combed and curled and wore it as a wig, with a little ritual sprig of fresh leaves tucked into her veil, to keep her husband happy. And her gown is always of pure dyed cloth. I'm sure she'd want a whole new outfit to greet the legate in.'

I nodded. The pontifex was whispered to indulge his younger wife. That was not altogether surprising perhaps, since his hoped-for job depended on it. The Pontifex of Jupiter must have a wife, and if he loses her—to death or desertion—must resign his office. Discreet divorce is not a possibility. A few lengths of costly cloth must seem a small price to pay for the lady's loyalty. 'All the same,' I said, 'I am surprised the news about the legate's visit has travelled quite so fast. It's evident the whole town knows already.'

Gwellia said, 'Perhaps not quite the whole town yet, citizen. I think, from what he was saying, that Honorius Optimus was one of the first people to hear. And he came here straight away. He said he was anxious to have his entry-pavement repaired before everyone else in Glevum heard the news and wanted to do the same.'

I smiled. That was unlikely to happen now—though it might have done, without this temple corpse. Whenever a dignitary visited the town, there was always competition to entertain him. Sometimes by moving out altogether and lending him a house (though that was a signal honour), but everyone who aspired to be anyone vied to provide banquets, dancers, poets, even lunch—anything, where the host could be seen in the great man's company. And of course every banquet-giver (and his wife) wanted new murals and decorations, and, if not new mosaics, at least mosaics in excellent repair. A pavement-maker may find himself suddenly in great demand.

But not on this occasion. My patron was at this instant in his apartments, writing a message to the imperial ambassador urging him not to come. I wondered whether I could confirm this contract with Optimus before he discovered the change of plan, especially since Marcus's commemorative niche would now presumably not be wanted either.

The thought of Marcus recalled me to my duties. 'Speaking of clothes,' I said briskly, 'I must change my own. I am to call on Marcus this afternoon. I shall need my toga. I am to be there about the eighth hour.'

'How are you supposed to judge what time that is?' Gwellia asked, practical as ever.

It was a reasonable question. She and I were

not brought up to 'hours'. The Romans operate like that, dividing the period of daylight into twelve equal parts, but I had no fancy waterclocks or time-candles, so I could only gauge the time by the position of the sun. When it was cloudy, like today, it could be very difficult to guess the 'hour'—especially in wintertime, as now, since obviously the hours get shorter with the days.

'I shall simply have to get there as quickly as I can,' I said. I could wait for Marcus: he must not wait for me. I made towards the staircase. 'Junio, you can help me into my toga. And bring a bowl. I'll have some of that clean water to rinse my face. Gwellia, my dear, you can do the same. I know that, until we get to market, you have no other garments of your own, but you will find an old tunic of mine underneath the bedding. It's rather torn and patched, but at least it's clean. Well?' I added, as I saw her stricken face. 'What is it? What's the matter, Gwellia?'

'It's that tunic, master!'

'What about the tunic?' Surely she was not embarrassed by the thought? It was a bit too big for her, perhaps, but otherwise there was little to show that it was a male garment.

'I . . . I'm afraid I've torn it up to replace your bedding with. I've put down new reeds, and thrown away the old . . .' She gestured to the pile she had been carrying when I came in. 'I found the tunic. It seemed old and

87

discarded, so I cut the seams and used it to make the bedding comfortable.'

She was biting her lip. And she'd called me 'master' again, I noticed. She was calling me 'Libertus' only a few moments earlier.

I debated a moment how to answer her. 'I sometimes wore that tunic into bed,' I said at last, 'while Junio washed the other one. I don't know what I'm going to do instead.' I raised my eyebrows at her, and she looked at me, blushed, and laughed.

'What did you do with the old bedding rags?' I demanded.

There was the suspicion of a pert twinkle in those beautiful brown eyes. 'What do you think I used to wash the floor?'

There was no possible reply to that, so I made none. I simply went upstairs to change—into an attic where that feminine touch had been at work again.

A little while later, full of a late lunch of bread and cheese and draped uncomfortably in my toga, I was on my way to Marcus's apartments, with Junio at my heels. Meanwhile Gwellia (dressed rather fetchingly, I thought, in a spare tunic of Junio's) was making a hasty visit to the clothseller's stall before the market closed. Indulgent of me, Marcus would doubtless say, since I had given her some money for a length of cloth, but I had also asked her to keep her ears open for any more gossip about Fabius Marcellus. If anyone could acquire that kind of information, I told myself, it was my clever wife.

CHAPTER EIGHT

Marcus did not keep me waiting long. In fact, no sooner had I been shown in to wait, and offered the customary plate of sugared figs and a beaker of watered wine, than Marcus burst into the receiving room. He was agitated. I could see that from the way he strode in behind his slave without even giving the lad time to announce him.

This unexpected entrance took me by surprise. I put down my drink and struggled to my feet. He waved aside any attempt to make the usual obeisances.

'Ah, there you are, Libertus,' he said, as if he had been searching for me from attic to ground. 'I have despatched the letter to Fabius Marcellus. So tell me, what did you discover at the temple after I left? Sit down at once and give me your report.' He stretched himself on a comfortable couch and gestured to the carved stool which I'd just vacated.

His manner was so urgent that I found it difficult to confess that I'd discovered nothing. 'I regret, Excellence, I have nothing to report. No sign of a hiding-place for a body, still less—'

I was going to say 'a murderer', but he made

89

a gesture of impatience. Whatever was troubling him, it was not that.

'So you found no body. I was afraid of that.' He helped himself absently to a fig. 'Or perhaps I was secretly hoping that you wouldn't.' He bit into the fruit. 'I need hardly tell you that nothing was discovered in the temple grounds—only an old beggar in a ditch behind the grove, right in the corner of the precinct wall. Found himself a perfect place to hide, it seems, and went there once too often. Must have been there a month or more—it's hard to say. They tell me the rats have eaten him. I've given orders to dispose of it.'

Into a paupers' grave, he meant. Piled onto a cart and tipped into an unmarked public pit, poor fellow—but at least it would be a proper resting place. Vagabonds who fall prey to thieves or wolves are often denied even that privilege.

Marcus brought me sharply back to the present. 'So, the question still remains. Was it a real body lying at the shrine or was it a visionary one? I don't know which is worse, old friend: to find the corpse of this legate in the temple, or to fail to find it when it should be there. If this *was* an omen from the gods, then Jove alone knows what trouble lies in store for us. If it was a real body, we are in trouble already.' He had been gesturing at me absently with the remains of his fig, but now he swallowed it and took another. 'My wife's

90

convinced it is this Icenian curse come true. What do you make of it all, Libertus?

I hesitated. The temple is not something I truly understand. I attend the public rituals at the Capitoline shrine, like any citizen (absence from these things is likely to be noticed), but these are not really my gods, and Marcus knew it. This doesn't make me altogether a hypocrite, or so I told myself. I worship the power of the universe: it probably does not matter to the sun spirit, for instance, whether you call him 'Apollo' or 'Cunomaglus'—and many local Celtic gods have now got Roman names. So I have always treated the Olympian deities, if not with reverence, at least with a certain respect.

But this disappearing body had not manifested itself at the shrine of Jupiter. It had happened in front of the Imperial altar, and whereas I was prepared to concede the potential power of Jove, I was extremely sceptical about Commodus's ability to offer miracles. However, he was my emperor, and it was very important not to say anything dismissive.

'You think it was a vision, Excellence? That ring was real enough,' I said at last.

Marcus nodded. 'Exactly, and that's what worries me. Page!' He turned to his servant. 'You may wait outside.' He waited until the boy had gone, then smiled at me triumphantly. 'You see that I have heeded your advice,

Libertus. I know that you are always warning me that slaves have ears.'

I gulped. This was even more serious than I'd thought. Usually Marcus was inclined to speak as freely in the presence of his servants as if they were not there, as Optimus had done with Gwellia. Like any other Roman, he seemed to believe that slaves—being mere possessions—were as incapable of independent thought as any other piece of furniture. But I had been a slave myself. I knew how easy it was for the blank-faced attendant in the corner to be following the conversation and, worse, how eagerly he will repeat it to his fellows afterwards. In a large household there is always gossip, and there is often someone, anxious to save his slave-price and be free, who might be tempted to betray his master to his enemies for the promise of a few *denarii*.

So I was not sorry that Marcus had dismissed his slave. What worried me was that he'd thought of it. Whatever my patron wanted to confide, it was evidently very sensitive indeed.

'What did you wish to tell me, Excellence?'

He looked at me and his hand went out to take another fig. It was a particularly large and sickly-looking one, but he bit it absently in half as though he were almost unaware of it. 'The question is, Libertus . . .' He took a deep breath. 'Do you suppose the Emperor has sent another ambassador to Glevum, secretly? Ahead of Fabius Marcellus, perhaps, and that is the ambassador who got himself killed today? I dismissed the idea previously, but now I'm not so sure.'

'Another legate in Britannia? Without your knowledge?' I shook my head. 'I am sure that is unlikely, Excellence. And—forgive me— what would be the point?'

He gulped down the fig. 'Perhaps he did send someone here, to spy on us? You know what the Emperor is like, all victory and honour be to his divine name. He suspects everyone. If he intends to honour the city, it would be very likely, don't you think, that he would send a spy to sniff us out beforehand? You see, that would explain everything. If someone had been lurking in the city, in disguise . . . ?'

The idea had not occurred to me, but now that he had raised the question, I could see the force of it. But there was a flaw in Marcus's reasoning. I tried to point it out as delicately as I could.

'But surely, Excellence, even if Commodus sent a spy—as I agree he very likely would—he would not have chosen an official legate for the job. An imperial ambassador causes such a stir—you said yourself that you would have heard if one had landed anywhere in the province. I'm certain, if the Emperor posted spies to Glevum, he would send them in some

93

less conspicuous guise. A travelling merchant perhaps, come to the market-place with goods from Rome? Even a well-placed slave or two?' I meant that there were almost certainly a dozen imperial informers in the town already, if not actually here in Marcus's house.

It seemed my patron was aware of that. 'Of course, I would have expected all of that. And naturally, I'm being very careful. You notice that I sent my slave away! Only that doesn't solve the problem. It wasn't a visiting merchant who was found dead this morning at the Imperial shrine. I would be less worried if it were. That corpse was an imperial ambassador—or at least the apparition of one.'

Something stirred in the recesses of my brain. I sat up sharply. 'I suppose we can be sure of that? The corpse was wearing "rich civilian clothing", the sevir said.'

Marcus stared at me a moment, then said thoughtfully, 'By Mithras, Libertus, I believe you're right. Meritus only concluded it was an ambassador because of the documents and seal. I don't suppose, for all his wealth, he's ever seen an actual ambassador before. After all, he was only slave-manager on a remote estate. And we have only his interpretation to go on.'

'Exactly, Excellence. A fine tunic, cloak and an imperial warrant don't make a legate, necessarily.' The more I thought of it, the more likely this all seemed. 'Supposing this was just a messenger? Part of the legate's retinue, perhaps, sent on ahead to make arrangements here?'

Marcus paused in the act of biting into the last remaining fig. He brightened. 'I suppose that is a possibility. A man may send an agent on ahead, and give him a document and ring to confirm his authority.' For a moment his face cleared, and then he frowned again. 'But it still does not explain how he got here unobserved, still less where in Dis the body's got to now.'

I was still thinking. 'Suppose that he was acting on instructions. He turns up at the temple—by appointment, do you think? Perhaps he did not put on his ring or show anyone his warrant until he got there,' I said slowly. 'Those may even have been his orders. It would make sense, if there was secrecy. An ordinary merchant, with a bag, would attract no more attention than any other wealthy traveller.'

Marcus leaned forward on his cushions. 'So . . . he took his documents and ring this morning, in particular, and presented himself at the temple? Why there, do you suppose? Perhaps to give a message to one of the priests? It seems an obvious conclusion.' He smiled at the cleverness of his own deduction. 'Thank you, Libertus, I knew that I could rely on you to make sense of the mystery.'

Of course, I had done nothing of the kind.

And even if this was the truth, it was not a comforting explanation. Certainly, the death of the legate's representative (if that was indeed what had happened here) was much less of a civic catastrophe than the murder of the ambassador himself, but it was no trifle, all the same. The man had still been carrying an imperial warrant, and any affront to that was a capital offence.

With some diffidence, I pointed this out to Marcus.

I had spoiled his moment of relief and he was impatient. 'So someone will have to pay for it. And quickly too. I'll leave that to you, Libertus. Obviously someone with access to the temple. Find out a little bit about the priests. And discover who knew Fabius Marcellus—since this was apparently to be a private meeting. I'll send to the ambassador again, and find out who it was he sent and why—he won't be best pleased, I'm afraid.' Marcus had seized on this interpretation, I noticed, and was now ignoring the uncomfortable possibility that the dead man was really someone of consequence, or a direct emissary from Rome.

I tried again. 'But Excellence, suppose the Emperor *had* sent an informer here—'

He cut me off. 'Libertus, you have never travelled here from Rome. I have. If Commodus had despatched a spy the minute after he sent that letter, the man could never have reached us in this time. The imperial post has fresh horses every few miles, and fresh riders when the others tire. And this murdered man certainly was not the messenger who brought the letter to me earlier. For one thing that rider was hardly more than a boy—I saw him myself: a great horseman, but no one would ever have taken him for a legate—and for another thing he stayed here overnight. I have just despatched him, with my messenger, back to Fabius Marcellus. So it wasn't him.'

'But did you ask . . . ?'

'If the *legatus* had sent another messenger? Of course I did. You're not the only one with intelligence, Libertus. I questioned him most carefully. But he knew nothing about it.'

I hoped that 'careful questioning' did not include the whip. Probably not. One cannot casually mistreat a legate's messenger. Which brought us back to that mysterious corpse. I frowned. 'But in that case . . .'

'You think Commodus might have sent a spy *before* he wrote to me? I suppose that's so. But why should the man wait till this moment to reveal himself?' My patron shook his head. 'Much more likely that the dead man was some secret messenger that Fabius sent. I'll write to him again, and see what he says. But, whoever it turns out to be, the same thing still applies, Libertus my old friend. You will have to make enquiries at the temple and see if you can find out why he went there today, and who it was that he was hoping to see.'

How in the name of Cunomaglus was I to do that, I wondered? 'But Excellence, this is a priestly matter. I can hardly become involved . . .'

'My dear citizen pavement-maker, you are involved already. It was only because of you that Fabius Marcellus was coming here at all. If it had not been for your discovery of that plot against the Emperor, His Divinity Commodus would never had deigned to honour Glevum with an ambassadorial visit. You can hardly back out of the consequences now.'

This was a view of such sublime injustice that it took my breath away. However, Marcus was quite right in one respect. I could not escape. Marcus Aurelius Septimus had demanded my services, and he was my patron and benefactor. Also, he was not a man to cross. And when he said he wanted me, he meant it: this time he'd been seriously alarmed.

I sighed. 'As you command, Excellence. But it will be difficult for me to interrogate the priests. I have not your social dignity.'

Even flattery did not soften him. 'Then I must rely on you to think of something else.' He was brisk.

I racked my brains, and inspiration dawned. Two pigeons with a single stone again. 'I have received a possible commission in the town. A

98

certain Gaius Honorius Optimus—perhaps you know the man? He wants me to repair a pavement for him. It seems that he knew Fabius Marcellus in the army. And his house is very near the temple. I have been to it before. Almost opposite the high priest's house, in fact. With your permission, I could take the job . . .'

Marcus's severe expression melted like a wax mask in the sun. He positively beamed. 'Of course, my dear Libertus. That will be excellent. Accept his commission, and find out what you can. And see if you can discover what happened to that body.' He stretched, suddenly indolent now that his previous panic was over. 'Always supposing that it wasn't just a vision, after all.'

It had become 'just a vision' now, I noticed. I said nothing.

Marcus darted a sidelong look at me. 'I promised my wife I'd make special propitiatory sacrifices, just in case.' Marcus had recently married a beautiful young widow, and she was now carrying his child. He was rumoured to spend a very un-Roman amount of time with her, and her word was becoming law in his household. I thought of Gwellia, and smiled.

Marcus took it for acquiescence. He stood up, and I scrambled to my feet too.

'Very well, Libertus, report to me tomorrow.' He clapped his hands, and his slave, who must have been just outside the door, came in at once. 'Fetch this citizen his cloak and slave, and escort him to the door.' His eye fell on the empty plate, and he frowned suddenly. 'And when he comes again, make sure he has more figs another time. It seems the citizen has an appetite for them. They always seem a little sweet to me.'

He nodded in my direction and went out, accompanied by the slave.

As I waited for Junio, I could not resist a smile. Marcus, as usual, saw what he chose to see. But really it was no smiling matter.

There were so many unanswered questions, that was part of the problem. That dreadful wailing, for example. None of our deliberations had suggested any explanation for that. I did not like it. Who was this 'legate'? Where had he come from? Who had sent him here and why? Who had killed him? And above all, what had happened to the body? Legate or no legate, he could not simply disappear. Somebody must know, but nobody was telling.

I sighed. This was not going to be easy. Since my patron insisted, I would have to investigate, but I ran the risk of angering some very important people—the priests, the imperial ambassador, and possibly the Emperor himself. To say nothing of the gods.

When Junio arrived, he helped me with my cloak, and we walked out into the street together. Outside the warmth of the apartment, the late afternoon had turned chill, misty and disagreeable, but I decided not to go the shortest way home. I wanted time to collect my thoughts, and also I could cast an eye over that pavement repair at the house of Optimus. If I contracted now to do the work, by setting a date to start and agreeing the fee which Gwellia had so skilfully negotiated, the contract would be binding under Roman law, and Optimus could not change his mind if Fabius did not come.

We skirted past the temple once again, and took the street which ran behind it, past the high priest's house. There was Optimus's dwelling opposite. Typical of the man and his constant preoccupation with walking a mile to save a quadrans, he had bought a mansion of the second rank. There it was, a spacious residence, but squashed between a barber and a pot-shop, with a door that fronted directly on the street. Unlike the pontifex's great house opposite, with its impressive gate and entranceway and glimpses of a formal court beyond, this building was closed in upon itself. Only a few small windows on the upper floor, and the iron grille through which the doorkeeper could peer, relieved the blankness of the wall which faced the street—except where someone had scrawled 'Vote for Linneus' in bold black painted letters on the stone.

I threaded my way through the waiting

101

clients at the barber's shop—the vogue for beards had never really caught on in the province, and shops like these were always filled to bursting with townsmen who had come to have their faces scraped, their nose-hairs clipped, their baldness treated, and their ears emptied of wax and then filled with the latest rumours in the town. There is nowhere quite like a barber's shop for catching up on the latest gossip. That might be very useful to me later.

I noticed the situation of this one, with approval, before I moved to Optimus's door and unhooked the iron rod to strike the bell.

CHAPTER NINE

Once we had got past the doorkeeper we were shown into the receiving room, a small antechamber off the atrium where visitors could sit uncomfortably on a bench and wait. There was a plate of rather ancient apples and a jug of very watered wine, of which we were vaguely invited to partake, but the prospect did not appeal. Optimus—with typical regard for money—clearly did not provide any other refreshment for his callers, unless they were very important, and there was nothing else to do but sit and look around.

My mosaic in the dining room still looked

good, I thought, glimpsing it through the inner arch, but otherwise the house betrayed its master's thrift. It had been built in the old-fashioned Roman style and the centre of the atrium was partly open to the sky. The gutters dripped into a sunken pool beneath, making the room disagreeably cold and damp. (Such pools were falling out of fashion in Britannia: one could see why on such a dismal day.) Under the shelter of the partial roof a fine carved table held a good bronze vase, but the wall decorations had been cheaply done—repetitious patterns in a poor paint which was already flaking.

A few damp pot-plants fringed the atrium pool, but by craning round the doorpost it was possible to glimpse the inner court and the more extensive formal garden there. Even that wasn't a great deal more decorative, if I remembered rightly. The master had been frugal here as well. I'd noticed on my previous visits that the box shrubs which formed the borders were thin-planted, and what should have been handsome flowerbeds were full of straggling turnips, leeks and other strictly practical additions to the kitchen. I leaned forward on my bench to see more clearly.

It was raining slightly, but someone seemed to have been tending to the garden, for as I idly glanced I sensed a movement. A figure clad in some long bluish garment darted swiftly into the shadow of the colonnade and disappeared into the rear apartments of the house. Some garden slave, most probably, caught in the rain and scuttling out of sight of visitors. Otherwise the garden was much as I remembered. I watched for several minutes but the figure did not re-emerge.

Then someone finally appeared to greet us. It was not Optimus himself, as I had half expected. It was the Phrygian steward who came hurrying out, all unctuous excuses and eagerness at the sight of a visiting toga. I stood up. The shock on his face when he recognised me would have been comic if it were not insulting. Of course, he had never seen me dressed in anything but a tunic.

'Why, thitithen! Libertuth!—it ith the pavement-maker, ithn't it?' The Phrygian, apart from his disdainful air, also adopted an affected lisp which made conversation with him doubly difficult. ('Lithputh' Junio and I had christened him between ourselves.) 'What bringth you to my mathter'th humble houth?' His words were those of conventional greeting, but there was nothing humble about either the 'houth' or the steward's manner, now that he had identified me.

'Greetings to your master Optimus. The Citizen Libertus presents his compliments.' I chose the formal responses purposely, keeping my tone deliberately brisk. 'I have come to see about a commission he was offering. Repairs to that faulty pavement in the entranceway. A hundred sesterces, I think it was agreed.'

He shook his head. 'I'm afraid you'd need to thpeak to my mathter about that. Unfortunately he ithn't here at prethent.'

That was a blow. Leave it too long, and Optimus might change his mind about his pavement, and I was relying doubly on this commission now. Not only would the money be welcome, but the house would give me a useful vantage-point over the high priest's dwelling and the temple beyond it.

The Phrygian steward must have seen my frown. 'I'm truly thorry that he wathn't here,' he went on. 'I do not think he wath ecthpecting you.'

I gave him a forgiving smile. 'I don't expect he was. I had business this afternoon with Marcus Septimus, and since I was passing the door, it seemed an opportunity to see the floor. It would speed matters, you see, and Optimus was in a hurry for the work to be completed. With a little preparation tonight, I could no doubt start work first thing in the morning. No matter. No doubt your master is expected soon,' I said. 'I am content to wait here till he comes.'

I expected some conventional response. Instead, Lithputh glanced nervously towards the court. No more than the hastiest of looks, but Junio had seen it too. I felt him stiffen at my side, and under the cover of adjusting my cloak he bent forward and caught my eye. He

105

raised his brows expressively.

I winked at him. 'Something is troubling you, steward?' I enquired of Lithputh, in a tone that was sweetly reasonable.

Lithputh flushed. 'Not at all. A pity your journey thyoud have been in vain.' His eyes strayed to the courtyard once again. He gestured towards the outer door. 'Another time, perhapth?'

The man was hiding something. He could not have signalled it more clearly if he had hung a swinging shop sign on the wall, like the one outside the potter's shop next door. I tried to recall that scuttling figure I'd seen. Who was it? I wished that I had caught a better glimpse. Optimus himself, perhaps—I had not had time to take a proper look, but I would have seen a toga, I was sure, and my impression was of a smaller figure than the old centurion. It wasn't Lithputh, either—unless he'd taken the trouble to go and change his clothes. He was still wearing the bright ochre tunic which I remembered as the household uniform. Ochre is cheerful, Optimus had told me, and it is not an expensive dye.

Lithputh was still trying to usher me out. I made another attempt to resist. 'I'm sure your master would not be pleased at losing the chance to have the work begun as soon as possible. I understand he was most emphatic about it.'

Lithputh licked his lips. His disdainful

106

manner had vanished like a tallow candle on a brazier. He thought for a moment. 'In that case,' he said at last, so agitated that he almost forgot to lisp, 'perhaps, if you would care to thee the pavement? I am empowered thometimeth to act on hith behalf. I am thure that thome arrangement could be reached.'

'Perhaps a small payment in advance? And a written bond from you, to guarantee the rest?' I said. That was impertinent. A written contract for work of this kind was almost unheard of in the Empire, and as for payment in advance! That was like buying a 'pig' of iron sight unseen, without having it assayed—a positive invitation to be cheated.

But if I had redoubled the asking price I firmly believe that Lithputh would have signed, he was in such a hurry to usher us away. By this time, naturally, I was more curious than ever.

I contrived to send Junio to do the measurements, while I remained in the ante-room to keep a stealthy eye on the courtyard, but there was nothing further to be seen. Lithputh left me in the care of the doorkeeper, and came back after a moment carrying a writing tablet, with the agreement for the commission scratched out in the wax—not the most permanent of records, but still a good deal more than I deserved. He pressed it with his seal-ring in my presence, and brought out some silver coins from his purse.

'Twenty thethtertheeth, pavement-maker,' he said, with a return to his old lofty manner. 'I will tell my mathter—'

'For the purchase of preliminary tiles only,' I said swiftly, slipping the sesterces into my pouch. 'Black, red and white ones, I presume? Like the ones he wants me to replace?' It was a silly question really, but I was looking for any excuse to prolong my visit.

Lithputh was not deceived. 'I imagine that will be what he had in mind. Tho now, if your thlave hath finithed meathuring?' He motioned to the door—and to the doorkeeper to see us out. 'We will thee you in the morning, thitithen.'

The doorkeeper was a stout fellow with a stick, as doorkeepers in this city tend to be, so I was not disposed to argue with him. I collected myself and my slave with as much dignity as I could muster and we made our way back onto the street.

It was raining hard by now, and the street was deserted. We would be glad of our cloaks, I thought, as I wound mine around me, and began walking briskly back in the direction of the workshop. 'Well,' I said to Junio, who was trotting obediently beside me, 'what did you make of that? The fellow was positively anxious to get rid of us. What do you suppose? That Optimus was somewhere in the house all the time?'

Junio peered up at me, his hood raised

108

against the rain. 'I hardly think so, master. Lithputh looked more guilty than anything, to me. But he would have lied for Optimus without a second thought, I'm sure. I think something else was troubling him. There was someone there, I'm certain of it. I thought I saw someone in the garden earlier . . .'

I nodded. 'I thought I caught a glimpse of someone too. Someone who was very anxious not to be seen. Was it a man or woman, did you see?'

Junio shook his head. 'I am very sorry, master. Wearing some sort of long bluish cloak, I think. Or it might have been a woman's robe. I can't be certain, it was all too quick. Tomorrow, when we go back to the house, I'll see if I can discover anything from the servants.'

'Mmm!' I demurred. 'You can try, by all means. But you know what Optimus is like— he doesn't keep half as many slaves as any normal man, and the ones he does have are kept so busy you never see them. I found that out last time I was working there.' It was true. Optimus had promised me some water for the mortar, but he'd left no pitcher and I couldn't find anyone to ask. In the end I had to go out to the public fountain and fetch some myself in my mortar bucket.

The thought of that bucket reminded me of home, and Gwellia who was doubtless waiting for us there. 'Come on, Junio,' I said, stepping over a slippery patch on the glistening pavement. Some citizen had brought his dogs this way. We had reached the main road now, and were about to cross. 'Gwellia is preparing food for us.' I glanced at Junio.

He tried to disguise it, but even under the hood I saw the look of disappointment in his face. Up until now, Junio had always prepared my humble supper, or fetched me something from one of the cooked food stalls nearby. I was about to say something comforting, but suddenly he interrupted.

'Look, master, look!' He jerked his head in the direction we had come.

I looked back. Sure enough, from the doorway we had lately left a tall muffled figure had slipped out and was already hurrying across the road away from us. The person—it was impossible to say at this distance whether it was male or female—was cloaked from head to foot against the rain, and the hood was pulled right down to shield the face. But as the figure turned away, the cowl billowed in the wind, and I thought I caught a glimpse of auburn hair.

It was, of course, impossible to be certain who it was, but—now I came to think of it— there was something familiar in the manner of the walk as well.

'Dear Mercury, I do believe that's Hirsus! Whatever was he doing in that house?'

'Who is he, master?' Junio turned to me.

'One of the Imperial priests,' I said. 'I saw him earlier at the Emperor's shrine. What is he doing here?'

But when we looked again, the hurrying form had disappeared. I sent Junio chasing after him, if only to try to find out where he'd gone—we could hardly go and knock on people's doors and start demanding explanations. Besides, I had no wish to alienate the priest. He was doing nothing wrong in visiting a neighbour in broad daylight and Optimus, of course, could entertain anyone he liked. But if it was Hirsus why had he gone to such lengths to avoid my seeing him? And if it wasn't Hirsus, who was it? It could have been anyone, even a woman, under the disguise of that long, hooded cloak.

Whoever it was, he had disappeared like smoke. Junio could find no trace of him, and nor could I, although we looked down every street around the forum.

In fact, we were very wet indeed by the time we finally got home.

CHAPTER TEN

Gwellia came out to meet us as we arrived. She had clearly taken my instructions seriously, perhaps as a way of redeeming herself for destroying my tunic earlier, and from her air of half-suppressed excitement it was obvious that she was bursting to tell me what she had discovered.

I led the way back into my unnaturally tidy workroom. 'So?' I said to her, as Junio helped me to remove my sodden cloak. 'Did you learn anything at the market stall?'

'Indeed I did, master,' she replied, bringing me a towel to dry my dripping hair. 'And I bought the cloth. At the stall you recommended. Good cloth they have in Glevum, too—but at such a price! Of course, I brought them down a little by threatening to walk away—they could not resist a sale—but it was a dreadful price, dear master. If you could construct a loom for me, in future I could buy a fleece and spin and weave my own. No doubt I could arrange something with the dyers . . .'

'And Fabius Marcellus?' I said gently, as Junio disengaged me from my damp toga.

'I did not learn as much about the legate as I hoped,' she said, rubbing my hair briskly with her clean dry cloth. 'But I learned a lot about the Priest of Jupiter and that Honorius Optimus of yours. Once the cloth-seller's wife learned that I was taken prisoner from the southwestern tribes, she couldn't do enough for me. Apparently she came from there herself.' She took my toga from Junio and began to fold it. 'Besides, I told her that I was new to the city, and that I'd come to her stall because I'd heard it rumoured that the wives of really important men came there to buy their cloth. She was only too anxious to impress me, by telling me what illustrious clients she had and how much she was in their confidence.'

I nodded encouragingly, but at that moment Gwellia's attention was diverted by the pot on the fire, which had begun bubbling urgently. She darted towards it, and rescued it with an iron hook. 'But see,' she said, gesturing towards where she had stood it on the stone hearth, 'I have prepared a stew for you—the kind you used to like when you were young—and it will spoil if you don't eat it soon. Besides, you should have something warm to eat. If you will be pleased to sit down at the table, Citizen Libertus, I will tell you as you dine.'

She lifted the lid of the pot as she spoke. Something was smelling delicious. I had forgotten that enticing aroma, and I was sharply reminded by a rumbling in my stomach that I had hardly eaten anything all day. How wonderful to have a wife again. I took her hand in mine and was about to say something complimentary when I noticed Junio, standing in the background and looking rather put out. Of course, he must be feeling superseded. I mustn't let my own joy blind me to his needs.

'Get yourself clean and dry too, Junio,' I said. 'And then perhaps some water? My feet are rather muddy from that wet walk through the town.'

It seemed to work. Junio brightened. He stripped off his cloak, and then went to get a bowl and some of the water he had brought in earlier. Of course I then had to submit to the tedious rigmarole of squatting on my own work stool and having my feet and hands washed like a Roman emperor (and carefully dried in what looked suspiciously like a piece of my old tunic). Meanwhile Gwellia placed a bowl in front of me and ladled out more stew than even I could comfortably eat.

I picked up my spoon and both of them instantly took up station at my side, ready to watch my every mouthful, and outdo each other in their efforts to refill my drinking cup.

I smiled wryly. With these two competing to look after me, life was becoming distressingly formal. Up until now, I would have eaten my supper with Junio squatting companionably at my feet, enjoying his own meal and ready to eat the leftovers from mine—though, of course, he would be ready at any time to leap up and fetch anything I wanted.

I wished that Gwellia could be equally relaxed. But she had been a slave for so long that she had firm views about a servant's place, and she was not comfortable sitting down to dine with me. When we were first reunited I'd insisted once, and she had sat obediently beside me, but the situation made her too embarrassed to swallow anything. I almost felt that I'd deprived her of her food. The experiment had not been a success and I had not repeated it. However, she was my one-time wife, and if she would not eat with me I could hardly allow Junio to take his customary liberties.

So here I was, sitting like a lonely emperor eating my stew alone, with both of them staring at me. I felt like one of the beasts outside the arena, when the urchins gather round their enclosures to watch them being fed.

I sighed. As soon as this temple enquiry was over, I promised myself, I would legalise the situation and marry my wife again. Then we would be equals, master and mistress in our own house once more—and I could indulge Junio if I wanted to.

'Well?' I said, when I had given the first mouthfuls of stew the attention they deserved. 'About the Priest of Jupiter? We called at Honorius Optimus's house ourselves.'

Gwellia settled her hands in front of her, an endearing trick I remembered from our early life when she had something interesting to tell. 'Well! You know the high priest has a younger wife—I remember you talking about her earlier this morning—how she is interested in dressing in the fashion, and getting round her husband's restrictive rules?'

I nodded. 'That's right. Everyone in town has heard of her, I think, although Junio knows more about her than I do.'

Junio looked at me gratefully, eager to furnish what he knew. 'She is chiefly famous for spending a fortune on her appearance. Some of the more serious citizens think it is unbecoming in the high priest's wife—it isn't dignified for her to be so frivolous. But most people make a joke of it. They say, for instance, that there is more black soot on Aurelia Lucilla's eyes than on the temple lamps, and more myrrh in her perfume flasks than was ever burned in the ritual censers.'

Gwellia looked at him unsmilingly. 'Well, and no wonder too, poor girl. Imagine— dragged away when she was no more than a child to marry an old man she'd never seen, in a country she'd hardly heard of.'

I looked at her in surprise. It was a long time since I'd heard Gwellia express herself with such vigour. This was more like the wife I used to know, ready to defend the rights of victims anywhere. 'A foreign country?' I asked.

She nodded. 'Indeed, or so the cloth-woman told me. She had it from one of the maidservants, who calls at the cloth stall very often. The pontifex does not like it—if he were a flamen his wife would have to wear simple, homespun clothes, but Aurelia Lucilla will have none of it. Apparently she keeps a maid whose only job is to buy dyed cloth and to attend her robes. What a lucky life!'

I smiled. 'To have a servant only for your

116

clothes?'

She looked surprised. 'I meant to spend your life with nothing more to do than to choose fine wool and sew a bit, and then sponge your mistress's stains with lavender and brush her hems each time she wears the gowns!' She broke off. 'I don't mean you, dear master—but when I think of what some of my owners demanded of me!'

I winced. Gwellia never spoke much about her life as a slave. It still pained me to think of all the indignities she must have endured. But giving her that assignment in the market had been a good idea. It seemed to have given her back her confidence to speak freely to me—though she still lapsed into silence if I looked at her too long.

'Go on,' I said, turning my attention to the stew again.

She needed no further encouragement. 'And there is another maid whose only job is to prepare her unguents, and bring the sheep's milk for her beauty wash. That's because Aurelia's husband won't have goat's milk in the house: it is forbidden to the Flamen Dialis and he won't allow her to have it, either, so she insisted on ewe's milk instead. Claims that she had these luxuries in her father's house in Rome, and would not consent to be sent here to marry the old priest without them.'

The spoon stopped halfway to my lips. 'She comes from Rome, too? Now that I didn't know. I was aware that *he* did, originally.'

Gwellia nodded. 'From one of the oldest patrician families in the city. And so was she—and both their sets of parents were married in the old religious style. That is why he married her, they say. There aren't so many people who fulfil those requirements, but the old man needed a wife who did, apparently, if he hoped to be appointed to the flamen's post. The Emperor himself suggested the arrangement—since there was no other candidate in view.'

I swallowed another mouthful of soup. 'No wonder he was disappointed at being passed over as flamen. He must have thought it was a certainty, with the Emperor taking an interest in his chances.' Everyone knew that the senior priestly posts were largely political appointments.

Gwellia looked thoughtful. 'Of course, Marcus Aurelius was emperor in those days, and he may not have intended that at all. The girl's family was under his protection and he may simply have wanted to repay a favour. The girl was just of marriageable age, but apparently she had been a bit wayward at home—too many smiles for cavalry officers with good looks and no money—and her father was delighted to see her wed. At least that is what the clothwoman said. It seems Aurelia didn't want it in the least.'

'And she submitted?' It was a foolish question. Obviously once the Emperor had

118

made the suggestion it would have been impossible for either party to refusc.

Gwellia gave me a look which said more than any words. We both knew that few Roman families take a bride's inclinations into consideration—not when there is money, status and political connection hingeing on the match.

I said hastily, 'She laid down conditions, though, you said?' That was much more unusual.

Gwellia nodded. 'They were accepted readily enough. The would-be priest was not short of money, and all he really wanted was a wife who'd last his tenure through. But he didn't get the flaminate.They offcred him the priesthood here instead. Though even now he hasn't given up hope of being appointed, one of these days, when the current flamen dies.'

I was doing some rapid calculation. By Celtic standards Romans marry young—a girl can be a wife as soon as she is twelve. That meant Aurelia was now perhaps twenty-two or -three. Young enough beside her husband, certainly, but still a little older than I'd guessed. 'Of course,' I said, aloud, 'I hadn't thought of that. The Flamen of Jupiter must have a wife, and if he chose her before he came to Glevum . . .? She must have been married to him for many years.'

Gwellia leaned forward, as if the walls were listening. 'It all depends, citizen, on what you

119

mean by married. Poor girl. The cloth-maker says that in fact she is barely wife to him at all—the old man is too terrified of losing her in childbirth to come anywhere near her. He'd never find another wife with her qualifications, and then he could never be flamen. Or that's what the household slaves report. But that's not all. Do you know who the young lady was?'

I looked at Junio. He was more in touch than I was with the chatter of the town. But he shook his head.

'Who was she?'

'None other than the niece of that very Fabius Marcellus you are expecting here.' Gwellia produced this sentence with a flourish, like a *praestigiator* at a festival conjuring a coin from a spectator's ear.

Like the magician's trick, it made me gasp. 'Fabius is her uncle? Surely not. If her family were favourites of Marcus Aurelius . . .' I hardly needed to complete the sentence. All the world knew that almost the first act of Commodus, when he attained the imperial purple, was to remove his father's favourites by exiling or even executing the most important men in the city—especially after an early assassination plot hatched by his own household. 'Fabius would hardly be singled out as a *legatus* now, if his family supported the old emperor.'

'He might be these days, master, with respect,' Junio put in. 'Look at His Excellence the Governor Pertinax. He was out of favour, wasn't he, at first—and then brought back when things were difficult?'

The boy was right, of course. Pertinax had once been exiled in disgrace, but—since Commodus's personal favourites proved themselves, one by one, as treacherous and unreliable as their master—he had been reluctantly reinstated and even given the governorship of this troublesome province. And now he was about to be promoted to still higher things.

I looked hopefully at Gwellia, but she shook her head. 'If Fabius Marcellus was ever out of favour, I don't know. But when Optimus knew him in the legions he was already rising fast, we know that—and that must have been in Marcus Aurelius's time.'

That was well argued, and I should have thought of it. I had been teaching Junio to help me in my deductions, and now here was Gwellia out-thinking me. I nodded, in what I hoped was a judicious manner. 'Exactly so. It seems Fabius Marcellus has somehow managed to continue in favour, despite the change of emperor. I wonder what service he provides Commodus?' I pushed aside my plate and allowed Junio to refill my water beaker. 'And speaking of Optimus, as we were, you learned something about him too, I think you said?'

'He has a big house very near the temple—' she began. I couldn't resist interrupting. 'As I know, since we have just visited the place.'

She flushed. 'Of course, master,' she said humbly, and I felt ashamed. 'It is merely that, being so close to the temple, it is also close to the chief priest's house. Of course Optimus has a wife, she followed him around the legions and he married her as soon as he was free of the army, but she is no longer young. While Aurelia . . .'

I was so astonished that I jumped up from my stool. 'You mean that Optimus and the chief priest's wife . . . ?'

'Nothing as strong as that, dear master. This is women's gossip, that is all. Only Aurelia's servants say that last year Optimus came to the high priest's house to arrange a sacrifice, and was invited to take refreshment with the pontifex—that is a signal honour, as you know. Aurelia was there, they say, and Optimus and she were very conversational—though the old man was too self-absorbed to see what was under his nose. Since then, there have been several "accidental" meetings—when Aurelia goes out into the street, or takes a litter, it's odd how often Optimus is there. It is even rumoured that his steward was seen delivering a letter to her once.'

I thought of that cloaked figure in the ex-legionary's garden. Junio, had you heard anything of this?'

'Not a whisper, master.' Junio sounded as surprised as I was. 'If there was the slightest scandal—or worse, if Aurelia was to leave . . . that would be the end of any hope of his becoming flamen. He'd have to resign his office in disgrace.'

Gwellia shook her head. 'I don't believe there's any chance of that. The two have apparently been exceedingly discreet—and really there's very little for anyone to see. They never do anything but smile and nod, and there has never been any other communication between them—at least as far as the servants are aware. But Optimus has started coming to the temple regularly, and bringing thunderstones for Jupiter. Though again, he has new business interests to protect—that's why he wanted that sacrifice in the first place—so there may be nothing significant in that. In fact there may be nothing in any of it, except servant talk—those maids of Aurelia have nothing else to do. But I thought that all the same you'd like to know.'

'I would,' I said. 'You have done well. And now, I think, I will prepare those tiles for tomorrow and then retire to bed. It will be getting dark soon and I need time to think.'

I knew that Gwellia would not consent to eat while I was in the room, and Junio would appreciate that stew as much as I did. I assembled my equipment speedily. I had a length of border-pattern mosaic, already made up and fixed to a strip of linen backing—a sort of pattern piece for clients. I could use that as a basis, I decided—lay it on one side of the passageway and tile the other side to match. It was an easy pattern, and I had the template made. With the help of that I could finish the whole entrance in a day or two—that would please Optimus.

I collected everything I'd need, ready for the handcart in the morning, then led the creaking way upstairs, and allowed Junio to help me into bed.

He was impatient to talk things over with me. 'So, master, you have learned a lot today. You have discovered several motives for the murder of the Emperor's ambassador. Optimus was a rival of Fabius Marcellus, and jealous of his advancement in the army—suppose that he had access to the temple, through Aurelia perhaps? She might well have helped him, too—it sounds as if she did not love her uncle, since he was instrumental in a marriage that she did not want to make. Perhaps she even encouraged Optimus? Or even killed the *legatus* herself?' He broke off. 'But I see that I am reasoning amiss. You look doubtful, master.'

I shook my head. 'I can see why either Optimus or Aurelia would want to kill the legate. But I'm sure that body in the temple wasn't Fabius. It seems more likely that it was a messenger. Why should anyone kill him? And more than that, where is the body now?' I looked at him. 'Go on downstairs and have your supper, Junio. You must be hungry and I want to think.'

My deliberations did me little good. I turned the problem over and over but no solution came. Perhaps Gwellia had gleaned some further information. I would ask her when she came—as my slave-cum-wife she consented always to lie beside me, and that part of life at least was sweet enough.

Downstairs I could hear her chiding Junio, and scrubbing the dish I had used with a handful of damp sand.

I turned over with a smile, and waited for my wife to come to bed.

CHAPTER ELEVEN

Gwellia had nothing further to report, and though we talked till far into the night no inspiration visited my dreams. I rose early, breakfasted on the oatcakes and water which Gwellia had prepared for me the previous night, and—having loaded everything onto a handcart and thrown an old sack over it—I had set off with Junio for Optimus's house before the sun was well over the horizon.

Even at this time of the morning the streets were already busy. We came upon a group of schoolboys, dragging their feet outside the building where the *paedogogus* had his rooms.

They went in as they caught my glance, and through the open window space we could distinctly hear one of them swearing that the household dog had chewed his writing tablet, and the master roaring for the whipping-slave (who was still cowering outside the door) to come and take his master's punishment.

Towards the centre of the town stall-holders and shopkeepers were opening shutters and setting out their wares, and as we turned towards the *macellum*—the area of market stalls behind the forum—we twice had to avoid sullen butcher-boys with staves, who were driving their animals down the narrow side streets. The air was alive with moos and baas and bleats, and we had to be very careful where we trod. (It didn't deter the purchasers, however. As we followed one lad and his herd of scabby sheep to the freshmeat market stall, the first customers of the day were already gathering.)

Apart from a laden donkey or two, and the occasional handcart like my own, the roadway was empty of waggons and carriages—wheeled transport is not permitted within the walls during the hours of daylight. Of course, it is a different matter after dark: the streets are full of creaking carts, and a ragged urchin was even now busy scraping up last night's manure into a makeshift bucket, no doubt hoping to sell it somewhere for an *as* or two. We negotiated our handcart around him, through the carriage ruts, and it was still only about the first hour when we presented ourselves once again at Optimus's house.

I was in my tunic this time, naturally, so no courteous delay awaited us. Strange what a difference the absence of a toga can make. No sooner had the doorkeeper admitted us than the Phrygian steward came bustling out to tell us how inconvenient it was going to be to have the entranceway repaired, and to inform us that we couldn't leave the handcart there. He watched us sulkily as we unloaded it, and despatched Junio to 'hide it' in the stable at the back.

'It ith ecthtremely awkward,' he complained. 'My mathter Optimuth hath important callerth—and if you've got the floor tileth up, I thuppoth we shall have to thend them around to the thervantth' entranth! That'th undignified enough, without them falling over a trademan'th cart!'

I realised that this was a veiled rebuke, and a reminder that today I should have come in by the servants' door myself, but I said nothing except, 'We shall be as swift as possible. Even quicker if you have a slave or two who could help us lift the broken tiles—and I shall need clean water later on for the mortar, and to clean the surface when the new pattern has been laid.'

The Phrygian steward looked appalled—perhaps at the prospect of the household's

127

supplying some of the unskilled labour for the job—although it is not uncommon in my trade, especially when a household wants a pavement in a hurry. 'I'll thpeak to Honoriuth Optimuth,' he said, with his most self-important air, and disappeared.

Junio had come back by this time, and was already on his knees with a sharp implement, removing the damaged border tiles. I set to work beside him. The pieces had been so poorly set that they lifted easily, and by the time a terrified little kitchen slave had arrived to help us—lugging a wooden pail of water that was half as big as he was—we had almost completed one side of the hall.

Junio showed him what to do, and I got out my wooden template and my measuring stick and began the work of making up the border to replace the edge we'd moved. It was a tricky business. The pre-formed pattern would fill most of it, but the piece had not been created for the space and the placement of it had to please the eye, before additional tiles could be arranged to fill in the remainder of the gap. But first the area must be prepared, and once the mortar layer was laid it was important to set the work in quickly, before the surface dried—preferably without having so much cement mixed up that the excess hardened in the bucket.

While I was busy with my calculations, someone struck the entrance bell outside. I was dimly aware of it, and of a murmured conversation, but I paid scant attention—remembering that Optimus was expecting 'important callerth' who had no doubt been duly directed to the rear entrance in the lane. Perhaps, in the light of that hooded visitor the night before, I should have been more alert, but I was so intent on centring my pattern that I noticed nothing, until a deliberate cough intruded on my consciousness.

I raised my head.

The Phrygian steward was at the inner doorway, his lips set in a disapproving line. 'Your pardon, pavement-maker.' There was something insolent about his tone. 'I do not want to interrupt your work, but there ith thomeone here to talk to you. An urgent methage from your patron, it appearth.'

I got to my feet, wiping my dusty hands on my tunic. 'A message? Here? From Marcus? What has happened now?'

The steward only shrugged and stood aside, and I went out to find the messenger.

He was waiting for me at the rear entrance, and was cloaked from head to foot against the rain, which had evidently begun to fall again. All the same, even at a distance I felt I'd seen the man before. As I approached, and he pushed back his hood to bow towards me, I realised who it was. 'Why, you're the temple slave who came to fetch us at the bath-house yesterday!'

129

He nodded.

'Something is amiss?' I asked. It looked as if there was.

He had been anxious yesterday, but he looked, if anything, still more anxious now. He was pale and seemed to be actually sweating as he said, 'A thousand apologies, citizen pavement-maker, for disturbing you again. I was sent at first to His Excellence your patron, but he told me to come and find you here. You are to leave everything and come at once.'

That would please Optimus, I thought. But Marcus Aurelius Septimus took precedence over a mere pavement. There was no question but that I would have to go. 'What's happened now?' I was already taking off my leather apron, and my mind was whirling like a donkey-mill.

The young slave ran his tongue around his lips and glanced about, as if afraid of being overheard. 'You will see.'

'Something at the temple?'

That nervous glance again.

I stopped, in the act of dusting off my knees. 'Not the bod—' I was about to say 'the body of the legate', but I caught the expression on his face, and was suddenly aware of the presence of the steward, still lurking silently behind me. I nodded, to show the temple slave I understood. If news of yesterday's disaster had not yet reached the town, I had no desire to be the source of it. 'Very well,' I said. 'Tell His

Excellence that I'll be there, as soon as I've had time to wash myself.'

The temple slave nodded, and left the way he'd come. I watched him for a moment, then swivelled round—thereby surprising the Phrygian steward, who was tiptoeing away, and trying to pretend he wasn't.

'You heard that,' I said, to make it clear I knew that he'd been listening. 'I am summoned to His Excellence, and need to make myself respectable. I have water waiting in the passageway.' I began to lead the way towards it.

'And what about my mathter'th pavement?' he complained, trotting after me.

'I will leave my slave to go on working while I'm gone. I have made the calculations, and he can manage here without me for an hour.' I had no idea how long this errand would take me, but I thought that this might placate Optimus, should he arrive and start to ask for me. We were back at the passageway by now, where Junio and the kitchen slave had almost finished moving the damaged tiles. I left the kitchen slave to prise out the rest as I took Junio aside and gave him my instructions. I also told him where I was going, and why.

'You think they've found the body, master?' he murmured in an undertone, holding the water bucket for me as he spoke.

'Something of the kind,' I whispered back. 'Let's hope it isn't something worse. The

131

temple slave wouldn't tell me any more, with the steward listening, although whatever it was seemed to have frightened him half out his wits.'

Junio bent closer, lifting the water, and taking the chance to murmur in my ear. 'Perhaps, since you are summoned to the temple, this really is an opportunity sent us from the gods. That kitchen slave has had a dreadful time. He hates his master and the steward too. I think he might talk to me some more—I might even discover who that caller was. But he won't say a word while you're about—you are a master, so you frighten him. I'll see what I can find out while you're gone.' He raised his voice. 'Now, if you're ready, master, to rinse your face?'

I nodded, and dipped my head into the water bucket. I came up spluttering, ran my fingers through my hair and eyebrows, and rubbed myself briskly in my cloak. It wasn't perfect for attending Marcus and the temple, but I was as ready as I'd ever be.

'I'll come back as quickly as I can,' I said to Junio, loudly enough this time for everyone to hear. 'Mix up some mortar, and then you can lay out that pattern on the linen base. You'll see I've marked the place where it should go. Do you think you can manage that?'

Junio gave me his wide, cheerful grin. 'I should hope so, master. I've had the most exacting tutor in the Empire.'

I aimed a playful cuff at his ear, and left him to it, aware that the kitchen slave was gaping like a frog.

It was no great distance to the temple, even from the rear entrance of the house, but it was raining enough to make me very glad of the veranda over the entrance and the ambulatory. The temple slave was there to greet me, together with Trinunculus who seemed to have appointed himself my especial guide. In the distance I could see Meritus and his attendant priests all huddled together at the entrance to the Imperial shrine. Of Marcus and the pontifex there was no sign.

'This is a dreadful business, citizen,' Trinunculus said, with only the faintest sideways glance at my ungentlemanly attire. 'It has caused quite a stir, I can assure you.' He waited for me to wash my hands again in the sacred water bowl. 'No doubt you know by now what's happened here?'

'You have found the corpse?'

Trinunculus looked startled and shook his head. 'If only it were something so simple.' He glanced towards the temple slave. 'He didn't tell you?'

The slave boy flushed, but he answered steadily enough. 'There was someone listening. And the pontifex instructed me to say nothing at all . . .'

Trinunculus silenced him with a nod. 'Very well. In that case, citizen,' he said to me, 'you'd

133

better come and see things for yourself.'

All this secrecy was making me thoroughly uneasy, and as we crossed the courtyard I turned to Trinunculus for an explanation. I knew his love of gossip and he was clearly bursting to tell me, but something—perhaps the mention of the pontifex—had silenced him, and he resolutely said nothing until we had almost reached the entrance to the Imperial shrine.

'There you are, citizen,' Trinunculus said. 'You can see it with your own eyes.'

He stood back, and I approached the shrine. Only one half of the screen door had been fully opened, and the little group at the entrance had to step back to let me in.

I am not normally a nervous man, but I confess that I was almost overcome by fear. Nobody spoke. Only Scribonius kept up a quiet sing-song chant—muttering charms and incantations, I realised, to keep the evil influences at bay. Meritus stood stock-still, like a human mountain, shaking his head as if in disbelief, while Hirsus had his hands pressed to his mouth and was gibbering faintly. By this time the hairs on my back were stirring with disquiet, and the palms of my hands were uncomfortably damp.

I swallowed hard, and peered into the religious gloom of the shrine. I was preparing myself for almost any horror: dismembered bodies, monsters, sacrilege. What I was not expecting was that—at first sight at least—everything in the temple seemed exactly as I'd left it.

I took a step forward.

'There,' Meritus murmured. 'On the floor. We found it this morning when we first came to the shrine.' He paused, swallowed and looked around, as if some malign presence might be listening, before he went on. 'I think you know we washed it yesterday.'

I looked where he was pointing, and I felt my veins run cold. There on the shadowed tiles before the altar, in the self-same place where yesterday I had seen Hirsus kneel and soil his priestly robes, was the ominous, dark stain once more. And yet I had watched, with my own eyes, as a temple slave had knelt and scrubbed all trace of it away.

I have seen death, even murder, many times, but this was something else. Something unnatural, unhuman and unclean. 'A curse on all things Roman?' Was that it? I felt my spine tingle, and my breath come short. But the priests were watching me. I had to do something.

I sent up a prayer to whatever gods there were, then knelt and touched my finger to the floor. It came up sticky and it smelled of blood. Fresh blood.

Unreasoning terror took my power of speech. I looked at Meritus. He shook his head helplessly. I tried to rise, but my knees seemed to be made of melting wax. Behind the altar the huge bronze statue of the Emperor gazed down at me, its cold face cruel and unforgiving. I put my hand upon the base to raise myself, then drew it sharply back again and found myself somehow on my feet.

'Uuugggh!' I had not meant to, but I'd cried aloud. More blood. Dear Mercury! My hand was red with it, and with something else—something that looked like scraps of human flesh.

It was too much for me. Blank terror made my stomach heave. I fought my way out of the temple, past the priests, and plunged my hand into the ceremonial bowl. The purifying water streamed with red.

Then I turned aside and was violently sick into the trees.

CHAPTER TWELVE

Too late, I recognised the effect of that. I'd desecrated a sacred place. I hadn't meant to, but that's what I had done. Not merely a sacred place, but the Imperial grove! I was wondering rather groggily what the punishment for that might be, when I came to myself and realised that I had become the centre of a little tableau.

All four priests—Trinunculus, Scribonius, Hirsus and Meritus—were lined up in a row and were staring at me with exaggerated expressions of dismay, like a comic chorus at the theatre. This, though, was no laughing matter. Apart from making an exhibition of myself, I had transgressed the laws of reverence, and could expect the anger of the god—or at least, his priestly representatives. That was no supernatural matter. News of this would reach the divine imperial ears, I could rely on that, since the Emperor has informers everywhere.

I waited, half expecting to be marched off to a cell. But though there was a visible affront, none of the priests made any move at all. Sometimes it is useful to have a powerful man like Marcus as a patron, I thought—or perhaps it was simply that, after the other desecrations of the shrine, my accidental indignities made little difference.

Whatever the reason, the sevir Meritus was the first to regain his composure.

He murmured something to Scribonius (checking the proper rituals, I guessed) then signalled towards the amubulatory, and I saw that the temple slave who'd fetched me had taken up his station there, waiting for further instructions. I blushed to realise that he must have been watching my antics with astonishment.

Now, however, the sevir clapped his massive hands and gestured with his head. The fellow disappeared at once, but in a trice was back again with half a dozen other of his fellow slaves.

What followed was an impressive demonstration of temple discipline. Meritus merely nodded here, and gestured there, and within moments all the slaves were hard at work, pouring out the polluted water from the bowl—round the outer altar where it mingled with the blood of sacrifice—rinsing the bowl itself, refilling it, and cleansing the desecrated precinct with clean sand. All this without the chief sevir uttering a single word.

When the slaves had finished, Meritus moved at last. He waited for everyone to withdraw and then he lifted the draped portion of his purple robe to form a hood—a clear sign that he was about to officiate. Then, and only then, he strode dramatically to the altar, raised his hands and in ringing tones he called down the mercy of the gods. The two assistant priests stood by: Hirsus wildly scattering purifying oils while Scribonius solemnly wafted sacred 'fire' by waving smoking incense in the air.

And all this was because of me. I could hardly have created more of a stir if I had been a corpse myself.

I glanced at Trinunculus, who was not taking part in the ceremony, and gave him a feeble smile. He whispered something to one of the departing temple slaves, who scampered off, and reappeared a short time later with a cup of watered wine for me. I was still feeling shaken and I drank it gratefully.

Trinunculus sidled over to me. 'Are you feeling better now, citizen?' he asked me in an undertone. 'I'm sorry you had such a shock. I would have warned you what you'd find—but that messenger was listening, and the pontifex himself had given strict instructions that no one was to say anything until you'd seen the blood yourself. He thinks the very mention of a corpse is unlucky, of course—since a flamen may not hear or speak of one.'

I nodded. I'd learned enough about Roman superstition to know that.

The young priest went on murmuring, with evident relish this time. 'Also there is a story about some kind of curse—and he told me that the more you mention that the more you strengthen it. I don't know if you've heard about it? Some executed leader of the Iceni calling down vengeance on all things sent from Rome?' Even the pontifex's warning, it seemed, could not prevent Trinunculus from passing on an interesting story.

Scribonius was frowning at us, through his incense cloud. We should not be gossiping like this. I nodded hastily, avoiding words, but Trinunculus refused to be subdued. His whisper, if anything, became more penetrating.

'I'm not surprised it made you feel unwell. That blood gave me a shock when I saw it, I can tell you, though I was more or less ready

139

for what I was going to see.' He saw my look of surprise and grinned. 'Of course, I shouldn't have known about it either. But one can't stop rumours in a place like this. Once the stain was found everyone in the temple was whispering about it.'

I turned to him, struck by a sudden thought. 'Who discovered it?' My voice was louder than I meant.

He made a little face, and nodded towards the Imperial seviri, who were on their knees by this time, their foreheads pressed into the dust. 'All three of them at once, I understand, though by rights it should have been Hirsus on his own. Usually on low days he opens up the shrine.'

I nodded. Every day is either auspicious or non-auspicious in the Roman calendar, *fastus* or *nefastus* to some extent—so much so that the civic calendar depends on it. Therefore (unlike public ceremonials, where different participants have specific jobs, so that the man who anoints the statue is not the same man who carries it in procession) within the temple priests may sometimes take it in turns to perform the rituals, according to the degree of seniority required to avert ill-luck.

'So what happened this morning?' I was about to say, but the Imperial priests had risen now to their feet, and were processing round the altar, doing something ritual with fire held aloft.

Scribonius hissed at us as he passed. 'If you must talk while we're purifying, kindly move away.'

We did as we were bidden, and went to stand a little further off. 'I suppose after yesterday's events, everything was unlucky and the day required special sacrifice?' I said to Trinunculus, in a more normal tone. 'That's why all three of them performed the rites today?'

He nodded. 'Partly that, of course. None of them even returned home last night—Hirsus was positively quivering with fright, and much too scared to sleep here in the robing room alone, as the duty priest would normally have done. He wouldn't go into the shrine by himself this morning, either, although Scribonius wanted him to do it—kept saying that if the rituals were not performed strictly according to the calendar it would mean even more bad luck, and take longer than ever to atone.'

That was interesting, I thought, glad to find my mind was functioning again. Did Scribonius have some reason for wanting Hirsus to go alone? I looked at Trinunculus questioningly. 'And is that right?'

'There may be a basis for it, somewhere in the rules—Scribonius knows the priestly regulations inside out—but I suspect that partly it was because he didn't want to go in there himself. And of course Hirsus was

141

almost hysterical with fear. I don't know why he wants to be a sevir. He's been frightened of his shadow ever since he came, and he's terrified of Meritus—who's twice his size, of course. But even that would not make him go into the shrine alone today. There was almost a rebellion until Meritus agreed that they all three should do it together.'

I nodded. 'So that is what they did?'

'I believe so. And the moment they went into the shrine, there it was—a bloodstain, back in the very place where it was yesterday. At least, that's what I understand. I didn't see it personally. The first I knew of it was Hirsus screaming.'

'Where were you at the time?' I had to ask the question.

'In the main temple with the pontifex. We had our own rituals to perform, of course. This business has been a desecration of the entire temple, not just the Imperial sanctuary, and the whole complex needed the most abject rituals,' Trinunculus answered me with dignity. 'Of course it is worse at the Imperial shrine. Meritus spent hours yesterday performing cleansing rites, and I understand they kept up prayers all night. But it doesn't seem to have done a lot of good. This morning, there the bloodstain was again.'

He spoke with such feeling that I was moved to ask, 'What do you think, Trinunculus? This reappearing stain? Is it a sign, a warning or a curse?' He was a priest after all, I thought, even if only a fairly junior one.

'To tell you Jove's truth, citizen, I don't know. I'm glad I'm not a sevir in the Imperial cult, that's all. When you join the priesthood you expect mysteries, of course—but nothing in my training covers this.' He seemed to speak from the heart, but I noticed he had evaded the question.

I persisted. 'But what is your opinion?'

He looked at me. 'Well, citizen, if this is a vengeance curse, why should it suddenly strike now, when nothing has happened all these years? More likely this is some sort of warning sign—because one of the gods is angry. I believe the high priest thinks the same; he is beginning to talk about a formal investigation into the morals of the Imperial priests, since it is in their shrine that the manifestations have taken place.'

'Their morals?' I enquired, in surprise.

'The way that they have kept their vows, I mean.' He leaned forward, confidentially. 'If anything is found against them, it could be serious. You heard what happened in the Imperial City, years ago, when one of the Vestal virgins was struck by lightning? Investigation showed then that some of the other Vestals had transgressed their vows. Several men had to be executed before the gods were finally appeased—and the women themselves were actually walled up, I think.'

It seemed likely, from what I knew of the matter. Vestal virgins are protected by their calling from anyone's laying violent hands on them—so that, if any of them were condemned to death, it was always by being bricked up alive in a confined space, without food or water, until they presumably perished of their own accord. Eventually.

I was still contemplating the horror of that fate when a discreet cough behind me captured my attention. I turned. The seviri had finished their rituals of purification by now, and Meritus was standing there, already pushing back his hood. I was conscious once again of his enormous height.

He stepped forward to speak to me. 'I apologise for that interruption and delay, citizen. It was necessary, as you understand.'

'I am the one who should apologise,' I said.

'Or propitiate, perhaps?' he said, and I realised that I had not escaped entirely unpunished, after all.

'Perhaps a little offering? A pigeon, maybe, or a dove or two?' Something inexpensive, was what I really meant. Priests are generally inclined to suggest gold and silver, if one leaves the choice of offering to them—as no doubt 'Lucianus the wretched' had discovered long ago.

Meritus gave me a condescending smile. 'Perhaps a pair of pigeons would suffice but I think a white lamb might be more suitable. To be offered on the next auspicious day. In the meantime, I must make a sacrifice myself, and we must ask the pontifex to cleanse the inner shrine with fire. If this is the working of a curse—as seems more and more likely—we are in the hands of the great immortals, beyond the scope of my more humble prayers.' He shook his head. 'It is all too horrible. And at the Imperial shrine as well! I am coming to think the pontifex is right. It cannot be safe to have the legate here. However, that is not for me to judge.'

'It's up to Marcus Septimus,' I said mechanically. I was thinking of nothing in particular beyond the cost of pure white lambs—always at a premium because of their value as a sacrifice.

Meritus, though, seemed to interpret my remark as a reminder that I had status here. He made hasty show of deference. 'Will it be acceptable, do you think, to have the slaves wash down the temple floor? Or did you wish to look at it again? Scribonius thinks it should be cleansed at once, but the pontifex and Marcus Septimus were very clear that I should do nothing in the shrine until you agreed.'

That would endear me to Scribonius, I thought—civil authority taking precedence over religious ritual. Yet, if anyone could tell me about the sacred rituals, there was no doubt that Scribonius was my man. Somehow I would have to win him over.

I glanced towards the small, balding priest, who was indeed glaring at me in a most unfriendly manner. I nodded affably in his direction. 'I'd be very glad to take another look,' I said to Meritus. 'But I have caused impurity enough. Perhaps if the assistant sevir would accompany me, he could advise me what I can and cannot touch, and so prevent me from doing anything else accidentally impious? I understand he is an expert on the rites?'

Scribonius kept the sober frown on his face, but I could see that I had flattered him. 'Admitting a person other than a priest is bound to desecrate a holy place,' he grumbled, but he took a taper and led the way back to the little temple in the grove.

He did, though, make me stop outside to ensure that I was thoroughly rubbed with ashes and sprinkled with water before he permitted me to set foot inside the shrine again.

CHAPTER THIRTEEN

This time, since the initial shock was over, I was able to pay more attention to my surroundings. I forced myself to look round carefully. At first sight, there appeared to be no alteration from the day before. Just the altar, the statue, the wall paintings, Augustus in his niche—and of course that bloodstain on the statue and on the shadowed floor. But surely...? I took a step forward.

Scribonius moved to prevent me. 'Citizen?' He said it doubtfully.

I wished I was wearing more official robes. I doubt if he would have stood in the way of a man in a toga. 'The inner door,' I said. 'It has been unfastened.'

He went ahead of me, holding the taper high. I was not mistaken. The heavy bolt, which yesterday had been so firmly closed, was now pulled back, so that although the door rested in the same position it was no longer fastened shut. It had been carefully done—if I had glanced more casually I would never have observed it in the shadows. I exchanged looks with Scribonius.

He said nothing, but we moved in unison. We pushed at the door together and it opened at our touch. Outside under the columns, however, there were scuff marks on the ground, as if the swinging of the door had marked it recently. I opened and shut it once again—it was moving freely enough now.

Scribonius looked at mc helplessly. 'I know what you are thinking, citizen, but you are wrong. I didn't do this. I didn't open the bolt, or arrange the blood, and I don't know anything about this moving corpse at all.'

He sounded so defensive that I turned to face him. 'I can see that someone went that way, and was unable to pull the bolt shut after them. Why should I suppose that it was you?'

He shook his head. 'I have said too much.'

'You have not said enough,' I told him crisply. 'I repeat, why should I suppose that you, in particular, might be involved in this? You must have a reason. Everyone else seems to suspect the hand of the gods.'

Scribonius glowered. 'I think you know the reason very well. Trinunculus will have told you, if no one else. One might as well keep water in a sieve as try to keep him from spilling information. It's perfectly clear why everyone will suppose that I have been involved. Weren't my forefathers rebellious Iceni, executed after the rebellion and their wives and children sold?'

I gulped. So that was what Trinunculus had meant by saying that Scribonius had to be particularly careful because of his 'background'! The famous Iceni. They had become a legend in the province—a byword among the tribes for their resistance to the Roman occupation force. The spirited rebellion under their warrior queen Boudicca had been doomed, of course, but they had torched Londinium and harried their conquerors for years, before they were finally subdued and their leaders put horribly to death. The very reprisals which had allegedly called down this curse.

'The Iceni?' I said inanely.

He rounded on me. 'How do you think I came to be born a slave? My family were cultured men, minstrels and poets, generations of them—but they were herded up and those that were not tortured to death were sentenced to the mines. As I am sure you know. After all, you are a Celt yourself.'

He spoke of his inheritance with pride, and when I looked more closely at him I could see that there was Celtic blood in him, though I guessed that there were Romans somewhere in that ancestry too. Patricians, probably—the build was too slender for a Celt and the nose too long. That was not surprising, of course. Everyone knew for what purposes the Romans liked to use their female slaves. I had only to think of Gwellia to remember that.

I changed the subject hastily. 'Do you speak Celtic?' I enquired, using that tongue myself.

He glanced around as if the walls were listening. 'I do not understand what you are saying, I'm afraid. I never learned to speak my native language. I was raised in a Latin-speaking houschold all my life. And only the highest quality of Latin too—my master was a grammarian and orator, and very strict about our speech.' He moved a little closer, and added, in a fierce mutter, 'And do not try to trap me, citizen. The Romans do not trust the Iceni to this day. You know that it would do

149

me harm if I appeared to be conspiring with you in a tongue which no one else can understand.'

'And yet you serve the Imperial cult?' I said.

The hand that held the taper trembled a little. 'Of course. It is the only way of proving my allegiance and having any influence at all. I was succeeding too. I had hoped, before all this . . .' He gestured towards the bloodstain on the floor. 'I have the necessary capital, and I've been freed. I hoped I might rise to the *equites*, or that at least my son could hope to join the knights. You can't imagine how much work I've put into it—ensured that nothing that I did could be construed against me, studied all the documents, learned all the correct rituals, made all the right offerings— and now, I suppose, it will all have been in vain. No emperor will look favourably on me, after this. Even if these horrors prove to be the work of the gods, I shall be suspected of somehow bringing their wrath down on the shrine—just because it was an Icenian who laid the curse. More likely someone will decide that I am actually guilty of carrying it out myself. Dear Mars . . .!'

He was right, of course. The idea had even occurred to me. But he had frightened himself by voicing the thought, and there was a danger that he would lapse into silence altogether. I did my best to appear supportive.

'So you suspect a human hand?' I said. 'So

do I, especially now I know that door's been opened up. The gods would hardly need to move the bolt! But if they didn't do it, who did—that's the question. That catch could only have been pulled back from the inside.'

'I can't imagine, citizen. When we left the shrine last night the place was empty. We locked the door, and opened it this morning with the key. How could anyone have slid the bolt?' He looked around nervously. 'Perhaps this is the doing of the gods, after all. We must have transgressed the rituals in some way.' He did not sound convincing or convinced.

I looked around. There was still no hiding-place in the shrine that I could see. I put a hand on the statue, avoiding the sticky patch, and tried its weight. It rocked, but did not shift its position. I did the same thing to the altar stone. That brought Scribonius hurrying forward, instantly, yelping like a scalded puppy.

'Citizen, the altar! You have defiled it with your hands.'

Of course I had. I should have thought of that. Doubly defiled it, probably, because despite my splashings in the sacred water pot my fingertips still bore traces of where I'd touched the blood.

I looked down at the stain on the floor again, and something caught my eye. There, in the shadowed recess at the altar's foot. I felt the hairs prickle on my neck. 'Give me that taper here,' I whispered. My voice would hardly answer my command.

'You should not be kneeling there.' He was still fussing, his thin voice quivering with anxiety. 'Not without a proper sacrifice.'

He was too late. I was already on my knees. And I did not need Scribonius's taper to see the object which my shaking hands had found.

I held it up into the light. It was a ring. A legate's ring. Identical to the one I'd found there, yesterday; the one I'd last seen in Trinunculus's hands.

I stood there in the gloom, looking from the object in my hand to Scribonius. He was staring at it with a kind of fascinated horror, and little moaning noises were issuing from his lips.

'Do you know something about this, Scribonius?' I asked him softly.

He raised his head then and met my eyes. When he spoke, his voice was strained and high. 'I know nothing about it, citizen, except that . . .' He glanced at the ring again, looking rather as I imagine I had looked when I put my hand down in that sticky mass. He shook his head. 'Except . . . Nothing! . . .'

Faced with that kind of half-confession, I have often found that confrontation is the most efficient strategy. I tried it now. 'You know something that you have not confessed to me! Is it about the disappearing corpse, the bloodstain, or the ring?'

He shook his head impatiently. 'I have done nothing, citizen. But perhaps I am to blame. I am an Icenian, after all. I can't escape from that—and perhaps that's why these things keep happening.' He sighed. 'I have tried to persuade myself otherwise—that the curse could not be manifested through me without my knowing it—but even I cannot deny this evidence.' He glanced at the ring, which I was still holding in the gloom, and looked away again as though he could not bear to see it.

I was surprised. A moment ago Scribonius had been completely in control of himself. What was there about this ring that had unmanned him so? 'You have seen this ring before?'

'I saw it yesterday,' he said. 'First when you found it at the shrine, then later when Trinunculus brought it back to us. The pontifex refused to handle it, he said, so Meritus told him to put it in the sacred water butt, as a propitiation to the gods.' He shrugged, as if giving up a struggle. 'But that's not the really important thing. The truth is, I'm sure I've seen it once before. On the finger of that legate who was murdered all those years ago. He came to dinner with my master once. I was a young man then, and I never saw him again—but that ring is very like the one he wore. The way that eagle doesn't sit quite straight, you see? And then I heard that he'd been set upon and killed. I don't know why I should remember it, especially, except that he was so very proud of it. But of course no one else *here* has ever seen the ring before, so that uneven eagle would have no significance for them. That is what upsets me, citizen. Its reappearance must be meant for me!'

I stared at the ring. It *was* the same one that I'd seen before. I had noticed the imperfection earlier. 'But surely . . .'

He gave a bitter, sharp, uncertain laugh. 'You do not know the sacred writings, citizen. I do. It is clear from them that a man *can* sometimes be what they describe as "the unwitting tool of the gods", the channel through which the deities pour out their wrath and work out their purposes.'

I stared at him. 'Did you put this ring here?'

'Of course not, citizen. But it manifested itself when I was here. Just as the blood did earlier. Oh, dear Mercury! I knew that it was an unlucky sign yesterday, when Hirsus dropped the sacrificial knife. He is such a feeble creature, he seems incapable of doing things correctly. And I allowed him to rush the purification rituals. Then I connived at unconsecrated persons entering the sanctuary. It serves me right. The recorded precedents are very clear!'

As one of the unconsecrated persons he was alluding to—and one who had desecrated the sacred grove, as well—I could see that I was troubling him by simply being there. Any moment now, he would decide that the reappearance of the ring was somehow connected with *my* presence—after all, I had found it twice. And if he persuaded the other priests of that, I would be in serious difficulty. Not only would I have to make more propitiation to the gods (which would certainly be expensive, and possibly even physically painful) but I would assuredly be banished from the shrine. Yet there was a great deal more that I needed to discover. Somehow Scribonius must be persuaded to let me stay— and even to help me if necessary.

I thought quickly.

'I wonder what the pontifex will say when he hears that these things are happening around you?' I murmured, with a pretence at sympathy.

'I know what that pontifex will say!' He sounded petulant. 'That I am ill-omened and not fitted to continue as assistant priest. After all the effort I have made. And to think that I was worrying about my promotion to the *equites*! If this is proved against me, I shall be never be a knight. I shall be lucky to get out of this alive.'

I could think of nothing adequate to say. He was probably right—as he pointed out himself, he knew the priestly code better than I did. After all, military messengers are sometimes executed for bringing their generals bad news in the field. Doubtless the same principle applies to priests. There was, however, one ray of comfort I could offer him. 'But it was to Meritus, surely, that the body first appeared?'

Scribonius brightened visibly. 'You are quite right, citizen. It was.'

'Perhaps I can say so to the pontifex, if he tries to argue that you are one of these "unwitting instruments of the gods"? Or even a deliberate one.'

He emitted that moaning sound again. 'You don't believe that, do you, citizen?'

I shook my head. 'That you are an unwitting instrument? Not for a moment, I assure you, sub-Sevir Scribonius.' I was prevaricating. If he was an instrument, I thought, he would not be an 'unwitting' one—but my words appeared to calm him.

'Thank you, citizen. If you would really speak to the Pontifex . . .? It is clear that he respects your judgement. See how he deferred to you yesterday.'

'If I am to help you,' I said severely, 'I shall need your help in return. There are things about this temple that I need to know.'

'If there is anything that I can do—anything at all—to help in your enquiries, be sure that I shall be delighted. Rituals, customs—anything that's not forbidden by the laws. Where would you care to have our talk?'

'Here, where we are unlikely to be disturbed. Put down that taper and come and sit beside me.' I patted the marble floor invitingly.

'But citizen, the temple . . .' he began, and then tailed off. He put down the taper where I had indicated, prostrated himself before the statue of the Emperor, kissed the altar, smeared his forehead with the ashes from it, and finally came to squat gingerly beside me, moving his robes carefully to avoid the stain.

I regarded him coolly. 'You can begin,' I said, 'by telling me exactly what happened here last night. I understand you all slept at the temple. Where, and when, and how was it arranged?'

Scribonius looked startled, as if he were surprised that I wanted to know anything so mundane, but he answered readily enough. 'There is a room set aside in the outbuilding for the officiating priest who is on duty here at dawn—usually that is Meritus, but sometimes on low days it is Hirsus, and occasionally the honour falls on me. Meritus has a house nearby, of course—it is required of a sevir that he resides near the temple for his year of office—but it is convenient for us because we live farther away, and he himself often prefers to stay the night before. The previous sevir used to do the same. So there is always a mattress and some blankets here, and of course the temple slaves have sleeping spaces too—it was not difficult to find a place. Naturally, with the events of yesterday, it was thought proper for us all to stay. There was always to be one of us awake—to keep the sacred fire alight on the outer altar, and to offer propitiatory prayers throughout the night.'

'So,' I said, trying to disguise my growing interest, 'any one of you might have come out into the courtyard and opened up the back door to the shrine? While the others slept?'

'I suppose so, citizen,' he answered doubtfully, taking up his taper again and holding it up to look at the offending bolt with lugubrious interest. 'But no more so than any of the slaves. Or Trinunculus, for that matter: he lodges with the pontifex, and the house backs directly onto the temple enclosure. I suppose it would have been an easy matter for any of them to slip in here unseen.'

Or Aurelia, I thought. Or even—with her help—Optimus. I sighed. There seemed little hope of finding a solution here. Then I remembered something. 'But the front entrance to the shrine was locked. Who held the key?'

'Meritus, usually. But last night Hirsus should have had it, since he was to open up the shrine at dawn . . .' He hesitated.

'You say he *should* have had it,' I prompted. 'That suggests he didn't.'

Scribonius's prim face flushed. 'You are quite right, citizen. He was terrified of even touching it. In the end Meritus put it on top of

158

the storage chest where the robes are kept—and as far as I know it was there all night.'

'Is that in the room where you were sleeping?'

'We slept in different chambers, citizen. Meritus was in the inner cubicle, and Hirsus and I had partitioned spaces in the slaves' quarters. The chest is in the robing room between the two.'

'So anyone could have reached that, as well?'

'Anyone who had access to the temple, and knew where it was put.'

'And who was that?'

'The pontifex, certainly—Meritus asked him where the key could properly be left—and I believe that Trinunculus was there, as well. Or any of the slaves, again.' He shifted uncomfortably. 'Is there anything else you wish to ask me, citizen? I should not be absent from my duties for too long.'

'Not at the moment.'

'In that case, citizen, if you will permit . . . ?' He was on his feet in an instant, going through his elaborate performance at the shrine again.

I stood up myself, put out an automatic hand to help myself—and narrowly missed touching the bloodstained plinth once more. Suddenly, for no reason that I could explain, the full horror of the last two days came over me, and I was overwhelmed by a desire to get out of there—away from disappearing corpses, mysterious bloodstains and supernatural reappearing rings.

I made the sketchiest of obeisances to the Imperial Divinity and hurried out, gulping the honest clean fresh air like a prisoner released from a fetid dungeon.

Scribonius was looking at me in astonishment, and I felt abashed. Out here in the daylight my fears seemed laughable. I tried to regain my dignity.

'Of course, I may need to call upon your help again,' I said.

'It would be a pleasure, citizen,' he assured me, although his tone said otherwise. He had not missed my moment of superstitious fear, and was clearly losing confidence in me.

'I won't forget to speak to the pontifex,' I said, attempting to reassert what credibility I had. 'I think you said there was a back way from his house into the temple. Can you take me there?'

Scribonius gave me a look which said more clearly than any words that I was not dressed for visiting the high priest. 'If you are certain, citizen?'

'I don't mean to call on him like this. Only I should like to see the route. It may help me to work out what happened here last night.'

Scribonius still looked doubtful, but he took me there. Behind the central temple on its plinth, a narrow path led to a small gated opening in the perimeter wall. The gate was slightly open even now—only an inch or two, but by peering somewhat inelegantly through the gap I could see that it led into a peristyle garden beyond: a very ornate affair with fountains, arbours, statues, shrubs, a pool and narrow ornamental beds. I craned my head a little further round to get a better view, and drew back instantly.

There was a lady sitting in a grotto opposite—clearly a lady from her clothes and hair, although she seemed to be unattended in the garden. She was frowning over some document, written on a piece of folded bark, but as I pushed my head round the gate she half raised her eyes. There was no doubt that she had noticed me. But—and this was the astounding thing—instead of summoning a slave, and having me brought in for questioning, or even challenging me herself, she turned immediately away, pulling her mantle up to hide her face before I could really look at her.

I had just time, as I retreated in embarrassment at being seen, to register that she had done the same.

CHAPTER FOURTEEN

'Citizen! You will offend the gods!' Scribonius's whispered protest startled me. 'It is not proper to spy upon the pontifex!' He gestured me urgently away from the gate. 'It is an affront for anyone outside the household to see the pontifex without his official robes. There are enough ill omens in the temple as it is.'

After that embarrassing moment—when I was sure that I'd been seen—I was only too pleased to leave, and I allowed him to usher me back along the path. He was clearly as anxious as I was to have me away from there, and I had to walk quickly to keep up with him.

'Suppose the pontifex had spotted you!' he chided, in that schoolmasterly voice of his, when we were safely out of earshot and skirting round the central temple to the west. His tone suggested that even if I was not afraid of gods, at least I should beware of earthly powers.

'The pontifex is in the temple still,' I reminded him. 'I was hardly likely to surprise him in the garden.'

Scribonius did not look impressed. 'All the same, citizen. Someone might have seen you, and told him about it. Then I should have been blamed for that, as well as everything

162

else. After all, I am supposed to be escorting you. Suppose there was someone in the garden, for example.'

'There was someone sitting in a grotto,' I admitted. 'Though whoever it was seemed eager to avoid my eyes.'

Scribonius's frown deepened. 'One of the garden slaves, I suppose,' he said, after a moment. 'I doubt he will report the incident—he'll be too afraid of being caught out sitting down. The chief priest likes his garden slaves to work!' He was still striding down the path at an alarming pace.

'I suppose they have to,' I said, rather breathlessly. I was struggling to match my step to his. 'It's a very elaborate garden. Not the sort of thing that you'd expect.' Scribonius looked at me quizzically, so I hastened to explain. 'I thought the old man was so busy observing rules and denying himself in case they made him flamen some day that he had little time for material pleasures, such as gardens.'

Scribonius slowed at this, and permitted himself a smile. 'So you know about his flaminial ambitions? Of course. But the peristyle is not for the pontifex's pleasure, citizen, it is for his wife's. She is very partial to the garden, and of course whatever she says is like an imperial command. The old man can't afford to offend her, or that would be farewell to his hopes of ever succeeding to the flaminate. Especially now.' He gave a short mirthless laugh. 'Trinunculus says the poor fellow already has more servants attending his plants than his person.'

That was interesting, I thought. Scribonius was in awe of the high priest's power, but he was still capable of disrespect, at least on the subject of Aurelia. 'Why do you say "especially now"? Because of the happenings at the shrine? Surely they don't affect Aurelia?'

Scribonius seemed about to speak, but then he frowned. He looked at me sideways, made a doubtful clicking sound and shook his head. He looked so like a shifty market trader deliberating a dubious bargain in the forum that I was emboldened to persist. 'I think you should tell me everything, Scribonius, if you wish me to put in a good word for you . . .'

He glanced around him nervously, and ran an anxious tongue across his lips. 'I suppose it is no real secret, citizen. The fact is, the imperial messenger brought word, when he came to tell us Marcellus Fabius was on his way. I don't know if he told your patron too, but no doubt it will be common rumour soon enough . . .'

'What will?' I said impatiently. He was still hesitating, so I added, 'Look, Scribonius, if this concerns the running of the temple, my patron will have to know in any case, since he is the highest civic authority hereabouts, and nothing can be decided without consulting him. And if

164

this is something that you could tell Marcus, then you can tell me. His Excellence made me his representative, you heard him: and the pontifex himself expects you to help me in any way you can.'

'I suppose so, citizen. Well, you see . . . the thing is . . .' he took a deep breath, 'the current Flamen Dialis is ill . . . dying . . . It is supposed to be a temple secret, for the moment.'

He glanced up at the image of Jupiter on the pediment, as though expecting retribution for having said so much. There were no thunderbolts, however, and after a moment he continued, 'Of course, when one flamen dies, another must be appointed, and there are few enough priests in the Empire who meet all the qualifying criteria—not only concerning himself but his wife and parents too—so our pontifex must think he had a realistic chance, this time.'

I nodded. 'I see.' I remembered what Trinunculus had said. 'The right patrician background, the right kind of temple marriage, all that kind of thing? And an unbroken marriage record too?'

Scribonius looked at me with renewed respect. 'You know about these regulations, citizen? So few ordinary citizens do. The requirements are extraordinarily strict—do you know the office was left open once, for years, because they could not find a man who met them all? And of course, it isn't everyone who wants to live a life like that—all those things you're not allowed to do—even with all the wealth and influence it brings.'

I nodded again. 'So, His Mightiness the pontifex . . . ?'

'Exactly, citizen. He has worked all his life for an opportunity like this. But these events . . .' he waved his hand towards the Imperial shrine, 'you can imagine what the effect of that will be. It will be seen as an omen against him from the gods. And that will make two of us whose dreams are shattered by all this.'

'You think he is unlikely to get the position now?' That was something I had not considered.

Scribonius shook his head. 'I think it will be impossible. He has ordered sacrifices and purification rituals of the gravest kind, but even he cannot believe that it will help. No augurer in the Empire could overlook a set of signs like those. It will spell the end of everything for him. He may even find himself removed from serving at the temple here, and sent somewhere even more remote—or removed from the priesthood altogether on some excuse.' He swallowed, his throat working visibly, like a toad's. 'Unless . . . Oh, what's the use of pretending! Of course he won't allow that to happen. I know the pontifex. He'll try to find some other scapegoat, and pin the responsibility for it onto him. And it's not hard to guess who that will be.' He paused and looked at me. 'So you see why it's important that you speak to him for me, and remind him that it was Meritus who found the body first. I know that you were shaken by what I said back there but you will do that, won't you, citizen?'

I was silent for a moment. It was true, I had been shaken—not by what he'd said, but by a sudden fear that this whole business defied analysis, and that some deep unexplained and sinister power was at work.

Scribonius began again, almost babbling by this time. 'I will offer votive tablets for you, citizen, make special sacrifices. I know what kinds of offerings please the gods and I'll ensure the animals are flawless and pass the *hirospex*. I'll petition them for riches, women—anything you like.'

That brought me back to rationality. The idea of the small, staid, balding Scribonius earnestly petitioning the gods for a selection of willing virgins on my account was enough to make me smile. 'Ask them for guidance for me, if you must,' I said. 'And make sure your offerings are made at the central shrine. Judging by all those prayer tablets from Lucianus, petitions to the Emperor don't seem to do much good.'

Scribonius looked up at the statues in the courtyard again. My irreverence clearly troubled him a lot. However, the gods remained immovably on their pedestals, and nothing came to strike me dead. 'Lucianus is a melancholy case,' he said unhappily, and led the way up to the outer gate. Before he reached it, however, he stopped in surprise. 'What are all these people doing here? Someone has been gossiping. News must have leaked out somehow to the town.'

He was right. Some rumour had clearly found its way beyond the gates, because quite a little crowd had gathered, and were crowding round the entranceway. Not merely curious onlookers, but people with an air of panic and unease. Some of them were clearly terrified. One or two women were actually wailing, and men were waving votive plaques, or carried sacrificial birds in wicker cages. The temple slave whom I had seen before was now outside the gates, attempting to keep the rabble back, and only just succeeding too, although his temple uniform ensured him some respect.

He was standing on a small four-legged stool, and trying to address the mob, and they were listening to him, though there were mutterings.

'You must keep away,' he was saying. 'There are ill omens for you at the temple now. Go back to your homes, and make your offerings there. There must not be a riot here, or we shall feel more than the gods' displeasure. The Emperor will hear of it. So go away. Leave matters to the priests. Sacrifices are being offered as I speak, and when the auguries are read the pontifex and the authorities will work out what to do. Your entering the temple will only make things worse.'

The truth of his words made my spine prickle. This was what Scribonius had also feared. If there was a civil disturbance at the temple, then the whole city would have cause to fear. In fact, when the Emperor heard what had happened here already—as he assuredly would do—there could be very unfortunate results for everyone. Commodus took Imperial worship personally.

Fortunately, the slave's little homily was having some effect. A few of the crowd were still muttering discontentedly but others were beginning to drift away.

'This is the handiwork of the gods,' the slave said again. 'Leave proper propitiation to the priests. There is nothing you can do here for the moment.'

I turned to Scribonius. 'If this *is* the hand of the gods,' I murmured (we were still inside the ambulatory, so that only he could hear), 'perhaps there is nothing *anyone* can do. However, I am still inclined to seek a human agency. I remember that opened bolt and that unprotected key. Make your sacrifices, just in case, to placate the deities—but keep your ears and eyes open too. That is the best way you can serve the temple.'

He nodded, doubtfully.

'Farewell, for now at least.' I left him to it,

and made my way out past the slave and through the gate.

A little gaggle of people still lingered there, reluctant to disperse. As soon as they saw me they surrounded me, asking a hundred questions and tugging me this way and that, all shouting at once, their voices high with panic. I could see in their faces that unreasoning fear which had possessed me earlier.

'What's happening, tradesman? Why have they called on you?' One of the wailing women accosted me. I did not know her, but she'd seized me by the sleeve and forced me to stop and talk to her. I was wearing a simple tunic, of course—if I had been wearing my toga, she would never have dared. 'What's happening in there? A demon with four heads they say. And someone saw a shower of stars last night. Are we all doomed?' She gave my arm a little jerk, as if she could shake the information from me.

Her terror was infectious. I knew that if I closed my eyes, I would see that reappearing stain, hear that inhuman moaning sound, feel the sticky warmth of blood upon my hands. I began to find my own heart thumping hard, and a cold sweat running down my spine. Besides, they were all swarming round me now. I've always had a fear of mindless crowds. But there was little I could say to calm them down. I was as mystified as they were. But it would not do to show it.

As I was trying to compose myself, a second

crone began plucking at me on the other side. 'And is it true there was a visitation from the gods?'

'A monstrous spectre with a face like death?' That was a third, pulling at my shoulder.

A man in a tattered tunic thrust his red face close to mine. 'Don't try to fob us off with lies. We heard that awful moaning yesterday.'

This was getting out of hand. It would not take much to start a riot. I had to do something. I strove to recollect myself. 'These things are exaggerated in the telling,' I said firmly, shaking myself free. 'Some serious events have happened at the temple, it is true, but there is a simple human explanation— which you will be told. But not today.' I only wished I was as certain of that as I sounded. 'The priests will tell you at the proper time, but first, of course, they must consult the auguries. Now, I am going back to attend to my work, and I suggest that you all do the same.'

The temple slave had got down off his stool, and now flashed me a grateful smile, as if we were accomplices in a convenient lie.

Yet there *was* an explanation, I told myself fiercely. There had to be. If these unearthly events had occurred at the altar of Mighty Jupiter, perhaps my terrors would be justified. Even a Celt like me would have recognised the workings of a supernatural hand. But they had happened at the Imperial shrine, and surely that was quite a different matter? Commodus was officially a god, of course, but I had never had the slightest belief in his divinity, much less in his ability to perform miracles and signs. Surely, rationally, I couldn't accept it even now?

I felt a little calmer at the thought, and that confidence must have communicated itself to the crowd, because they began to drift away. I couldn't explain my reasoning to them, of course—I value my scraggy neck too much. It would not have taken much, in the mood that they were in, to turn the mob against me, and what I had just thought was treasonable, as well as impious. The punishment for that was horrible, though it might have caused amusement to the crowd. If Fabius Marcellus the legate ever did visit the city, I had no wish to form part of the civic entertainments by facing the beasts in the arena for his delight. I am an old man, and my sense of humour about these things is not what it was.

I elbowed my way out through the remnants of crowd, and went resolutely back to Optimus's house. One or two of the stragglers followed me, still plucking at my sleeves and questioning. I was glad to arrive at the back door of the house, where I could get away from them.

Especially since I had no answers to give them. If there *was* some human explanation

172

for what I'd seen, I had no idea what it was. I needed time to think.

I rapped sharply on the wooden gate, and the doorman let me in.

CHAPTER FIFTEEN

This time, when he greeted me, the doorkeeper seemed noticeably more relaxed. 'Citizen Optimus got tired of sending important visitors round to the servants' door,' he informed me cheerfully. 'He's gone off to hold his meetings in the public baths.' He chuckled. 'Taken that Phrygian steward with him, so you can find your own way through the house if you like. Save me having to get up, and leave the back door unattended.'

'Thank you. I think I know the way.' I hurried off before he had time to change his mind. I wanted to take the opportunity of being unattended to have a quick look in that inner courtyard garden where I'd seen the hooded shape. Not that there was very much to see. The colonnaded walkway I had seen the day before; a few uninteresting plants; a collection of poky storerooms at the back, full of amphorae, sacks and barrels; a sort of two-storey outhouse for the slaves; a *lararium* to the household gods, and a small courtyard with an oven in it, where bread and cakes were evidently baked without the threat of setting fire to the kitchen. Just like a dozen other dwellings of its kind.

I might have investigated further, but at that moment a woman emerged from one of the bedrooms off the colonnade. She was short, well fed, well coiffured and well dressed, and accompanied by a pretty slave girl carrying a tray of unguents. This must be Optimus's wife. She stared at me.

'I've come about the pavement, lady,' I explained.

She nodded vaguely and I went quickly on into the front section of the house.

It was almost a relief, after the pressures of the day, to walk into that calm interior and to think about a piece of floor which was not occupied by disappearing corpses or reappearing blood. The only bodies in the passageway, when I arrived, were those of Junio and the kitchen boy, and they were clearly very much alive. Both were on their knees, facing away from me, occupied in laying tiles to a template under Junio's vociferous command.

'Not there, you stupid oaf, you'll put your hand down on the wet cement. A little further right. That's it. And now another—pass me that red one, quick! Before the mortar sets! Come on! Did they breed you from a tortoise and a snail?'

I recognised something of my own style in

this, and could not contain a chuckle. The kitchen slave heard me and scrambled to his feet, red-faced, brushing his dirty hands diligently on his apron.

'What are you . . .?' Junio said, and then he turned and saw me too. He stood up in his turn, a slow reluctant smile on his face. 'There you are, master,' he said. 'I did not hear you come.'

'So I observe,' I said, trying to sound severe. 'Judging by the sight that greeted me!'

The kitchen slave looked anxious, but Junio only grinned. 'Master, you have come back half an hour too soon. Another little while and we'd have finished the job.' Now that I was not confronted by a pair of tunicked bottoms, I could see the border they had been working on. He was right. Most of the missing tiles had been reset by now and a good job they had made of it—though there was a slight imperfection in one corner, and they had created a lot of dust and chippings in the process.

I said, 'It's an improvement on the previous pavement, certainly. That corner piece, you could have used a smaller template there—but it will do. I think I can disguise it.' I tied on my leather apron as I spoke (it had been folded on the floor nearby) and got to my own knees, creakily. 'If you let me have those last few tile pieces there, and some water perhaps, so we can wash it down . . .' My last remark was

175

intended for the kitchen slave, but he had already seized the bucket and was gone.

'Master, what happened at the temple?' Junio asked eagerly, as soon as the boy was out of earshot. 'Have they discovered something new? What did they want you for in such a hurry?' He was already collecting up the tesserae I'd asked for.

I told him, briefly—omitting my sacrilegious moment in the grove. 'So, you can see, I have made little progress. Not like you—I see you've had assistance all the morning here?'

Junio nodded. 'Lithputh gave orders that the boy was to help me until you came back—decided that someone should keep an eye on me, I think. I got the feeling that he knew what I was planning, and did it to stop me wandering about unsupervised and questioning the other slaves.' He put the pieces he'd collected into a pile, and stood nearby to help. I looked up at him, inviting him to think about the task. 'Red, in that corner, do you think?' he said.

I held a tile or two above the floor to try out the effect. He had a good eye—red was exactly right. I nodded, satisfied. But I was still interested in Lithputh. 'It wouldn't make much difference how many slaves you saw. If Optimus or his steward had anything significant to hide, surely one servant would know as much as any other?' I spoke from experience. 'It's hard to keep a secret in a household full of slaves.'

Junio shook his head. 'Perhaps not in this household, master. Lithputh rules it with a rod of iron—quite literally a rod sometimes, I hear. Out of frustration, I suppose. It seems he's been trying for a long time to save up and buy his freedom—but you know what Optimus is like. Phrygian stewards may be commonplace in Rome, but they're a luxury item here—and Optimus must have set the price unreasonably high. In any case Lithputh can't afford it. And his master fines him for all breakages and "wastage" in the house—so even that price rises all the time. It's clear his master doesn't want to let him go.'

'And Lithputh takes it out on all the rest?' I guessed.

Junio nodded. 'Beatings for everything, from breaking plates to "standing gossiping"— and he has his spics—so naturally, if there is the slightest problem, everyone blames everybody else, and no one confides in anyone. There's a real household atmosphere of resentment and mistrust.'

'At least when Lithputh is about,' I said, remembering the doorman's manner. I put down the tiles and began to scratch the pattern in the mortar. The paving task that I had set myself was complex—an inner curve to minimise the flaw and link the new work to the old, and a final small medallion shape to draw the eye away. Curved lines are always more difficult than straight, and it must be done before the mortar dried.

'There!' I said at last, sitting back on my heels. 'That will do, I think. Now we can start filling in the tiles.' The task must have needed all my concentration because it was only now that a thought struck me. 'All this about the household, the slave boy told you that? *You* seem to have gained his confidence, at least.'

'I'm not part of the household,' Junio grinned. 'All he wanted was a sympathetic ear. He was only too anxious to pour out all his woes.' He was passing me the tiles one by one, anticipating my needs.

'Which were . . . ?' I prompted.

'The poor boy was only purchased recently, to replace another kitchen slave that died. He is terribly ill-suited to the job. His name is Kurso. He was a child slave and playmate to a rich man's son before, but then his master went to school and so he wasn't needed any more. He's had a dreadful time since he arrived. He dropped a serving dish the first hour he was here—he had not known that it would be so hot. Of course, they punished him—and that made it worse. He's grown so terrified that he's clumsier by the hour. The other slaves avoid him—they think he brings bad luck.'

'Perhaps that's why Lithputh selected him to come and help us?'

'I expect so, master. Unfortunately, though, if there is gossip in the household, he is the one least likely to have heard it. He seems to have spent much of his time locked in a cellar, either waiting for a beating or recovering from one. Poor boy, he has no skills at anything. I'm surprised that Optimus chose to purchase him. Though Kurso was healthy, young and cheap—no doubt that appealed. But he's not stupid, master, though they think he is. He isn't clumsy if he isn't scared. I showed him what to do here, and he was very quick to learn. Especially when Lithputh left us alone. I think Kurso even quite enjoyed himself.'

'And so did you, you impudent young scamp,' I told him. 'I heard you giving orders like an overseer!' That sounded sharper than I meant, and I hurried to add, 'To some effect, at least. He seems to have been very helpful here.'

Junio's face cleared, and he grinned. 'Helpful in more ways than one. One can learn things even in a cellar. As I promised, master—I think I may have some real news for you—' He stopped suddenly as the boy came back into the room, red-faced and struggling under the weight of the heavy bucket, which was filled right to the brim.

'Ah, Kurso! The water!' I said, getting to my feet. 'At last!'

It was the mildest of rebukes, but the effect was startling. Kurso turned a painful shade of red, stepped backwards, and slopped half of the bucket's contents on the floor as he set it

179

down. 'I'm sorry, citizen,' he blurted, with a little sob. 'I did not mean to be so long—and now I've spilt it.'

'You'd have been quicker with a lighter bucket,' Junio said.

'Lithputh is back. He saw me coming to you with the pail and sent me back to fill it properly. Said I was a lazy little swine and to fetch a proper bucketful next time. I'm sorry, citizen.' His lip was trembling.

Poor child, I thought. That bucket was almost as heavy as he was. And, of course, he dared not spill a drop. Junio says you have been helpful here,' I said, giving him what I hoped was a reassuring smile, and reaching out to take the water pail.

Kurso misunderstood. He was expecting a blow. He dodged backwards, kicked the pail and almost overset the thing again. He stood there against the wall, gazing at me, breathing fast.

Junio rescued us. 'Well, my master has come back now, Kurso. I think you should go and be about your duties. Thank you for your help. If you have finished with that pattern, master, I'll make a start at cleaning over here.' He picked up the brush that Lithputh had provided and turned away, scrubbing the fresh-laid tiles as if the water had been poured out there on purpose.

Even then Kurso looked at me, too terrified to move without permission. I nodded, and he scuttled off in reverse, still bowing, as fast as his legs would take him. (People talk lightly about unfortunates who have learned, from bitter experience, how to run faster backwards than forwards. In Kurso's case, I realised, it was true.)

I waited until I was sure the boy was gone before I said to Junio, 'Poor child. But I think you said he may have told you something significant?'

He put down the brush at once. 'I did, master, and it seems that you were right! About it being Hirsus in the garden here last night. Of course I can't be absolutely sure— Kurso didn't see the visitor, and naturally I couldn't press him too much for details.'

'It wasn't Optimus's wife, at any rate,' I said. 'I met her a little while ago, and she is much too short and fat. So what did Kurso say? Be quick and tell me, Junio. Lithputh will be here any minute.'

Junio resumed his scrubbing and took a deep breath. 'Well,' he said, 'it's like this . . . Kurso was chained up in a store outside one day, waiting to be whipped for something he'd done. They left him there for hours. He thought at first it was done to punish him, but Optimus had come home unexpectedly, and it seems in all the rush they'd genuinely forgotten him. They'd left the door a little bit ajar—fortunately, or he might have suffocated —but no one came near him all the afternoon.

But later, when it was getting dark, he heard a noise.' He paused dramatically.

'Hirsus?' I said, anxious to get to the point.

Junio shook his head. 'I can't be sure. Kurso himself didn't know. He only knows he heard a voice—a whispering, he said, and what sounded like the chink of coins. He thought it was his master's voice he heard, and he was petrified. Decided that Optimus was tired of him, and was in the process of selling him back to some slave-trader. Not that Kurso was happy in the household, but things could be a whole lot worse, of course—if he got sold on to the mines, or something—the more so if they sold him in disgrace. Naturally, he wanted to know what was happening. He couldn't hear a word of what was said, and he was chained so he couldn't really move, but he did contrive to shuffle up a bit and got a small glimpse through the door.'

'And what did he see?' I said impatiently. 'Who was with Optimus?'

'That's just it,' Junio exclaimed. 'It wasn't Optimus at all. It was Lithputh. And he was talking to a priest. Kurso is absolutely sure of that. It was getting dark, and he was peeping through a crack, but he is absolutely adamant. He'd seen the man before, he said, over at the temple—and anyway he recognised the robes.' He grinned. 'Sounds like an Imperial priest to me! Any of the other priests would wear a toga, wouldn't they, even the High Priest of

Jupiter.'

'I suppose they would!' I worked it out aloud. 'Impossible to tell them from any other citizen, in the dark—except perhaps for that flaminial hat?'

My slave looked doubtful. 'Kurso didn't say anything about a hat. I got the impression he couldn't see the face—he would have been kneeling on the floor, remember. But definitely he mentioned "priestly robes".'

'Not someone from the Mithraic temple or the Osiris cult?'

Junio shook his head. 'From the temple opposite, he said. "And in the cloak he looked so slight and slim he might have been mistaken for a woman." Those were his very words.'

'It does sound like Hirsus, then,' I said. 'No one could take Meritus or Scribonius for a girl. So, what did Kurso do?'

'Nothing,' Junio replied. 'He simply held his breath and tried his hardest not to make a noise and after a while the two men went away. But here's the thing I thought would interest you. The priest wrapped himself up in a hooded cloak, he says—just like the figure we saw yesterday—and (this is the most extraordinary thing) Lithputh himself went out to the gate, and personally let the caller out. Kurso is sure of that. Lithputh would have a key for the back gate, anyway, of course.'

I stared at him. 'Where was the doorkeeper?'

'Who knows? At the front door perhaps? Anyway, Lithputh went back to the house, and Kurso was left to wait again. Nobody came for him for days—by that time he was starving and shivering with cold, and he was almost glad to have his beating and get back to his work.'

'I wonder what Lithputh and Hirsus were up to?' I said, putting the last scraps of tile away and collecting up my tools. 'Who was paying whom for what? And why meet secretly in the dark to do it?'

Junio thought about this for a moment. 'Hirsus bribing Lithputh, perhaps, to let him come into the house again—like yesterday? Kurso didn't seem to know—or care, once he knew that they weren't selling him! He only told me any of the story because I stopped to eat some of that piece of bread and cheese we brought. He looked at it so longingly, I asked if he was ever hungry. And then it all came out— how he'd been locked up and starved for days.'

All this talk of bread and cheese reminded me that it was now long past midday and I had not eaten anything myself. The floor was almost finished now—only those last few tiles that I'd put in remained to be cleaned off, and that could not be done until they'd set, so I asked Junio to pass me the remnants of the food.

He did so, rather sheepishly—there was not a great deal left. ('The poor boy looked so ravenous, master,' Junio said apologetically 'and I thought that you'd be eating with the priests.')

I had to wait while the mortar dried, so I ate my unexpectedly frugal meal, leaving Junio to load up our things and bring the handcart round to the front door. I didn't offer to help him—that would teach him to give away my lunch!—and I was just finishing the last few crumbs of cheese when Lithputh came back into the room. He looked displeased to see me squatting there.

'Thtill here, thitithen? I underthtood from your thlave that you had finished?' He looked at the floor. 'I thuppothe the work ith thatithfactory—it didn't theem to take you very long. You were away for half the morning, too, the doorman telith me. I hope you don't ecthpect my mathter to pay you the prithe that he agreed—when he provided half the labour and you're thimply thitting there?'

'I agreed to do the job within a day,' I said, blessing Gwellia's astuteness. 'And I've completed it in less. If anything, I should increase the price.'

Lithputh looked singularly unimpressed by this, and I could see that I was in for a long dispute before I saw my money. I was about to argue—my slave's work is mine to sell—when it occurred to me that Lithputh might have an interest in seeing me paid less. As steward of the purse, he would doubtless have the opportunity to pocket some of the difference

185

himself.

Perhaps that's what made me confront him then and there, and say, conversationally, 'Perhaps we could ask the temple to arbitrate between us? It was they who summoned me away, and I understand that you are friendly with one of the Imperial priests?'

I was aware of the door behind him opening, but I did not glance towards it. If Lithputh had anything to say, I was only too glad for Junio to witness it—especially if Lithputh didn't know that he was there.

Lithputh didn't have anything to say. He stood there silent, looking shocked.

'Well?' I urged him. 'Isn't that the case? Hirsus the priest has been here, more than once?'

It wasn't Junio at the door, I realised. It was Kurso, and if Lithputh had not been so intent on me, he too would have heard that sharp intake of breath. But the Phrygian steward was too transfixed by my words to be aware of anything else.

'Hirthuth!' he exclaimed, with evident astonishment. 'How did you come to hear of that? Did one of the houthhold tell you? Or have you been thpeaking to the prietht himthelf?'

'I did not need to hear from anyone. I have the testimony of my own two eyes. I saw him leaving yesterday, shortly after I left here myself.' I said this thinking to reassure Kurso,

186

but when I glanced towards the door the boy had disappeared. Lithputh was still staring at me. I went on, 'And since I didn't see him in the public rooms, I deduced the priest had been entertained here privately.' It sounded a bit lame, when I said it, but the effect on Lithputh was remarkable.

'Ah!' he said. His manner had changed abruptly, and he almost squirmed. 'Well then, I thuppothe you'll have to know . . . It'th nothing of importanth, really—just a buthineth matter between Hirthuth and my mathter.'

'What kind of business?' I demanded. I was genuinely curious. What did a miserly ex-legionary like Optimus Honorius want with an assistant Imperial priest and one-time slave?

Lithputh flushed and looked more embarrassed than ever. 'That I can't tell you, thitithen. If I knew the anthwer, which I don't, my lipth would thtill be thealed. I am a private thteward, after all.'

'I'll speak to Optimus about it,' I said, and hoped it sounded like a threat. 'When I talk to him about the fees, perhaps? I shan't leave here until that matter is resolved.'

'Ah, ath to that,' Lithputh began. He sounded suddenly conciliatory, as I'd hoped he might. 'My mathter ithn't here at prethent, but ath thoon ath he comth back I'll thend it after you. I'm thure we can—'

But what we could have done, I never learned. At that moment Junio burst into the

187

room.

'Master,' he said, without waiting for permission. 'Can I have a word?' He glanced at Lithputh. 'For your ears alone, citizen pavement-maker. It may concern your patron . . .'

Lithputh sniffed, and looked affronted, but he left the room.

I turned to Junio. 'Bad news from Marcus? You look terrified!'

He shook his head. 'Nothing to do with Marcus. I said that because I wanted to speak to you alone. Master, I think you'd better leave. The front way, too, as quickly as you can. There's a crowd of people out there, massing at the back—quite a little group of them, all shouting and calling on the gods. The mood is getting ugly: some of them are armed with sticks and stones. I don't know what's provoked this, master, but something clearly has. I heard them shouting at the doorman. They know you're in here—it's you they're looking for.' He gulped. 'It's something to do with the problems at the temple. You've brought down divine wrath upon the town, they say—and only your death will satisfy the gods.'

CHAPTER SIXTEEN

An armed mob! Looking for me!

For the second time that day I felt my blood run cold. I had been alarmed by the seemingly supernatural events I'd seen, but this was a far more pressing threat. I have seen what angry crowds can do. Even the Roman authorities are afraid of riots—especially religious ones. See how they persecute the Druids. And the founder of the Christians was put to death—though the provincial governor was reluctant to do it, if the accounts are true—precisely at the demand of an angry mob like this.

Of course, I was a Roman citizen, which helped—but if the rabble got hold of me, dressed as I was in working clothes, I didn't suppose they would stop to ask questions. Even if I survived their sticks and stones, and claimed my rights, they would probably haul me to the authorities and demand a trial on a charge of sacrilegious treason. And if that happened, not even Marcus or Pertinax could save me—all I could do was appeal to the Emperor, whose temple I had accidentally desecrated! Commodus thinks he's Hercules and will not tolerate any slight to his divinity: men who do not show appropriate respect to an Imperial shrine often end up as fodder for the arena beasts. I could face worse vengeance than the mob's.

But they had to catch me first. Under Roman law there can be no trial without the accused's being present. If only I could smuggle myself out of the house and get away! I thought of appealing to Lithputh for help, but that was no use. I had seriously unsettled him and I suspected he would cheerfully betray me to the crowd.

'Do something, master,' Junio urged.

But what?

In the end I got away in the handcart. It was not the most comfortable journey of my life, huddled on a pile of broken tiles and cowering under a piece of filthy sacking, and it was all Junio could do to push my weight, but it was the only solution I could think of.

It was a near thing, even then. Junio had the cart at the front door, where he had been loading it in full view of passers-by, and we had to choose a moment when the front street was clear for me to slip out and clamber on. As I did so, someone came out of the potter's shop next door and Junio threw the cloth over me just in time. I must have made a grotesque-looking heap, but fortunately no one paid any attention to the slave—whom they had previously seen innocently loading tiles—pushing his laden cart away.

He pushed me halfway across the town. I swear I felt every carriage rut and cobble, and by the time he paused in a little lane behind the market to let me climb painfully down, I was so shaken and bruised that I was beginning to wish I'd taken my chance and tried to talk my way out of the mob.

I said so to Junio, as I stood in a disused doorway picking pieces of tile out of myself and trying to shake the stone dust from my hair. 'I suppose I brought this on myself by talking to that crowd at the temple gates. Some of them followed me to Optimus's house. I might have known they wouldn't go away. They'd heard rumours from somewhere of strange things at the temple, it had all got hugely exaggerated, and I suppose they think I know more than I admitted to. Perhaps if I'd just tried to talk to them . . .'

Junio shook his head. 'I don't think so, master. From what the doorkeeper said to me I don't think this was an opportunity to chat! The mood was pretty ugly in the street. And if these were the men who followed you at first, they must have gone away and come back with their friends! This lot did not start to collect until about an hour ago—then apparently they all turned up at once. And not because you hadn't told them things! They wanted you, they said, because you were causing these events—by going in there and angering the gods! The gods demanded blood, they claimed.'

It was stupid of me, I suppose, but I had not seen the danger. It had occurred to me that

Scribonius, for example, might suddenly decide that all the misfortunes at the temple had been brought about by my presence, but I simply had not considered the possibility that the people of the town would think the same. And if they were eager to appease the gods they wouldn't be content with merely beating me and offering expiatory sacrifice. They seriously intended to kill me.

It was a sobering thought.

Of course, killing a citizen was a serious offence, unless they could show 'just cause' before the law. But perhaps they thought they could. Everything I'd said to them outside the temple could be turned against me and used in their defence. My assurance that there was an explanation for events *could* be construed as blasphemy against the Imperial gods. And if Scribonius and his fellow priests joined in—explaining how I'd desecrated the shrine and generally occasioned all these auguries—then murdering me to protect the city could almost be seen as a civic duty!

I felt my old heart lurch a beat or two.

Things were not looking good. It was only a matter of time before the rabble worked out who I was, and came to try to find me where I lived. In fact, I would not have put it past Lithputh to have put them on my tail already, once he discovered I'd escaped. I cursed myself for an idiot. Why had I antagonised him like that?

I looked up and down the lane, but there was no sign of pursuit: no distant cries except the normal ones of commerce, and nobody in sight except a lethargic peasant with a donkey, passing the corner with his panniers full of turnips, together with a bored lad—probably his son—leading a thin and most reluctant pig. It was the picture of tranquillity. But I knew better than to trust appearances. I'd won myself a little time, that's all.

I did the only thing that I could do. 'Go quickly,' I said to Junio. 'Find Marcus and tell him what has happened. Insist on seeing him yourself—don't be content with messages. Say those were my explicit instructions. Go now. Run.'

Junio hesitated. 'But master, what happens if they find you here? Who will protect you if I leave you?'

It was rather endearing, this willingness to face the mob for me, though what defence he would have been—one small lad against a crowd with staves and stones—it's hard to see. I swallowed down a lump of gratitude.

'I don't intend to face them,' I declared. 'I'll take a litter and go home, to warn Gwellia of what has happened here.' I was working out my strategy as I spoke. 'I'll change into my toga—they won't be looking for a citizen, not yet—and make my way back to the high priest's house. He'll have a proper view of this, and won't be led by superstitious fears.'

Junio was nodding. I devoutly hoped that what I was saying was true.

'If necessary I can shelter there—and at the very least, it will calm the crowd. If they want some sort of expiation from me, who better than the pontifex to handle it? Tell Marcus he can reach me there. Quickly, before they come and catch us here.'

This time he did go, only pausing to say plaintively, 'But master, how will you manage your toga without me?'

It was a reasonable question, in fact. I am notoriously inexpert at draping that cumbersome garment—but I'd have to manage somehow when the moment came. For now I had more pressing problems.

The first was the cart, which I disposed of by the expedient of calling after the sullen boy with the pig, and bribing him to walk it home to my lodgings. It was not an ideal solution, the boy looked as if he would sell the cart, the pig and his father to the highest bidder, and I knew that if the mob caught up with him he would betray me without a qualm. But I had no time to worry about that.

Instead I turned my attention to trying to find a litter for hire, but—as usual when you really want one—there was none to be had. If I went back towards the forum there were no doubt litters waiting two or three abreast, but that would have taken me back in the direction of my pursuers.

I wasted several minutes searching. I had been hoping for a covered litter, which would hide me from the street, with a couple of fleet-footed boys to carry it, but not a single litter of any description came my way. I was becoming increasingly alarmed, imagining that I could hear the cries and noises of pursuit, and in the end I abandoned the attempt and simply scurried home on foot, keeping to the back streets and alleyways and hurrying as quickly as I could.

I knew that I was making myself conspicuous. The sight of an elderly man half running through the lanes was enough to make the beggars stare, but I hurried on, not stopping even when my sandal lace came undone. By the time I reached my workshop I was panting with exertion.

'Why, citizen master, whatever is the matter?' Gwellia put down her broom of bundled twigs as I came in, and hurried over carrying a stool.

She set it down invitingly, but I shook my head. I took her hands and—between gasps—told her the story.

'Sit down,' she said. 'I'll fetch your toga for you. You wait here.'

I was in no state to argue, and I did so, glad of a moment to recover.

She disappeared upstairs and was back in an instant. 'Stand up!' she instructed, and I obeyed. 'Lift your arms, so!' She wound the

195

toga round me, almost as deftly as Junio.

'You've done this before!' I said, and she smiled grimly. 'Many times. It was a part of—' She broke off. 'Listen! What was that?'

I had already heard it and my heart sank. A sound from the corner of the street. The savage, heart-stopping sound of an approaching crowd, baying like a pack of hunting dogs. I looked around wildly, with some confused idea of concealing myself underneath the table, or trying to climb out of the window-space and hide.

My wife surprised me.

'Sit down,' she said. 'Quickly, on the stool. Here. Tip your head right forward—let me get to it. Don't argue, husband . . . master . . . there's no time!' She picked up a handful of ash from the fire and part of the dust she'd been sweeping together, white with marble dust and stone, and to my astonishment tipped it on my head and rubbed it roughly on my face and beard.

'From a distance that will have to do. Your skin looks chalky and your hair is white—' She broke off. There was a disturbance right outside the door, and cries of 'This must be the place! Look at the stone piles outside!'

'Quickly!' Gwellia hissed at me. 'There's no time to get away. Pull your toga up to form a hood.' She quickly did it for me as she spoke.

'I'll look as if I'm about to offer sacrifice,' I protested.

196

'Will you stop arguing! The really old men sometimes wear their hoods when they're in mourning, especially the pious ones. That's why I put those ashes on your head. Now, that will have to do. They're coming through the outer shop this minute! Pretend you're choosing a memorial pavement—here, look at this pattern book. Leave this to me.' She thrust the pile of vellum sketches into my hand and swung around to face the entranceway. 'What is the meaning of this intrusion, gentlemen?'

I glanced up under my hood. There were two of them, pushing forward into the doorway, ruffianly-looking fellows in coarse tunics, with ragged cloth tied around their feet for boots. The rest of the mob were clearly outside in the street, balked by the partition which screened the outer shop: I could hear the shufflings and murmurings.

'Well?' Gwellia said again. 'What do you want? You haven't come here to buy pavements, I suppose! And now you have alarmed this customer! And him a respected Roman citizen!'

Too late, I realised what she was up to. I'd thought of using my toga as a temporary disguise, myself, but to try to pass me off as someone else, here in my own house! It was a loving, clever, desperate thing to do. Brave, too. The crowd would not take kindly to attempted tricks. They might easily turn their anger onto Gwellia too.

But there was nothing for it now. I squinted at them through dust-reddened eyes and tried to look as Roman and inoffensive as possible. I didn't need the ash to make me pale.

The larger of the two intruders, a big broad-chested fellow with a head like a battering ram and thick dark stubble on every inch of skin, flicked a brief glance at me and looked away. He had a stout stave in his hand, and looked as if he knew how to use it, but Gwellia's challenge had taken him by surprise.

'We're looking for the pavement-maker,' he snarled, looking her up and down in an unpleasant fashion. 'Where is he? Don't try to lie. We know his workshop's here.' All the same, he'd lost something of his aggressive swagger.

Gwellia gave a little snort. If I had not known better, I would have believed it when she said, 'You want to see the pavement-maker? So do we! This poor citizen has been sitting here, I don't know how long, waiting for my master to return. But does he? Not a bit of it! And guess who'll be in trouble if we lose the commission?' She laughed bitterly.

'Never mind all that,' the fellow said. 'What's happened to your master? And who is that?' He gestured at me with the stave.

Gwellia glanced at me. 'Don't worry about him, he's deaf. Can't hear a word unless you shout, poor man.' She dropped her voice. 'Poor old fellow can't make up his mind. I

198

think he's . . . you know . . . but who cares? He pays. I only wish my master would come home. He went out this morning to repair a pavement for a rich man somewhere in the town. Don't ask me where, I'm only a domestic slave, I've never seen the place. Why? What's he done?'

The other man, a fat, freckled ruffian with a shock of bright red hair, waved the baton he was carrying, excitedly. 'Only affronted the Imperial gods, that's all! And mighty Jupiter as well! There've been the most dreadful happenings. Visions of murdered corpses at the temple, bloodstains—all sorts of things. Sudden icy winds and moaning sounds. Last night there was a shower of shooting stars— dozens of people saw it!—some of the soothsayers had warning dreams, and water in the sacred pools turned red!' He laughed lugubriously. 'I tell you, I've bought myself an amulet to ward off evil spells. And if you work here, you'd better do the same. It's him that's bringing all this bad luck down on us.'

Grizzle-head nodded. 'Brought this curse back with him from Londinium—Mars alone knows what he got up to there. Apparently it all started the moment he got back. He's bringing divine vengeance down on Glevum. Just when the imperial legate's due to come. If we're not careful he'll destroy us all.'

Gwellia had been listening to all this with an expression of dismay.

'I can see why you want to talk to him,' she said. 'But just be careful how you deal with him. You could find yourself in trouble. Believe me, I know! His patron is Marcus Septimus, the governor's personal representative in Glevum—your amulet won't save you from him. Besides, my master is a ci—' She hesitated. I am convinced to this day that she was going to say 'a citizen', and then thought better of it . . . 'a serious favourite of the governor himself!'

The redhead looked uncomfortable. 'No one told us that.'

'What difference does it make?' his companion said disdainfully. 'Doesn't matter who his patrons are. It won't save him if the gods are after him.'

Gwellia nodded. 'Strange that the deities should bother with such an unimportant man,' she observed. 'More likely to be about that legate, you would think.' She spoke tranquilly, but I was almost hopping on my seat. The murmurs of the crowd outside were getting louder now, and it was clear that they were becoming impatient.

'That's what a lot of us were saying,' the red-haired man agreed. 'But the man who told us this was adamant. He had it from the augurers themselves. Do you know why the legate was coming, anyway? Because of something that the pavement-maker did! So, however you look at it, it's all your master's fault.'

'He's in serious trouble in any case,' Grizzle-head put in. 'Optimus Honorius is after him as well, for enticing away a little kitchen slave. And it's no good calling on his wealthy friends. I'm not afraid of them, compared with the immortal gods. He's bringing danger on us all, that's what. Wait till we catch up with him!' His voice had risen to a shout, and he was waving his stave threateningly.

I had already started up. 'What . . .?' The response was startled out of me, and I was on my feet. I almost blurted 'kitchen slave' but stopped myself in time. I thought I had betrayed myself, but Gwellia stepped in.

'Now see what you have done, storming about like that! Frightened my poor customer away. Well, it hardly matters now. I don't suppose my master's likely to come home— not with all that crowd outside his door. In any case, if there are several lots of you, he's probably been picked up somewhere else by now.'

The two men exchanged glances. 'How do we know your master isn't hiding upstairs all the time?' the big man with the stave said, rather belatedly suspicious.

'Go upstairs and look, by all means. Do you two want to come in here and wait? This citizen is leaving anyway. Perhaps you could send one of your friends outside to go and find him a litter? I should send the rest of them away, if I were you. Tell them to go and look for my master somewhere else. I told you, he won't come here if he sees a mob out in the street.'

There was a whispered consultation, then, 'All right. We'll wait. No funny business, mind!' And the red-haired one went out to pass on the news. The crowd were definitely restive by this time. We heard him hollering to make himself heard. There was a great deal of shuffling and shouting and imprecation, but a few minutes later the fellow reappeared.

'We've found out where the pavement-maker is. Or rather where he was. A boy has just turned up here with a cart—says he met the fellow in the town, and was promised money if he wheeled it here. He described the place, an alleyway behind the market stalls. I've sent the others down there to search. Our pavement-maker can't have gone far; the lad was swift. I gave him a few *quadrans* for his pains.' He smirked.

It was a travesty. I had already paid, and—far from being quick—there was time to have wheeled the cart round the city twice! But the boy's indolence had turned out usefully for me.

The bigger man nodded. 'Then I might as well go down to the market, too. You stay here for a bit, in case, but it doesn't sound as if our man is coming here.' To my amazement, he turned and left the room. Gwellia's trick seemed to have succeeded. Only the red-headed man was left, and he was nothing like as threatening.

It was tempting to make a run for it, but he now stationed himself at the partition door from where he was attempting to watch both us and the street. Gwellia caught my eye and I subsided back onto the stool. Better to wait quietly and hope for my transport to arrive.

I waited, not daring to breathe, for what seemed eternity. At any moment, I was sure, my guard would come and take a closer look at me. He did glance towards me once or twice, as if suspicious, but nothing happened and in the end he went out to the street. For a long moment nothing went on happening.

Then all at once he reappeared around the partition. He came towards me, dangerously near. I closed my eyes, expecting the worst. His freckled hand fell on my shoulder and I winced.

'The litter's outside, citizen,' he bellowed in my astonished ear. 'Litter! Outside! Understand?'

I nodded, too shaken to speak.

The man didn't move.

'What now?' I wondered, privately, and the realisation dawned. I was supposed to be a wealthy Roman citizen! I fished out my purse and offered him a coin. That was an embarrassment—I had only a bronze *as* or two about me, beyond the litter-hire, but I gave him one and he took it grudgingly.

'Blind as well as deaf,' I heard him mutter, and then he moved aside. He really was about to let me leave! I could hardly believe my good fortune.

He watched me sourly as I shuffled to the door, still in my role of aged citizen. The litter was filling up the lane outside, and the crowd was gone. I could have howled with relief. 'The high priest's house!' I muttered to the slaves, as they lowered the litter and I climbed quickly on.

Too quickly? From the inner doorway of the shop my would-be captor could be still watching me. Had my sudden sprightliness alerted him? I was too afraid to glance behind me as my bearers hoisted me.

'And be quick about it,' I ordered, and they set off at a run. My makeshift hood, made from the loose end of my toga, dropped backwards as we went, revealing me more clearly.

But no one came lumbering after us. No shouts of 'Hey you, come back!' I closed my eyes and prayed to all the gods—Roman and Celtic—I had ever known.

If we could only reach the corner, I was safe, at least for now. Even if he came after me he'd never catch me then: he was fat and slow and my bearers were fast—and hoping to be generously paid. The litter lurched and swayed

like a coracle in a storm, but I held on grimly
for my life until we were safely out of sight
around the bend.

CHAPTER SEVENTEEN

As soon as we were out of sight I sat back
heavily. I was safe—for the moment, anyway!
But even as I felt relief wash over me, I knew
that I could not really afford to relax for an
instant.

If Junio was right, my pursuers would not
give up easily. They were probably already
on my trail. And if they found me . . .! I
shuddered. Think, foolish pavement-maker,
think!

I tried. It was not easy while struggling to
keep my balance on a wildly rocking litter, but
I tried to put my fear aside and to think
rationally about the day's events. While I was
in the workshop I had been too terrified to
give a moment's consideration to anything
beyond getting out of there, but now that I
turned my mind to it I began to recognise for
the first time the full horror of my
predicament. I was effectively a fugitive. Half
the town was looking for me and even the faint
protection of my toga was no longer a disguise.
I could not go home, there was nowhere in the
city I could hide for long, and the town gates

would certainly be watched. Nowhere was safe. What was I to do?

I was concerned about Gwellia, too—and guilty. In making my escape as I did, I had left her at the mercy of that red-headed idiot with the stick. I could only hope that he would think a female slave too trivial to waste his time upon. Or, since he was convinced I was an evil-bringer, perhaps he'd be too concerned with chasing me! I sent up a prayer to whatever gods there were that—for whatever reason—the mob would not go back to the workshop and mistreat my poor ex-wife. But I wasn't confident. Misery darkened my despair. She deserved better of me—without her quick thinking I would never have escaped. My own brain seemed to have deserted me entirely this afternoon.

It certainly had. Dear Mercury! I sat up suddenly—so suddenly that I almost fell off my perch. Why hadn't it occurred to me before? The stories which that red-haired man had told! All those tales about signs and omens! Most of the information was correct! He was not just repeating wild imaginings, like the mob I'd spoken to this afternoon. He'd known about the corpse, the blood—the 'water turning red'. So where on earth had the information come from?

Not from the temple, surely? Everyone there had been sworn to secrecy by the high priest himself—even Trinunculus had tried to be discreet! But—I had to face it—how else could the rumour possibly have spread? No one outside, except myself and Junio, had any inkling of the truth. Not even Marcus could have known all of this morning's happenings.

And there was something else. If the crowd were looking for somebody to blame, what had possessed them to alight on me? Why not Scribonius, for example? He seemed a much more likely candidate. He was an Icenian—and there was that legend of a curse. Or the visiting legate perhaps, as Gwellia had suggested?

Because the augurers had told them it was me. That's what the ruffian had said. I hadn't taken too much notice at the time—but suppose that it was true? Even if the augurers had said nothing of the kind, surely the whisper must have started at the temple? It was not the kind of thing the populace would make up by themselves—most of them had never heard of me. This was not like rumours of Fabius Marcellus's visit, which had spread through the town like a bakery fire. Or was it? That had become common knowledge, too, when the messenger had come only to Marcus and the priests.

If there was someone deliberately fomenting this, it would explain everything. Someone within the temple! Or someone with access to its dealings. I found myself shaking my head in disbelief. Everything pointed in that direction, and the more I thought about it, the more certain I became. This outcry against me was no accident. Someone was trying to frighten me off—or worse. I had made an enemy somewhere at the shrine.

Yet here I was, being conveyed of my own free will back in that direction. The realisation gave me a nasty shock. Unlike the Christians in the arena, who are said to actively embrace their fate, I have no taste for martyrdom. Yet where else could I go? It was getting late by now, and the mob were looking for me in the streets—and no doubt had watchers waiting at the gates.

We had reached the centre of the town by now, and I struggled to sit up a little more, ready to call to the bearers and have them set me down. I would stop outside the forum after all. With a little luck I could make it to Marcus's apartment, over the wine-shop opposite. It was a risk, but it was not very far away, and if I was quick about it I should be safe from any rabble there.

But as we rounded the last corner into the central square, we met a scene that made my stomach churn.

A small crowd had gathered outside the fish-market. The worst kind of crowd. There were a few respectable cloaks and tunics among them, but for the most part they seemed to be the dirtiest and most desperate of the poor—peasants, beggars, vagabonds and

208

thieves. They were being addressed by a man who was standing on the plinth of a statue by the road. He was largely hidden by the mob, but fragments of his impassioned speech reached my ears. 'Root him out . . . a danger to us all . . . clear message from the gods . . . insult to the Emperor's shrine . . . Celtic rat . . . no more than he deserves.'

The crowd muttered and roared in agreement, hanging on his every syllable. He gestured to make some energetic point, and as he raised his head I caught a better glimpse of him.

I tried to flatten myself on the litter. He was too engrossed in his own oratory to notice me, but I would have known that grizzled battering ram of a head anywhere—even without the stave the speaker carried in his hand. It was the ringleader from my kitchen earlier—and he had wasted no time in finding himself an audience. This was clearly not just the crowd that had first accompanied him.

He was reaching his peroration now.

'Are we going to find him?' he hollered as I passed, and 'We are!' they all roared back.

'This is witchcraft!' one desperado called, and the mob took it up. 'Stop the sorcerer! Dead or alive!'

It was a sickening moment. Witchcraft is a capital offence—it undermines the state. Whole families have been decapitated for the crime, and buried with their severed heads between their knees. And being a citizen is no defence.

I let the litter take me to the high priest's house after all.

I was seriously uneasy by this time, especially as there was a little knot of people gathered opposite, outside Optimus's house. These were clearly wealthy citizens, quite a few of them in Roman dress, and they stopped to watch the litter as it drew up, and I got out to pay. They were looking at me oddly, I was sure, and my heart was in my mouth when one of them nudged his companion, nodded towards me and whispered something in his ear. I was expecting to be hailed at any minute, but no one accosted me, and I reached the front door without incident.

I knocked. The slave who kept the door pulled back a wooden shutter, and looked at me for what seemed an age. Surely I was not imagining it? The man was unwilling and suspicious.

I was desperate to get inside. 'I am the Citizen Longinus Flavius,' I heard myself saying, afraid that somebody was listening. (It was true, in case anybody questioned it. Those are my first two official Latin names, although no one ever calls me by them.) 'I have business with the high priest and with Marcus Aurelius Septimus.'

The doorman's hostile expression did not waver. His eyes never left me for an instant, but after a moment's further hesitation he opened the door at last and let me in.

'Through there,' he muttered ungraciously, by way of greeting. He made no attempt to call an attendant for me.

I went in the direction he had indicated, and found myself in the high priest's atrium.

It was not a welcoming room—more like something in a public meeting hall than a private residence. I felt almost as if I had stumbled into a courtroom by mistake. It was extremely intimidating, in my agitated state.

White statues and an ornamental central pool (which must have been filled and drained by slaves—the room was, quite sensibly, roofed against the Glevum winter snows); a huge mural on the walls depicting a rather gruesome scene of white bulls being led to sacrifice; and a shrine to Jupiter in a corner niche. Beside it, through an open door, I glimpsed an even grander space beyond. Hardly a comfortable room.

But this was not a courthouse, I told myself. Merely a private atrium designed to daunt. Around the walls there ran an elaborate but extremely ugly frieze, depicting a parade of sacrificial birds, and the same pattern was repeated in the (admittedly well-laid) mosaic of the floor. It must be a strange business, I thought, practising to be Flamen Dialis all your life.

The furniture was on a massive scale as

well: all clumsy, oversized and gilt. There was a huge carved wooden bench for visitors—too high to sit comfortably upon—and a gilded table set in front of it, on which there was already a dish of unleavened bread and honeyed dates, some drinking cups, and a pitcher of what I took to be the customary watered wine. An open door led to the garden and the inner wings beyond.

I was hesitating over what to do when a small slave, who had been standing unnoticed by the wall, came forward to invite me to sit down.

'I will try to find somebody to receive you, citizen, though I am not sure where my master is. We received an imperial messenger earlier today, and the pontifex has been closeted with the governor's personal representative ever since. And he has problems at the temple too—as no doubt you are aware. Nevertheless, I'm sure he'll see you when he can. Please partake of the refreshments while I go to find someone to announce you to.'

I sat down, grateful to be safely here, even if I could expect a longish wait. I waved aside the offer of the sweetmeats, though. I was far too upset to eat even the dry bread, let alone the honeyed dates—however much of a luxury Marcus would have thought them. Preserved Roman fruit is always too sweet and sticky for my taste.

The slave boy was looking at me oddly—it is

not polite to spurn such hospitality—so I did allow him to pour me something to drink. Not wine, as it turned out, but water—which in general I prefer. However, this water had that unmistakable stale smell and yellow tinge which results from the current Roman fashion of storing it for months, or even years, to 'improve the quality'. I prefer my water straight from the spring, as nature intended it, and in my anxious state I could not stomach this. I feigned a sip or two, but as soon as the page had disappeared I tiptoed over to the pool.

There was nobody in sight, and I poured the liquid guiltily away, before going back to sit uncomfortably on the bench.

And then there was nothing else to do but wait. I have grown accustomed to waiting in my life, but today I found it difficult to sit patiently. I was as restless as water on a griddle. It is conventional, of course, for an important man to make you wait a long time for an audience—the more important the man, the longer the wait, and men don't come much more important than the pontifex. And if he was 'closeted' with Marcus it would be twice as long. Thanks be to the old gods of sky and stone that this second imperial messenger had left the city earlier in the day! If Commodus's representative had been greeted by a shouting mob at the temple gates, I shuddered to think what the punishment would be—both for the city and for the unfortunate pavement-maker who'd occasioned the unrest.

I tried to compose myself, but I couldn't help getting up from time to time to glance uneasily towards the street. I half expected the mob to come thumping at the door at any minute.

'You do not care for our refreshments, citizen?' A female voice behind me made me start. Had someone seen me tip away my drink? But before I could say anything the voice went on, 'Oh, please, do not look embarrassed. I can hardly blame you. Who but my husband would greet his guests with only water and unleavened bread? The dates should be a little better—or I hope they are. I ordered them myself.'

I turned. A woman had come in through the inner door, and was standing by the shrine, looking at me with frank, kohl-fringed brown eyes, and wafting a cloud of perfume in her wake.

CHAPTER EIGHTEEN

I did not need anyone to tell me that this was the high priest's wife. Nor did one have to be a rune-reader to see how she had gained her reputation for waywardness and frippery. Not that she was necessarily extravagant or vain.

214

What this woman visibly lacked was *pietas*, that most feminine of Roman virtues, compounded as it is of modesty, devotion, loyalty and reserve.

She was obviously long past the first flush of youth, as I had calculated earlier—perhaps as much as twenty-five or -six—but there was nothing remotely matronly about her. She still had the awkward, eager air of a woman half her age. She was slim and muscular—none of your graceful Roman curves—and though she had done her best to make herself look fashionable by the application of powders and unguents, no amount of white lead and lupin powder on the face, red wine Ices on the cheeks, or even grease and lamp-black round the eyes, could quite disguise that big nose and determined chin. She held herself casually, too, like a child, with no attempt at grace or elegance.

She reminded me of a young colt I used to have—in the days when I was young and free and had my choice of horses: it was healthy and lively and from first-class stock, but rather a trial to possess, being rather too inclined to nip unwitting passers-by and a little too spirited to take kindly to the reins.

'I am Aurelia Honoria,' she said, coming across the room towards me. She galloped over, I noticed (still thinking of the horse), rather than gliding in the approved feminine manner, and instead of modestly shunning

215

private company with her male visitor she waved her page impatiently away.

I found myself staring at her in surprise.

I must have passed her sometimes in the town—Glevum is not a large *colonia* and, as a dignitary's wife, no doubt she went out visiting her peers. Perhaps—being de facto High Priestess of Jupiter—she even performed private domestic rituals for them. Possibly she even sometimes attended the baths, although naturally a woman of her class would not frequent the market, since she had slaves to make her purchases. But I did not remember ever seeing her. Of course, like any well-born Roman wife, doubtless she always wore a veil in public places, and travelled in a covered litter or a private chair—but all the same it was surprising. Even when I had disturbed her reading in the garden (I was sure at once that this was the same person) she had instantly covered her features.

This was the first time I'd seen her face to face.

If I had seen her before, I would have noticed her. She seemed such an unlikely wife for the withered old Priest of Jupiter—not only in her coltish manners, but in her dress. Her stola was of the finest woven stuff, dyed amber and embroidered with silver, and worn over a tunic of the deepest green. Her hair was dramatically dressed, thick black locks coiled up in the latest style, and her make-up must have cost her handmaids many hours. But her neck, ears and hands were bare of any jewellery. That was unusual enough for a wealthy Roman wife, but what made her look particularly odd was a small apologetic wreath of wilting leaves tucked in among her hair. Given her lack of any other adornment it looked extraordinarily out of place. Altogether she was a strange assortment, with her graceless movements and fashionable dress.

My surprise was making me forget my manners. I bowed one knee to greet her. 'I am the Citizen Longinus Flavius, lady,' I began. 'They call me—'

She cut me off with a gesture. 'Oh, I know who you are, Libertus. My husband was expecting you.' She had a surprisingly pleasant voice, girlish and humorous, and I found myself unexpectedly warming towards her. No one could ever call her beautiful but there was a frankness in her manner which gave her a certain fresh attractiveness. 'He will be here to greet you presently, when he has finished fussing with his incense.' She spoke with such feeling that I was moved to smile.

Tactless! I suppressed the grin at once, but I realised she had noticed it. I tried to cover my embarrassment. 'No doubt the rituals are tedious, lady, when one is forced to live with them all day.'

Her response astonished me. 'Tedious? It is a form of torment. And so unnecessary too! If

217

my husband had been appointed flamen, as he hoped, perhaps all these restrictions would be acceptable, but he does not even have the post! And yet he insists on these petty regulations—not only on his own life, but on mine! Preparation for the role, he calls it. Preparation for the netherworld, more like! And it's not one thing, or two, it's everything! Look at this room!' She gestured to the mural I had noticed earlier.

I muttered something about 'impressive painting'.

'Impressive?' She almost snorted. 'What woman wants to spend her life with that? And only bulls depicted, you notice! No "inauspicious" goats or horses, only bulls. And that frieze! We can't have graceful vines or ivy patterns, like anybody else, because they trail and that would be unlucky, wouldn't it, given the flamen's intolerance of bonds and knots? Only, of course, he is not the flamen, yet! Or ever will be now, as far as I can see. In the meantime, I have to live with that. Isn't it the ugliest thing you ever saw?'

I was embarrassed. It was indiscreet and inappropriate, talking like this to a stranger. No wonder her family had found her 'wayward'! All the same I found myself increasingly liking this extraordinary creature, who had at least the rudiments of artistic sensibility. I remembered what Gwellia had said about the circumstances of this marriage:

how Aurelia had been dragged into it against her will, and how the pontifex was afraid to come near her in case she died in childbirth. It was impossible not to feel sympathy for her—a woman trapped into a childish role, caught in a kind of permanent immaturity.

I could see why the old pontifex indulged her—more as a daughter than a wife—permitting her extravagances in the market and allowing her to have a garden if she wished. I only hoped it was enough. This young lady was no shrinking flower—if she were too far from satisfied I could envisage her walking out, and causing a sensation in the forum by publicly demanding to be sent back home!

What I could not imagine was that discreet liaison with Optimus which my wife had hinted at. This Aurelia seemed quite the least likely person to attract that elderly, *quadrans*-pinching man, and the least likely to keep it quiet if she did.

Surely her love of spending money (which I found myself mentally justifying, as a trapped girl's appreciation of fine things) would offend his frugal miser's ways? Of course, she had powerful family connections; perhaps that was what attracted Optimus. Status mattered to him very much. But whatever did she see in him? I began to wonder if the gossip might be wrong. It sometimes was—as I had cause to realise today!

Perhaps she was simply grateful for a friend, I told myself, and the whole relationship was wholly innocent. On the whole I rather hoped it was. Even if Aurelia escaped exile and the disgrace of a divorce, surely consorting with Optimus was merely exchanging one misery for another? However, it was none of my business, and Aurelia was still chattering about the frieze.

'My husband paid a fortune to have it done,' she was saying. 'And look at it! A simple stencilled pattern would have looked far better.'

I heartily agreed, though I could hardly say so. 'You have a good eye, lady,' I said tactfully.

She smiled, actually colouring with pleasure. It transformed her face. 'Why, thank you, citizen. It is not often anyone pays *me* a compliment. I take it doubly kindly from an artist like yourself. I hear Optimus's pavement is quite spectacular. If only my husband had asked for your advice! But there! I am neglecting my duties. You have eaten nothing in our house. Can I send for something a little more to your taste? We only have unleavened bread, I fear. A flamen cannot touch or come into contact with yeast—so, naturally . . . !' She gave me a wry smile. 'But we could find some fruits, perhaps, or cheese? My slave is waiting, just outside the door.'

I shook my head. 'You are most kind, citizeness, and I don't wish to be discourteous, but just at the moment I don't think I could eat. Outside, in the town, there are armed men searching for me, wanting to kill me.' I found myself explaining as though talking to a child. 'All I want is to rest here, and to see your husband when I can.' I stopped, suddenly recalling what she'd told me earlier. 'Did you say he was expecting me?'

She nodded. 'That's right, citizen. Your slave brought word to us. He came here looking for your patron and told us what happened. He said that you were coming here.'

'Marcus Septimus was already here?'

'Indeed, because we had just received a messenger from Fabius Marcellus insisting that he will visit Glevum anyway.' She looked at me. 'Marcus has been with my husband half the afternoon. They're in the temple making a special sacrifice, so they can read the entrails and find out what to do.' She made a little face. 'I hate all that—sticking your hands into an animal's blood and looking at its innards. Thank Jupiter I didn't have to watch. But my husband felt he had to do it. He is taking this very badly, you understand? All these goings-on in the temple, and disturbances in the street. And with the legate coming too. He knows this is the end of his hopes of getting the flaminate.'

'I'm very sorry about that,' I said. I meant it sincerely. I was desperately reliant on the pontifex for help, and I was not going to endear myself to him if he saw me as someone who'd helped destroy his dreams.

Aurelia shot me a look. 'Don't be sorry on my account, citizen. I shan't be at all upset if this *is* the end. Perhaps then he will be persuaded to give up these ridiculous rules of his, and allow us to live a normal sort of life. There are restrictions enough in being High Priest of Jupiter, without adding to them of your own accord. I could wear my rings and necklaces again—he can't be in the same house with "bonds" like that!—and eat bread and beans and goat's cheese like anybody else. And get rid of this stupid wreath he makes me wear—because the Flaminia Dialis has one, of course. And wear my own hair, too, instead of this!'

To my astonishment she seized the piled black locks and tore them off, revealing them as a clever wig. Her own hair, dark, uncombed and wispy, fell around her face. I had been warned about her hairpieces, but the transformation was startling. Without her wig she looked younger and more vulnerable than ever.

'You see what I have to put up with, citizen? You realise, if he was appointed, I'd have to weave and sew all my own clothes and his—with my own hands? Not even a slave to help me. And go back to live in Rome, which I don't think I could bear. But the Flamen of

Jupiter cannot leave the city for more than three nights in a row. Or take his hat off at any time. Or even have an empty table in his house. He's got to be ready to make sacrifice at any hour of day or night! You know he already has the legs of his bed rubbed with earth, as the flamen does? It's perfectly disgusting. The gods alone know why!' She paused suddenly, sighed, and gave me a rueful smile. 'Believe me, I shall not be sorry if he doesn't get the job.'

I found myself saying gently, as though to a child, 'Let's just hope that he doesn't lose the job he has. You realise he might? If the Emperor holds him responsible for what has been happening here? It is his temple, after all.'

She looked at me in evident dismay. 'You think that's possible? By Hermes, citizen, I hadn't thought of that. Commodus can be . . . well—' She broke off, biting her tongue. Even she felt the need for some discretion here—no one criticised the Emperor in front of strangers.

'Swift in his punishments?' I suggested.

She nodded gratefully. 'Exactly, citizen. My husband is an old fool, sometimes, but I should not wish any harm to come to him.'

She always called him 'my husband', or 'the pontifex', I noticed. More deference to his would-be rank, no doubt, even when calling him a fool. I wondered how she referred to

223

him in private. Even the high priest must have a name. Perhaps, if a man wishes to be flamen, not even his family can use his *praenomen.*

I was about to make some conventional remark when we heard the opening of the inner gate and the murmur of voices in the garden court.

'Ah! No doubt that will be my husband now. By the way, citizen, I hardly like to mention this, but I suppose you are aware that your face is smeared with dust, and you seem to have stone chips in your hair?'

Great Jupiter, I had forgotten that. No wonder those citizens outside had stared at me. How could I meet the pontifex like that? And my patron was arriving too. I looked around wildly. I thought of using the water in the jug, but that was specially matured, and cost accordingly. My eyes fell on the ornamental pool, but before I could do anything the page came in.

'His Excellence Marcus Aurelius Septimus and my master have arrived,' he announced.

The two men came in, accompanied by the unmistakable odour of sacrifice—burnt feathers and fresh blood—and also by Junio, to my great relief, though naturally he was unannounced. I saw his eyes widen as he saw me and took in the ashes on my hair and face. He shook his head pityingly.

But it was too late now. I knelt to greet my patron, as I was. 'A thousand apologies,

Excellence . . .'

He waved his acceptance loftily. 'Very well, very well. Get up, Libertus.'

The high priest said, in that reedy voice of his, 'Ah, there you are! I hear you've become the centre of a storm. Dear me. Most unfortunate. However, since you're here, you can tell us all about it.' It was not exactly a welcome, but he held out his staff of office to be kissed.

I bowed over it. 'All homage be to Jupiter, Greatest and Best . . .' I began, but I got no further.

'Gracious Hercules, what's that?' Marcus exclaimed, but, with a sinking of my heart, I had already recognised the sound.

From the direction of the temple, clearly echoing around the high priest's garden court, there came that long, low, unearthly moaning sound again, like the desolate wailing of the dead.

CHAPTER NINETEEN

There was a moment's horrified silence. Marcus and Junio both turned to me, shock and dismay carved on their faces. Aurelia and her page looked terrified. Only the pontifex seemed unconcerned.

'That noise again,' Marcus said, after a little

pause.

'A noise? Ah! One of the temple trumpeters, I expect.' The high priest was vague. 'No doubt they're practising for later on.'

Behind him, Marcus met my eyes and shook his head. I scarcely needed the assurance. No temple trumpet ever made a noise like that. It moaned into silence and was still. Everyone breathed a sigh of palpable relief.

'All the same, Sacredness,' Marcus persisted. He spoke in the loud and measured tones which everyone used when talking to the pontifex, but he was courteous. The temple might be part-servant to the state in many things, but the priest was final arbiter on actual dealings with the gods. 'I think someone should make sure. Perhaps if . . . I thought for a moment that he was going to suggest that I investigate again, and I was horrified. I was in enough trouble already. If that had been his idea, he seemed to think better of it. 'Perhaps if Junio . . . ?'

'If you so wish, Excellence.' The pontifex was preoccupied with a pair of elaborate folding chairs, which a silent slave had brought and was setting down near the *impluvium*.

It was tantamount to an order from the highest sources, but all the same Junio looked towards me for permission. I would have been much happier not to have him leave my side, but in the circumstances I could hardly refuse.

226

I nodded and he bowed himself quietly out, while Marcus settled himself on the grander of the seats, and the high priest sat down fussily on the other.

Aurelia, instead of disappearing discreetly into the interior as most women would have done, sank down upon the visitors' bench and watched us with an air of alert curiosity, like a spectator at the games, or at a trial.

It felt rather like a trial. I was the only person, apart from the slaves, still on my feet. In any normal social situation, someone of my humble status would have been expected to sit somewhere inferior—as Aurelia had done—so that my head was decently lower than my betters'. If the room had reminded me of a courtroom earlier, the impression was ten times stronger now—and it was clear what role I was playing here. Marcus and the high priest were both senior magistrates, and even without bonds or chains (which, in any case, no one could wear in the presence of the pontifex) I felt like a man accused. Especially as I still had penitential ashes on my head.

What's more, I was beginning to suspect that this was how the pontifex intended me to feel. When he turned to me he seemed more pale and fragile than ever, but though his voice was cracked and feeble his glittering eyes were shrewd. 'Your patron and I have sacrificed a pair of doves and consulted with the augurers. We think a full procession round the town is

227

best—a proper torchlight ceremonial, that sort of thing—carrying small statues of the triad gods, and a threefold sacrifice at dawn. Marcus is arranging for the animals.' He rubbed his thin hands briskly, as though he were relishing the prospect.

Marcus nodded his agreement.

'We'll have the censers, dancers, pipers and cymbals too,' the old man went on happily. 'I've sent word to the households of all priests from the other temples of the Olympian gods. Trinunculus and several of the slaves are calling on the chief priests of Apollo, Mercury, and all the other patron gods of the major craftsmen's guilds. No doubt some of the priests will join the ritual. Dear me! That will ensure a good crowd at the shrine, and that should satisfy the populace. Nothing like a big religious procession to make the townsfolk think that something's happening!'

'It's most unfortunate the townsfolk have turned on you, Libertus!' Marcus leaned back on his chair, placed his fingertips together magisterially and addressed himself to me.

I said nothing. I could think of nothing to say. I was feeling increasingly uncomfortable.

Marcus smiled at me indulgently. 'Most unfair, I know,' he went on, in that brisk this-is-not-of-my-choosing tone which officials always use to convey unwelcome news, 'Especially as you were not even there when the first of these phenomena occurred. But people do seem to associate all this with your presence in the temple, or at any rate with your return to town.' He was interrupted as the page, on a signal from the pontifex, brought him the plate of honeyed dates. Marcus picked one up and bit it thoughtfully. 'And once they get an idea like that, an angry crowd is hard to reason with. Ah . . . wine!'

He broke off again as the slave poured a little from a ewer. It was already watered—no respectable Roman household would offer undiluted wine—but the pontifex motioned for it to be topped up with additional water from the jug.

My patron took a sip. 'Good water, this.'

'Oak-aged five years,' the pontifex said, tasting his own, and nodding his white head with satisfaction.

I did not need an augurer to read the omens here. This diversion was not merely a gesture in the direction of social convention. I was convinced that the pontifex was deliberately contriving it: partly to emphasise my inferior status—important visitors like Marcus merited wine and folding chairs, whereas I did not—and partly to add to my anxieties by keeping me waiting helplessly. If that was his intention, he was succeeding admirably.

The old man shot me a sly look, and then said silkily, 'You were saying, Excellence? About the crowd?'

Marcus took another date. 'Ah, indeed. The

crowd.' He seemed oblivious of these undertones. 'It seems to us, Libertus my old friend, that the best thing you can do is join the procession as a flagellant. It looks penitent, that sort of thing—and with the sacrifice, that should dispel the mob. I see you've smeared yourself with dust and ashes, so you're already half prepared for it.'

A flagellant! I felt myself grow pale. Of course self-flagellation was by no means unknown—young converts followed some parades, dressed in skins or ragged skirts, whipping themselves savagely until they fell bleeding and half-senseless to the ground. But for an ageing man? And it was no good doing the thing half-heartedly: some helpful member of the crowd would seize the whip and do the job himself. I swallowed. I might as well have stayed to face the sticks and stones.

'But Excellence!' I blurted. 'I have been the merest bystander.' I gave him a brief outline of my day.

He condescended an uncomfortable smile. 'Unfortunate for you, I know, but the imperial ambassador has decided that he's coming after all. It is essential that some gesture should be made. One must think of the greater good— the peace and welfare of the town.'

My heart sank. So there was nothing to be hoped for there. Marcus only retreated into that kind of social rhetoric when he felt forced into some course of action which he did not

230

like.

The high priest wafted all this aside with a wave of his thin hand. 'Citizen, it's no good you muttering your discontent like this. You did defile the sanctuary. Dear me! Some public gesture of atonement is required.' He looked at me with his pale, vague smile. 'Though we can arrange to administer it, if you would prefer.'

The public torturers, he meant. Men had been known to die under their floggings. I found myself babbling. 'As to my desecration of the shrine, that was an accident. And it was this morning, Mightiness, long after most of this had happened. I wasn't at the temple when that moaning first began. Or when the corpse was found. Or the returning bloodstain—'

The high priest interrupted me impatiently. The old man was as pale as ashes but he could be decisive when he chose. 'This is all very well, citizen, but it is no excuse. The crowd are superstitious, but there is justice in what they say. There have been supernatural happenings here, there's no denying that. I've been a Priest of Jupiter for thirty years, and I've never seen anything to equal it. And they are right. These things have all occurred since you returned to town. No, pavement-maker, don't protest. Even if you have done nothing deliberate, it is possible for a man to be the unwitting channel of the gods.'

This was what Scribonius had been frightened of. I felt my hands go clammy.

I was about to protest my innocence again, when something suddenly occurred to me: a danger I hadn't thought of before. Gwellia had come from Londinium with me, and it was the first time she'd visited the town. If the townspeople once learned of that, she would become a target too. If she wasn't already. The thought made me turn quite cold. If so, there was little I could do to help. She was officially a mere female slave, with none of the protections of a citizen. Better that I should take my flogging like a man.

I couldn't bring myself to speak the words, but I bowed my head submissively.

My co-operation seemed to reassure Marcus. 'That should dispose of popular unrest.' He took a thoughtful sip of wine. 'And win us a period of quiet, though it may not solve the problems at the shrine. Libertus is quite right; he has not been here all the time. But there are people who have. Any of the priests, for instance, pontifex. If we are looking for "channels of the gods", there might be other candidates . . .'

I glanced at him gratefully. Marcus was doing his best for me.

The pontifex was not so accommodating. He did not dare to contradict my patron outright, but his thin voice was querulous. 'Excellence, you have heard the augurers.

Someone's presence here has outraged the gods. The priests are in the temple *every* day. So why should these things suddenly occur?'

There were a dozen possible replies to that, but I understood the message. It was no use trying to justify myself. It was expedient for a 'culprit' to be identified.

The old man looked at me slyly. 'In any case, who else—' He got no further. Hirsus had rushed into the room, white-faced and shaking, his diadem askew. He brushed past me without a glance and threw himself before the rich men's feet. His red hair looked startling in that sombre room.

'Mightiness! Excellence!' He scarcely seemed to know to whom he should address his agitated bows. 'Excuse this unforgivable intrusion! Something most terrible has hap—' He saw me suddenly and his voice, already high with anxiety, rose to a tormented squeak, and then failed altogether.

'Something has happened? At the temple?' Marcus enquired drily. 'We heard it. That moaning sound again. We sent a slave over to investigate. Have you come from him?'

Hirsus shook his head. 'It's . . . it's . . .' He trailed off helplessly. He was staring at me and trembling so much he seemed incapable of speech.

Marcus was clearly losing patience. 'By all the deities, what is it, man?'

Hirsus opened his mouth again, but still no

233

words emerged. Instead he raised his hand in my direction as if to ward off blows and I realised that he was wearing an amulet under the folds of his elaborate robe. I had only glimpsed it, against the reddish hairs of his arm, but I could guess what it would be. I had seen similar things in the market many times. Pieces of auspicious herbs, no doubt, bound with a woven cord, and a silver image of some symbol of good luck—a phallus for example— dangling from the whole. Hirsus might be an Imperial priestling, but he was clearly not above using a magic talisman to protect himself from my evil influence.

In the presence of the high priest too, where knots and bindings of any kind were generally forbidden! It suddenly brought home to me with force how feared and hated I had suddenly become.

Still Hirsus did not speak. Indeed, it seemed as if we might have remained in ignorance for ever of what he had to say, had not Junio chosen that moment to return. We turned as one man to look at him.

He was looking almost as shaken as Hirsus, but his face was resolute. He shouldered his way past the slaves (who had been watching all this in astonishment from the inner door) and came to stand beside the central pool. He looked surprised to see the sub-sevir here, but he wasted no time in delivering his message. He did not pause to kneel or even wait for permission to speak.

'Mightiness, Excellence, master—forgive my bursting in.' He bowed his head politely to my patron and the priests, but he did not look in my direction. All the same I knew his words were meant primarily for me. 'There is a lot of trouble at the temple. When the slaves tried to go out, as you commanded, to summon the priests from other shrines, they found that crowds were massing at the gate—all demanding that Libertus should be brought to trial. Shouting and screaming for blood-sacrifice, and calling on the gods. The temple slaves can't hold them back for long. Someone should go to call the city guard. There bids fair to be a riot otherwise, and if the mob break in—who knows what they might do.'

He paused, and then at last he turned to me. 'All the same, master, I think you'd better come. There seems to be another body at the shrine.'

CHAPTER TWENTY

There was an audible gasp from everyone. Marcus and the high priest started to their feet. 'Dear gods!'

Hirsus gave a little moan of terror. 'It's true. That is what I came to tell you. Oh, merciful Apollo . . . !'

Marcus rounded on him. 'This is what you came to tell us?'

Hirsus nodded.

'Then,' Marcus said dangerously, 'perhaps you had better do that—since the high priest is not permitted to look upon a corpse. In fact, considering the danger from the mob, perhaps we none of us should go back into the temple precinct without the protection of the guard. Junio, go and summon them. Here!' He slipped his seal-ring off and gave it to my slave. 'Show this to the commandant. Tell him to send a dozen men—on my authority. Go!'

Junio looked reluctant (he knew that if there was trouble I'd prefer to have him at my side) but there was no arguing with Marcus. He made off obediently in the direction of the street door, and a moment later I heard the ring of his running sandals on the paving stones.

Marcus and the high priest resumed their seats, and my patron turned to Hirsus. 'And you,' he barked out, 'tell us what you know. Quickly too! Before we call on someone to help you find your tongue.'

If I had been the hapless little priest, already too petrified to speak, that extra threat would have been enough to deprive me of utterance for ever. However, he licked his lips and managed painfully, 'In front of the altar ... I went in ... lying there with blood all over him ... I ...'

He stopped, and glanced at me again.

My patron was looking seriously displeased. 'Go on,' he said icily to the priest. 'You saw the body lying there. What did you do?'

Hirsus shrugged helplessly. 'I . . . nothing . . . Meritus and Scribonius came. I was . . . they didn't . . . they sent me to tell you.'

The pontifex had been leaning forward intently, watching and listening to all this. A spot of colour had crept into his ashen cheeks. 'Speak up, man!' His rustling voice was hardly audible itself. 'A body, do you say? Was this before or after this noise they tell me about?'

Hirsus turned to him gratefully. 'Oh, after, after, Sacredness! That was why I went into the shrine at all. Meritus sent me in to light the censers. Scribonius said it should be done from the sacred fire—there's been one burning on the inner altar ever since it was cleansed.' He glanced at me. For a moment his indignation got the better of his fear. 'After this citizen had paid his visit there, and desecrated it again,' he finished bitterly.

Marcus glanced at me. 'Have you anything to say to that, Libertus?'

'I have a question, with your permission, Excellence,' I said.

Marcus nodded though the old priest looked displeased.

I turned to Hirsus. 'The body. Did you recognise the man?'

He made a helpless little gesture with his

237

hands. 'I could not see the face.'

'So it could be the same body as before?' Marcus had seen what I was thinking. 'How is the dead man dressed? As a legate?'

'Or a messenger?' I said, and saw the high priest pale. There had been another messenger today. If it was his body lying at the shrine, then all our fears about reprisals in the city could be multiplied a hundredfold.

Marcus looked sharply at the sub-sevir. 'Well, tell us, man. Is there a seal? A ring?'

Hirsus shook his head. 'I don't know, Excellence. I couldn't see. There seemed to be a cape . . . a hood . . . pulled over him. He is just lying there. Face down. And all this blood . . .' He broke off, shuddering.

'You're sure it is a man?' I put in. It was perverse. A few moments ago, when I had expected to be sent back to that accursed shrine, I had been afraid to go: but now that Marcus had decided otherwise, I was suddenly anxious to see this for myself.

This time Hirsus answered readily enough. 'A man? I thought it was. How could it be otherwise? There, in the inner temple? Women don't come in. I thought at first it was a penitent, one of the supplicants who sometimes come. In fact, I almost thought . . .' He met my eyes a moment and then quickly looked away as if I might bewitch him by my glance. 'I'm almost sure it was a man.'

'And he was bleeding? Did you see a knife?'

238

He paled again. 'No knife. Just blood. From head to toe. He looked like . . . like . . .' he shook his head, like a man trying to wake himself from a dreadful dream, 'some sort of sacrifice.'

'Did you touch the body?'

From Hirsus's look of horror, I might as well have suggested that perhaps he could have kissed a venomous snake. 'I did not, citizen. And if you had seen it lying there, in all that blood—after what's been going on in the temple these few days—neither would you have done.' He paused. 'Anyway,' he muttered sulkily, 'if any other strange manifestations occurred we were to fetch the senior priests, and not to go near anything ourselves.'

'What's that?' The high priest's voice was sharp.

Hirsus repeated what he had said—a little more loudly this time. 'On your strict instructions, Pontifex. Meritus told us yesterday.'

Marcus looked enquiringly at the high priest. 'And is this so?'

The old man had been looking vague, but he brightened visibly. 'Indeed, indeed, I did give the command. Dear me. A necessary precaution, we thought, Excellence. A matter for experienced celebrants. Of course, we could not guess then that a body would be found, but we thought it probable that something would occur. And I'm sure the principle was sound enough. If the gods are already angry, we decided, we should not add to it by interfering in their acts with unhallowed hands.' He nodded his white-capped head at me.

My hands, he obviously meant, but Marcus chose to ignore the implication. He turned back to Hirsus. 'So you found the body and went for help? Tell me, how did you come to discover it, exactly?'

'Your pardon, Excellence, I thought you understood. We were in the robing room, preparing—there is to be a procession, as you know—when Meritus came in saying that, after that dreadful moaning sound, he wanted both the censers lit and carried with the images. Scribonius agreed. He said they should be lighted from the sacred fire, and I was supposed to be the duty priest today. So I was sent. It is beginning to get dark as you will have noticed, gentlemen, so I lit a taper from the brazier, and went over to the shrine.' He had forgotten his nervousness by now—or rather it had made him garrulous, because he went on without a pause for breath. 'It was very dark inside the shrine, only the light of the embers on the altar, and I didn't notice that there was something pale glimmering at its foot. I almost fell over it. But as soon as I lifted my taper over it, I could see exactly what it was.'

He gulped again, but no one said a word.

240

We were all imagining, too clearly, what had met his eyes.

'Right in front of the altar, Excellences, where all the signs and omens occurred before. Stretched out full-length like a kind of sacrifice. And that bloodstain seeping over it. It was hard to believe it was a human form— just a package of something soft and warm and wet—'

'You did touch it!' I could not help myself. I interrupted him.

Hirsus shook his head.

'You must have done,' my patron said, with a triumphant look at me. 'Otherwise how could you know that it was warm?'

Hirsus shook his head again. He looked genuinely bewildered. 'Believe me, gentlemen, by all the gods! I would not have dared. And nor did Meritus or Scribonius when they came. We simply closed the shrine and sent for you. But . . . I don't know. I suppose I know what blood is like—I've seen it shed at sacrifice often enough—and this was new blood, freshly spilt. Great Mercury!' He swallowed hard. His pale face had taken on a greyish hue and his voice choked as though the memory had made him nauseous. 'It glistened in the taper-light . . . bright red . . . and had a warm smell, if you understand . . .'

Strangely enough, I thought I did, though Marcus was looking dubious.

'Excellence,' I said urgently, 'I think he's

241

telling us the truth. And if he's right, that is significant. If that blood is warm and wet there is a chance the man is not yet dead.'

Marcus and the high priest stared at me.

Hirsus gave a little sob. 'No man could lose that quantity of blood and live. Citizen, he was completely drenched in it.'

'All the same,' I said. 'I think that we should go to the temple now. Immediately. Without waiting for the guards. Suppose it is the legate's messenger? Bad enough that he should be attacked. Do you wish to have it said you left him there to bleed to death, with no one coming to his aid?'

If I had suggested that Jupiter himself was liable to descend at any moment, I could not have caused more of a sensation. Everyone leapt to their feet at once, and began their own manifestations of panic.

Aurelia started crying out aloud, 'We shall be ruined!' and tearing at her hair.

Her husband shuffled to the household shrine, pulled up his hood and began muttering incantations to himself—though, if he was hoping to avert evil influence, it seemed to me he'd left it rather late.

Marcus said nothing, but he had that tight-lipped look I knew. It meant that he was planning something. Usually something uncomfortable, involving me.

I was right. He tapped his baton on his thigh and gave me his most patronly smile. 'I suppose that you are right as usual, my friend. If there is any chance of what you suggest, there's no time to be lost. We shall simply have to brave the mob, and hope they haven't broken through the gates. The high priest cannot go, of course, in case the man is dead and he finds himself looking on a corpse. Nor me, for the moment, I'm afraid. I must consult with him and plan what can be done. We can hardly go ahead with the procession if there is a body in the shrine. You go with Hirsus and assess the situation. I will have the slaves bring torches, and I won't be far behind.'

I felt the hairs on the back of my neck prickle. When I had urged this I had envisaged a large party, with plenty of illumination and a dozen slaves. I'd never thought of going back there alone.

Bad enough that the mob was after me, but to walk through the temple precinct in the dark! A temple where strange happenings had occurred for days. All those shadowy statues and stone gods. Bloodstained altars and a chilling shrine where, at best, a bloodstained horror awaited me! At worst—I didn't dare to think of it. Compared to this, being a self-flagellant in a procession seemed almost desirable.

Hirsus seemed no more keen than I was. 'Excellence,' he wailed. 'I'm sure the man was dead. And how could it be a messenger? The temple grounds have been sealed off all day.

243

Besides, if Libertus is ill-omened and we take him to the shrine . . . Forgive me . . . Oh, blessed Mercury, we shall all be doomed!'

But it was too late. Marcus frowned, and tapped his baton on his palm impatiently. 'You heard me, sub-sevir.'

I had brought this on myself. Marcus had given his command, and there was no help for it.

Which is how I came to find myself walking alone with Hirsus, through the inner gate into the darkness of the temple grounds.

CHAPTER TWENTY-ONE

It was getting seriously dark by now. Dark clouds had blocked out whatever stars there were and the feeble light of the taper we were carrying only served to make our surroundings seem more mysterious. Also there was suddenly a damp chill in the air. I am a rational man—or try to be—but even to me the graven faces of the gods appeared to stir as our moving torch-flame flickered across them, and a hundred expressionless stone eyes seemed to be silently following our every move.

Beside me, Hirsus was panting with terror. I could see him fingering his amulet.

I could feel my own pulse racing. From

244

somewhere beyond the temple there came a faint, persistent roar. Too far away to be distinct, but rising and falling like the sea, with sometimes a high shout, louder than the rest. The crowd. I have heard them like this at the arena, shouting 'Kill the netman! Death to the trident-bearer!' I did not need to hear what they were chorusing tonight. I knew.

Ours was not the only light in the precinct, however. In the distance we could dimly see the shadowy silhouettes of slaves, coming and going beside the outbuilding, with lamps or burning torches in their hands. Further off, half shrouded by the grove, we could see the dull red light of an altar fire. A group of dark figures could be seen, and behind them the columns of the Imperial temple gleamed menacingly in the glow.

Hirsus, who had not addressed a single word to me, gestured towards all this with his hand. He was clearly too petrified to speak. It must be my presence, I thought suddenly, rather than his surroundings, which terrified him so. He must after all have crossed this courtyard a hundred times, and the shadows of the temple were his second home. I knew from Scribonius that the duty priest sometimes kept watch all night. Yet he was genuinely terrified. He really feared that I was cursed.

I turned towards him, intending to say something reassuring, but he drew back with such a sharp gasp of alarm that I thought better of it, and simply allowed him to guide me to the shrine.

Meritus was there, with Scribonius, and a whole team of temple slaves with lighted brands. They were ranged around the outer altar once again, and from the mingled smell of burning feathers, blood and fur, it was clear that they were offering continuous sacrifice.

Meritus looked up at our approach—or rather, looked towards us. In this intermittent light he looked bigger and more powerful than ever, as if one of the stone statues had climbed down from its plinth. He did not hurry, but completed the sprinkling of oils that he was engaged in, so that the altar flame leapt up and the sharp smell of frankincense mingled with the other odours on the air. Only then did he pull back his hood and come slowly towards us, moving with that dignified calm which gave him such solemnity.

'You have come back, citizen,' he said. 'I had feared, with the crowds . . .' He smiled, but even in the torchlight I could see the tension in his face. 'I am glad to see you safe. You have heard of the latest dreadful discovery to afflict us here?'

I nodded. 'I was in the pontifex's house. Hirsus and my slave brought word. A bloodstained body, I believe.'

Scribonius had finished muttering at the shrine, and joined us in time to hear my words. 'Blood-soaked would be a truer description!'

he said, with feeling. 'I have slit a sheep's neck for a sacrifice and seen less blood than that.'

'Or a man flayed.' Meritus nodded sombrely. 'I'm afraid that's true.'

'It's fresh blood, I understand?' I said. 'Marcus believes that this may be the legate's messenger. If so, this could be very serious for us all. And if he is still bleeding, the man may not be dead.'

'Of course!' the sevir said. He looked surprised. 'Why did that not occur to me? I'm sorry, citizen, I ordered that the shrine be sealed. I suppose, after the last time, I assumed the worst.' Another strained smile. 'I shall have to send Hirsus for the key. I wanted to contain the evil, as it were, keep it away . . . And, if I am honest, to make sure that the body could not disappear again—by mortal means, at least.'

It was my turn to look astonished. In the light of everything that had happened, why had that possibility not occurred to *me*? I looked at him weakly. 'I think we'd better have Hirsus fetch that key.'

Meritus nodded. 'Hirsus, see to it.'

For a moment I really thought the red-headed priest was going to protest, so unwilling did he look, but in the end he bowed his head and walked reluctantly away, accompanied by one of the servants with a torch.

The sevir turned to me. 'I did not know

whether to open up the shrine again and get the little statue out or not. It would be wanted for the ritual parade, but in the circumstances . . .' He sighed. 'I hoped for instructions from the pontifex. You know that he ordered a procession here?'

'I did. He wanted me to be a flagellant.' For a moment, I had a foolish hope. Perhaps, now, the procession would be cancelled and I'd be spared. But as soon as I had formed the thought, I knew that it was doomed. With another body at the shrine, the pontifex would think my penance more desirable, not less. And as for the crowds, when they once heard of it . . .! I listened to the rumbling murmurs in the street and shuddered. Was it my imagination, or were they louder now?

The sevir gave a thin smile. 'Well, we shall see. Let's hope that your famous reasoning is right, and that this unfortunate man is still alive. Though, I confess, I see no hope of it. Here is Hirsus coming now. I see he has the key.'

The sub-sevir was hurrying towards us, carrying the key on a metal tray. Even then he was handling it gingerly, holding it with the tips of his fingers and away from his body, as if it had been in the fire and was too hot to hold. He was clearly anxious to be rid of it, but Meritus did not take it from him. Instead he signalled for a lighted torch, then, holding the flame above his own towering head, led the way around the altar to the shrine.

We followed him, like a small procession in ourselves: Hirsus—still carrying the key—Scribonius, the other two torch-bearers and myself. The sevir made directly for the door, and the rest of us would have followed him, but Scribonius paused at the water bowl.

'Forgive me, sevir,' he said, in his pedantic voice, 'but we must not neglect the rituals. Particularly now!'

A look of impatience crossed Meritus's face, but he returned, and handed the torch back to a waiting slave. Hirsus, meanwhile, had plunged his hands into the water as if he could not wait to cleanse himself, but as he brought them out again he gave a wail.

'Merciful Apollo! What have I done to deserve all this? Look! Look! Oh, Mercury!' He had fallen to his knees and was sobbing wretchedly, his hands outstretched and real tears coursing down his face.

The rest of us looked at each other uneasily, and then Meritus gave a cry. 'By Great Jupiter! He's right! Look at the water there!' He seized the torch again, and in its light we saw what he had seen. The liquid in the bowl looked merely dark and shadowed, but Hirsus had plunged his hands in it and cupped them to bring water to his face. Streaming between his fingers in the torchlight was a little slippery string of something darkish and congealed, and round it the water was faintly tinged with red.

There was blood in the ritual cleansing bowl again.

Hirsus had turned away, retching, and I thought that he was about to repeat my morning's desecration of the grove. Meritus ignored him. He motioned for Scribonius to pick up the key which Hirsus had set down beside the water urn, and strode up to the door, still brandishing the torch.

'Open it,' he commanded, and we watched while Scribonius fumbled with the complicated lock. At last we heard the levers tumble, and Scribonius turned to look at us. His face in the torchlight was grim and set. 'Sevir,' he said desperately, 'the rituals! We none of us are cleansed.'

'Stand aside!' Meritus's voice was thunder. 'Stand aside, I tell you. What have you to hide?'

Scribonius looked despairing, but looking at Meritus's face he saw that it was hopeless to resist. He said helplessly, 'On your authority, then. So be it, Sevir Meritus. But if there is catastrophe, don't say I did not warn you. We defy the rituals at our peril.'

He looked back towards the water basin, as if he intended to wash his hands as a sign that he ritually cleansed himself from responsibility, in the way that priests and magistrates sometimes do. But—one could almost see the process in his face—the memory of what was in the bowl dissuaded him. In the end he simply fell back, and allowed Meritus and me to pass.

I admit that my heart was pounding and my throat was dry as the sevir pushed back first one door and then the other. In the interior, the embers of the altar-fire still glowed faintly, but the rest of the shrine was by now completely dark. He raised the torch, and I was almost reassured to see the faint glimmer of something pale and motionless, lying there huddled on the floor. Something covered in a cloth, a lifeless bundle at the altar's foot. Not a disappearing corpse, this time, at least. I felt a surge of something like relief.

'Let us have some more light, here!' Meritus commanded. Despite his fierce attempt at self-control, this ordeal was having its effect on him. His face was a mask of tension and alarm.

But he still held authority, and—although there was a dreadful chill about the place—the two temple slaves came in at once, holding their torches so that we could see. One of the boys, I noticed, was quivering so much that he could hardly hold the flame steady.

He was right to be alarmed. The bloodstained bundle on the floor was sickening. As soon as I could see it clearly in the light, I realised that Hirsus had been right. There was no hope of life. The blood was almost dry by now, great rivers of it, which had run down in all directions from the head, so that only small portions of the pale cloak could still be seen—mockingly pale against that darkening stain. The folds of stuff had collapsed upon themselves, and it was hard to believe that something so meagre and reduced had ever been a man. There was the faint stench of death upon the air, foul and rotten-sweet.

I moved a little closer, like a viper fascinated by the charmer's pipe. I could make out the outline of the man—there was the shape of the head, the arms, the knees, even a pair of bony feet barely concealed beneath the bloodstained cloak. But there was something unnatural in the angle of the back . . . And that smell . . . ?

I glanced at Meritus. He was looking at me fixedly and I knew that the same thought had come to him. He nodded faintly and I bent forward, mastering my terror, and lifted back the dreadful blood-soaked cloth.

This time it was Scribonius who screamed. 'Merciful Jupiter, have pity on us all!'

Hirsus, at the door, merely moaned and rocked himself. 'It can't be true,' I heard him mutter stupidly. 'It can't, it can't, it can't! Whatever else, he cannot have come to this!'

Even Meritus gave a strangled cry. 'Great Mercury!' and I saw that there was sweat on his brow, while the little slave who had been trembling before simply dropped his torch and fled whimpering into the night, careless of the threat of fire or of the overseer's lash.

I picked up the brand, almost without conscious thought, and lifted it aloft as if more light could somehow alter the truth of what I saw.

Under the bloodstained cloak there was nothing but a pile of bones, some of them with scraps of rotting flesh attached. Yet the shape of the once-living man was there—as if some supernatural power had come and stripped away blood and sinew where he lay.

CHAPTER TWENTY-TWO

How long we might have stood there, gazing stupidly at the horror on the floor, I cannot say, but we were interrupted by a sudden noise. A thunderous knocking sound, a bellow, shouts, and then—amazingly—a hush. Even the murmur of the crowd had ceased.

Meritus shot me a glance. 'Listen!' But we had no need of his instruction to make us strain our ears. Even Scribonius had ceased his chant to hear.

Fresh noises now. The clank of hobnails on the temple court, the measured tread of marching feet. I knew, with a sudden lifting of the heart, what it meant. Junio and the soldiers had arrived! Only a contingent of armed guard could have brought about that immediate compliance from the crowd, and gained such instant admittance from the slaves who held the gate.

As I looked out through the open doorway of the shrine they came into sight—a dozen soldiers under the command of a small, stocky man. He seemed to have forsworn torches and had marched them in darkness across the court, and was now drawing them up into a small formation, three abreast, beside the outer altar. The light of our torches glinted on their armour, on their drawn swords, and on the helmet, with the sideways plume, of the centurion in charge.

He finished barking his commands and stumped to the doorway of the shrine. But there he stopped. The army are, by virtue of their oath, obliged to worship the Imperial gods, and he seemed to feel that some gesture of respect was needed. Rather awkwardly, he pulled off his helmet, revealing a short-cropped head and swarthy face.

'Well then,' he said, in the deep guttural Latin that betrayed his Rhineland origins, 'what have we here? Which of you is Libertus?'

Hirsus found his voice again, and pointed at me triumphantly. 'That's him!' he cried in a high, cracked tone, as if the appearance of the guard had given him sudden confidence. 'He's the one who's brought all this about! Do your duty, officer. He has disturbed the safety of the state—brought down the anger of the gods—

and now the crowds are calling for his death. Under the old laws of popular acclaim, he must be tried before the people's court, or at least brought before the magistrates.' He looked about him, as if pleased by his own display of bravery.

'I have orders from Marcus Septimus to report to you, citizen!' The officer took a step towards me and in doing so appeared to see, for the first time, the raddled pile of bones on the floor. He looked aghast. 'Dear Jupiter. What in Dis is going on here? A dead body at the temple, I was told. Surely, by all the gods in Gaul, this can't be it?'

'It is, it is!' That was Hirsus again, babbling now as if he could not stop. 'This is immortal vengeance, officer. There was a body here—a proper body, not this heap of bones. I saw it with my own eyes, earlier. And so did both these other seviri here. And now see what the gods have done to it.'

The centurion paled. He backed away a little, and I saw his fingers tighten on his sword-hilt. 'Is this true?' He rounded on the priests. 'You saw it, both of you?'

'Not clearly.' Only a tremor in Meritus's voice betrayed the effort of his self-control.

Scribonius had lost some of his dry pedantic drawl. 'I did. I saw it,' he said urgently. 'Not the whole body, just a huddled cloak—but it was a body—I could see the leg. And the ankles underneath the robe.'

I looked at him, appalled. If that was true . . . !
'Sorcery!' The centurion let go of his sword and backed away. This is outside my powers, his expression said, as clearly as if he'd uttered the words. 'Did anybody else see anything?'

'I did, master!' That was Junio's voice.

I looked over and saw him for the first time, standing in the darkness at the entrance to the shrine, behind Hirsus and the smaller of the slaves. He could have come no further if he'd tried. There was not room in the little temple for us all.

'Junio!'

They stood back then, to make room for him, and he made his way forward, further into the shrine. Even then he hung back at the door, looking embarrassed and uncomfortable —this was not a place where freemen often came, much less humble pavement-makers' slaves. And only then as wretched penitents, come to present their prayers and offerings. No wonder Junio looked hesitant.

'Well?' the centurion demanded, more cocksure now that he had someone whom he could safely bully. He seized Junio by the arm and pushed him forward so roughly that he fell on his knees beside the macabre thing on the floor. Junio looked from the pile of bones to me. 'It is as I told you earlier, master—there was a dead body here at the temple. That is all I know. As soon as I discovered it I came to find you, and you sent me into the town to fetch the guard.'

The centurion aimed a half-hearted kick at him. 'Is that the man you saw? That's what we want to know. Speak up, slave, or we'll find ways of making you.'

I could see Junio thinking how best to answer this. The wrong answer, or anything that could be construed as blasphemy, could quickly have him whipped, and with the crowd baying for my own imprisonment there was little I could do to protect him.

'It is impossible to know,' he said at last. 'This could be anyone, if the gods have had a hand in it. But the body that I saw didn't look like this. And it wasn't wearing a cloak, either. It looked more like—I don't know—a priest. And if it's the same body, I don't know what it's doing here. It was outside, when I saw it—lying behind the temple in the grove!'

'Nonsense!' Hirsus's voice had become a squeak. 'This is some story you have devised, to save your wretched skin. And your master's too, no doubt. I must have been in the grove immediately before you—you followed me into the high priest's house—and I saw nothing.' Everyone was staring at him, and his pale face flushed. 'Ask Marcus Septimus,' he said. 'Ask the high priest, ask anyone.' He looked at me with loathing in his eyes. 'Ask this citizen, he was there!'

'It's true that I was in the high priest's house,' I said. 'And Junio followed Hirsus in.

But if my slave says that there was something in the grove, then I believe him.'

'Then he must have put it there himself?' Hirsus retorted. 'What was he doing in the temple court at all? I didn't see him there.'

'Nor did I,' said Meritus thoughtfully.

'I thought I saw someone in the grove,' Scribonius supplied. 'After Hirsus had found the body here. When you had gone with the attendant, sevir, to get the key and lock the shrine. I thought nothing of it until now—just supposed that it was one of the temple slaves going over by the back path to the pontifex. They were scurrying everywhere, at the time—taking messages about the procession that he'd ordered. But that person was moving, so it couldn't have been the body that Libertus's servant saw—unless, of course, he murdered him himself.'

'Perhaps there never was a body,' Meritus said wearily—and then, as Junio started to protest: 'Perhaps it was a vision. Or the body disappeared again. Perhaps what you saw was the spirit of this unfortunate man here, coming to haunt his bones. Anything is possible, with what's been happening! Jove only knows what we have done to anger the gods so much.'

'It's his fault!' Hirsus said, gesturing to me. 'Him and his accursed slave. The crowds are right, these terrors follow him around. And you know what you saw in the auguries.'

They were all looking at me again, openly

suspicious. It was as well Marcus had sent instruction that the centurion should report specifically to me, otherwise I believe I would have been seized immediately and marched away to jail. And as for my unfortunate slave, he would have been lucky to survive the night, subject as he was to a lower court.

I tried to remain rational and calm. 'Of course, the fact that Hirsus didn't see a body doesn't prove it wasn't there.' Hirsus looked angry at this suggestion of untruthfulness, and I added carefully, 'After all, his mind was full of what he'd witnessed here, and he had an important errand to perform.'

Hirsus subsided, but he still looked sulky and resentful. 'There's one way to resolve it,' I went on. 'Let Junio show you where the body was.'

There was a stir among the seviri.

'A troop of soldiers, in the sacred grove!' Scribonius exclaimed. 'Trampling on holy places, and profaning everything with their impious hands. It will take a year to cleanse it all again!'

'You heard Hirsus, citizen,' the chief sevir said. 'There was nothing there. No body. Nothing to be seen. And, as Scribonius says—'

'Even if it is not there now, there may be signs of where it was,' I insisted. 'And if it was as bloodstained as you say . . . what is it, Junio?'

He was still kneeling on the floor, signalling

259

frantically that he wished to speak, though in company he did not dare to interrupt.

'Your pardon, master.' He was frowning now. 'There was no blood on the body that I found. At least, none that I could see. But, master, look . . .' He gestured with his hand. 'Bring the torch a little closer here.'

I was still holding the brand and I did as he suggested. 'There!' he said. 'A smudge of blood. Over there, beyond the altar, see?'

There was. A smear of blood. Not a splash, as one might have supposed, given the bloodstained mass that was the cloak, but a smudge, a mark as if something bloody had been moved. I brought the light closer so that I could see. Everyone crowded behind me. There was another mark, and another yet, hard to distinguish in the flickering light. I moved a little closer with my torch, and there it was, fainter but just discernible, a trail between the altar and the inner door. And the bolt on the rear door was unsecured again.

Any doubts that all this might be something supernatural vanished. That bolt was open because someone had gone through the door and not been able to secure it again. And the blood had left a trail, however faint. So what about the earlier body, then? I glanced up at the three Imperial priests and at the giant statue at my side. It was too early to be sure, but a train of thought had just occurred to me. Something that I could test out by degrees.

I straightened up, and signalled my slave to stand. 'There you are, gentlemen,' I said. 'Proof positive, I think, that it was not the gods that moved that corpse you saw.'

'Right!' the centurion said. He seized my torch. 'You, slave' (that was Junio) 'come with me and show me where you saw this corpse of yours. Pardon me, seviri, for going through the back door, but I think it's necessary now. I'm sorry if it violates the shrine. I won't bring my soldiers this way.' He raised his voice. 'You, in the first rank, stand guard here. The others, meet me at the back and help me search. Bring a torch-bearer with you.' And he was through the inner door and gone, with Junio at his heels, leaving me with the three seviri in the shadowed shrine.

Scribonius was aghast. 'Look, Chief Sevir Meritus, what he has done! Is there no end to blasphemy? And for what? What will he find if the gods have done these things?' He looked helplessly at the ghastly remnants on the floor.

I shook my head. 'A trail of blood, an open door, and someone seen moving in the grove? Does that sound like an immortal hand to you?'

Sevir Meritus was looking at me fixedly. 'So you suspect . . . ?'

I met his eyes. 'I think there is a human intelligence at work. I suspected as much for some time, but now I'm sure of it. Someone is setting out to terrify.'

261

The sevir looked appalled. 'But why? And who?'

I shook my head. 'That's what I can't answer yet, sevir. Someone who wants to get rid of me, I think. Someone who started these rumours in the town.'

The big priest looked at me, and glanced at the outer door, where the remainder of the soldiers still stood guard. He dropped his voice warningly, as though afraid that they would hear. 'There is some truth in what they say, you know. I read the auguries this afternoon, and after what you did in the grove . . .' He did not finish the sentence, but he hardly needed to. I had been judged *nefas*, impious and accursed.

'So anyone who killed me need hardly fear the law? Of course that's true,' I said. 'That's why the crowd felt confident in hunting me. But who passed that news on to the town? Not you, sevir—you have not left the temple. So who did?'

He seemed relieved that I had eliminated him, and he hastened to be helpful as he said, 'No one has left the temple, citizen. Only yourself, the pontifex, and Marcus Septimus. Oh, and some of the temple slaves, of course. We have all been far too busy with our duties here. Even the legate's messenger did not come into the temple—he visited the high priest in his house.' He shook his head. 'Great Augustus, citizen, I do see what you mean.

How did the news get out into the—'

He was interrupted by a shout from the darkness behind us, and a moment later a foot soldier came running up, his sword clanking on his armour as he came.

'You had better come, gentlemen,' he managed breathlessly. 'We have found something by the outer wall.'

Meritus glanced at me, and as one man we followed him. Scribonius and the torch-bearer were not far behind, although Hirsus hung back reluctantly. I believe that it was only the prospect of being left alone in the dark with that desiccated corpse that gave him the courage to come at all.

We did not have far to go. The centurion and Junio were standing in the grove and at their feet lay something still and white. Two soldiers turned it over as we came, and in the flickering torchlight we could see clearly what it was.

It was Trinunculus, and he was dead.

CHAPTER TWENTY-THREE

He had been strangled. As I bent over him with my taper that much was clear, not only from his mottled face and bulging eyes but from the dark bruises visible around his throat. I turned back the folds of his elaborate gown

263

to examine him better. Poor young priest. Something swift and terrible had caught him from behind, and tightened inexorably around his neck until his swollen tongue was forced between his lips. There was a mark under the left ear where the ligature had been looped into a knot.

I shivered, and not only because the night was cold.

'As I thought, master,' Junio said, at my elbow. 'There was no blood on him.'

Junio had not known Trinunculus. To him this was just another body on the ground, but I remembered only too well the earnest, affable manner, the almost-too-great willingness to talk.

I nodded. 'I think Marcus should see this,' I said. 'Go and tell him, Junio. I don't know what's delayed him; he should be here by now.'

The centurion, who had been standing restlessly behind me watching all this, saw an opportunity to take control. 'No need for that, citizen. I've got soldiers here. Third rank, escort duty—' He stopped. There was a commotion at the inner gate, a group of moving figures and a whole galaxy of lights. 'Perhaps there is no necessity.' The officer seemed almost disappointed as he motioned his soldiers to stand down. 'That seems to be His Excellence now. And the high priest with him, by the look of it.'

I nodded. Even at this distance and through

the trees, I could make out a large embroidered canopy supported by the slaves, the torchlight dancing on the goldwork of its threads, and two figures sheltering under it. The canopy did not surprise me. It was obviously designed for use in the procession (such things were not unusual) and would be convenient if the threatened rain began. But the appearance of the pontifex brought problems of its own.

'Very well,' I said to the centurion. Experience has taught me that a confident manner is best in such situations, however uncertain one might feel inwardly. 'Have your soldiers carry this body to the robing room. It can be laid there and prepared for decent burial. I believe you have a bed there, Meritus?

The sevir nodded, without enthusiasm. I could sympathise. The presence of a corpse in the room, even briefly, would require expensive and extensive ritual to purify it again. 'But . . .' he began, looking to Scribonius for support.

The sub-sevir gave it instantly. 'The temple is no place for death,' he said. 'The body should be taken to its home and made ready for the funeral pyre. Anointers, and professional mourners, if there is no family to lament, with proper candles, grave-goods and a feast.'

'Trinunculus was lodging in the high priest's

house,' I pointed out. 'We can hardly take the body there without permission—the pontifex must not look on violent death. When it is properly prepared and cleansed, perhaps. It's possible the pontifex will even choose to read the rites himself. But in the meantime, we can't leave it here. For one thing it isn't fitting for a priest, and for another, the pontifex is coming. It's no less unfortunate to him to see it here.'

There was a certain amount of muttering, but four soldiers formed a platform with their shields, and the remains of Trinunculus were lifted reverently on to it.

'Go with him, Scribonius,' Meritus said softly and his balding assistant, who had been watching whey-faced, began an incantation as they lurched away.

The centurion looked at me.

'And get rid of that abomination in the shrine,' I said.

'But, citizen, the gods—'

'Are more offended by its presence there than they will be by its removal.' I spoke with conviction. 'Anyway, the responsibility is mine.'

He looked at once helpless and repelled. 'What shall we do with it?'

I thought a moment. 'Have them take it to the paupers' pit. I think that may be where our killer got it from.'

Meritus shot me a piercing glance. 'You think so, citizen?'

266

I nodded. 'An explanation has occurred to me. That body of a beggar that was found, which Marcus ordered should be taken to the pit—it was scarcely more than bones, from what he said. Everyone here must have known of that—and where else could such a thing be found? It would not be difficult to get it back; those places are not guarded carefully. One body more or less would not be missed.'

'But how did it get back here?' That was the centurion.

'Somebody must have carried it,' I said. 'Someone, obviously, who knew that it was there.'

'All of us knew that, citizen,' Meritus put in. 'I gave orders for the burial myself. But who could have gone out to bring it here? And when? With all the rituals, we have been occupied— and there were mobs of people at the gate—somebody would have seen!'

The centurion snorted. 'Of course they would. The whole idea's impossible. No one could carry a thing like that through the streets without attracting interest from the watch.'

Meritus looked thoughtful. 'Hirsus and Scribonius did go into the market, briefly, to purchase sacrificial doves—the pontifex had used the only ones we had in the temple. But there was no time for them to do anything like this. I was preparing to read the auguries, overseeing the cleansing of the shrine—you remember it had been desecrated again?—and by the time I'd finished they were back again. Besides, how could they have got through the gates with that?'

I had no answer, and I shook my head.

Hirsus began to wail. 'I did not bring it, citizen. By all the gods I swear. I would not dare touch such an appalling thing—'

I cut him off. 'It is appalling, and a sacrilege. That's why it must be moved, and quickly before the pontifex arrives. He and his party are already on their way. Do it—on the authority I hold. There is no time to lose.'

The centurion made off, still grumbling, and I heard him giving orders to the guard.

Meritus looked at me. 'The pontifex is not quite on his way. Something has delayed him. Look—they've stopped.'

They had. When I looked more closely through the trees I could see that the whole little procession opposite had halted. There seemed some sort of disturbance at the gate, though there was little noise. I looked at Junio, took my torch, and hurried over to investigate, with Meritus and Hirsus at my heels.

Once clear of the sacred grove it was easier to see the scene, though as I skirted round the shrine of Jupiter the shadows were so deep I almost lost my footing on a stone. By contrast with the torchlit scene ahead, the night elsewhere seemed blacker and more ominous than ever.

I could see them clearly now: the high

priest, wearing a ceremonial stole and with the little diadem round his brow shining against the whiteness of that ridiculous white cap, gesticulating feebly with his hand; my patron, holding himself aloof under the shelter of the canopy; and at least a dozen household slaves, some carrying the canopy, the others equipped with torches. And a struggling figure in a cloak and tunic—now being dragged forward into the light by another group of baton-wielding slaves.

I stopped at a respectful distance, out of the range of flying batons—I had no wish to find myself caught up in the scuffle. It would not take long. The prisoner was resisting fiercely, but he was no match for a retinue of slaves. Behind me, I heard Hirsus catch his breath.

At the same moment, I saw who it was. I turned to Junio, who was standing at my side. 'Lithputh!' we whispered, almost in unison.

The steward was struggling bravely but they had him now. He stood there, breathing heavily, his cloak ripped from him and his tunic torn. Then one of them hit him savagely across the back and head, and suddenly he slumped, all opposition gone. Two slaves took him by the armpits and dragged him like a sack towards the house, his feet trailing uselessly behind him on the path. A trickle of blood ran down his face and his eyes were closed, but even though his head lolled forward he was breathing still.

'They are not to bind him!' I heard the high priest say. 'Oh Jupiter, Greatest and Best! All this when we have a procession to arrange.' And he tottered off in agitated pursuit, followed by a number of his slaves. Only Marcus remained under the canopy, accompanied by two attendants with their lights. They too seemed ready to retrace their steps.

I stepped forward. 'Excellence?' I could not have timed it with more precision. At that moment a flash of lightning lit the sky and a rumbling growl of thunder followed it.

There was pandemonium. Slaves began rushing to and fro, wailing and shouting. 'Dear Hercules! The very voice of Jove!' one of them exclaimed, and Hirsus—behind me—began to sob. 'It is all fate. They will kill him. Everything is doomed.'

The first heavy drops of rain began to fall.

Marcus alone seemed unperturbed. He gestured me to come and join him under the canopy, though the slaves who were supporting it looked at me nervously.

'Nothing to worry about now,' he assured them breezily. 'We've caught the man who's responsible. Found him lurking here outside the gate, next to the pontifex's house! He must have been here all the time, my old friend. Not like you to overlook something like that. Still, what does it matter, since we caught the scoundrel?' He had that benevolent, self-

270

congratulatory air which meant that he was inwardly delighted with himself.

The slaves seemed somewhat—though not wholly—reassured by this, and when he added, 'Shall we go in and see what he has to say when he recovers consciousness?' they had recovered themselves sufficiently to walk back through the gate, keeping the cover carefully over Marcus's head.

It was raining really heavily by now, and I felt sympathy for poor Junio, who could only follow in the driving wet. Meritus, I noticed, had pulled up his hood, as though he were about to sacrifice again, but Hirsus was walking behind us like a man asleep—the water simply coursing down his face and mingling with his tears.

Marcus made no attempt to invite them to come and join our shelter. 'I presume this is our murderer,' he said cheerfully, as we picked our way back through the peristyle. 'I see his tunic-edge is smudged with blood. He must have been responsible for it all.'

I shook my head. I still could not believe it. 'Lithputh? I don't understand.' Water had seeped through the thick embroidered canopy and was beginning to drip uncomfortably on my head, while my hems were sodden with the bouncing spray, so I was glad when we reached the shelter of the house.

Marcus stepped through the door into the ante-room, leaving the shivering slaves outside to fold the canopy away. 'You know the man?' he said, without a backward glance, as the sudden withdrawal of the cover left me standing in the rain.

'He is the steward of Honorius Optimus,' I said, following him gratefully inside. 'The ex-officer whose pavement I was laying'—I was about to say 'yesterday', since it seemed impossible that so much had happened in a few short hours, but I caught myself in time — 'earlier today.'

I sat down on the stool provided next to his, and gave him an account of what I'd witnessed, while a pair of slaves removed our wet sandals and washed and dried our feet. I saw Hirsus and Meritus come in, drenched with the rain, and be shown a place to sit and wait their turn. Junio had not appeared—bundled away to the servants' waiting room, no doubt. I hoped that he was provided with a towel.

'Well,' Marcus said as—our warmed damp shoes having been returned to us—we were led away and the servants turned their attention to the seviri. 'This must be a relief to you. No need for public self-flagellation, now that the guilty party has been found. I'll have a proclamation made in the forum, since no doubt the procession will be delayed in any case. The thunder will be taken as a sign.'

I was tempted by this line of thought. If Lithputh was found guilty by popular acclaim, then Marcus was quite right, I would escape and this whole incident would quickly pass. Why not permit the Phrygian to take the blame, although it left so many questions unanswered? Why meddle with affairs which seemed to have so providentially arranged themselves? But the punishments for sacrilege were harsh—usually involving death by ordeal—and those for killing priests were harsher still. Lithputh was vain and self-important, but nobody deserved a fate like that.

Besides, I was beginning to develop a different theory of my own. I said as we were led towards the atrium, 'Of course, even if Lithputh was involved, he cannot have done all this alone. A man would have to be familiar with the rituals, and know his way about the temple perfectly. I wonder what Lithputh was doing at the shrine?'

Marcus was sharp. 'I should have thought that it was obvious. A bleeding corpse, a murdered priest—and then a man with bloodied clothes nearby? You have a better explanation, perhaps?'

He was rebuking me, and I deserved it, too. My suspicions were still not strong enough to voice. 'Not that I can think of, Excellence,' I said meekly, and followed him into the room.

Lithputh was there, still unconscious on the ground where they had thrown him face down in an ignominious heap. All the same, his arms were still restrained—a pair of hefty slaves had

273

hold of them, ready to drag him to his feet the moment he woke, as he was showing faint signs that he might do. A group of other slaves was nearby, and so was the pontifex, who had ignored the chair that had been set for him, and was pacing abstractedly before the altar. He turned to face us as we entered.

'Ah!' he exclaimed. 'At last! Be pleased to seat yourself, Excellence, and then, please gods, send for your troops and have them take this accursed slave away. We should lock him up, before Jove visits any more miseries on us tonight. And you are here too, pavement-maker! What's this I hear about a pile of bones? Don't look so startled, citizen. One of your torch-bearers has been telling me.'

The little slave who had fled the shrine, I guessed. I gulped, ready to tell the story once again, but Marcus (who had taken the proffered chair) was already telling it—how Lithputh had killed the messengers, and tried to hide his crimes by smuggling the first body from the shrine, and changing the other for the beggar's corpse. 'No doubt, if we had them search the public pit, we'd find the other body we were looking for,' he finished. He looked at me triumphantly. 'Well, Libertus, what have you to say? You disagree with my analysis?'

I did, on several counts, but I know better than to 'disagree' with Marcus, especially since Meritus and Hirsus were now being ushered in. Marcus did not like to be contradicted even

274

in private. In front of witnesses I must be a dozen times more circumspect.

'I'm sure you're absolutely right, Excellence,' I said. I gave him time to smile before I added, apologetically, 'In some respects.'

His smile grew tight, but I had done enough. He nodded.

'Had you considered, Excellence,' I ventured, 'that there might be only one body here?' An appeal to his intelligence was better than a simple explanation, as I knew.

He frowned for a moment, and then his forehead cleared. 'I see. You mean that the body yesterday might be the same one as the priests saw today?' I was aware of a tense hush around the room. Everyone was listening carefully to this. Then the smile reappeared, more broadly. 'Indeed it might! Perhaps the substitution was intended to take place earlier—after all, the body of the tramp was there! But why? Simply to terrify the populace?'

Marcus could be a clear thinker when he tried, though his account was not exactly accurate.

'Something very much like that, Excellence,' I said. There was a rustle of relief around the room.

'One body, then,' he said. 'Two if you include Trinunculus.'

I bowed my head. 'Exactly, Excellence.'

The high priest had whirled around. 'Trinunculus!' he gasped, and I realised with horror that this was the first the old man had heard of the death of his assistant priest. It had shocked him deeply, by the look of him—his face was whiter than his robes, and his pale eyes seemed to have lost their gleam.

This time it was Meritus who explained—his voice so resonant that even the pontifex could hear—'Strangled, Mightiness! Probably a cord, or band—the soldiers found him lying in the grove. He must, I now realise, have been coming here—there was an angry mob outside the gate, and it would have been difficult for him to pass. I know you told him, Pontifex, to summon other priests to the procession. I imagine he had simply hoped to go out this way. But this worthless wretch'—he gestured to the inert figure on the floor —'must have been loitering, and encountered him.'

'Who is he, anyway?' the high priest asked, his voice no more than a ghostly whisper. 'I seem to have seen him somewhere before.' He came forward to have a closer look, and the two slaves lifted up the lifeless form for him to see, then dropped it back cruelly, so that the head struck the floor.

'Lithputh,' I murmured, but Hirsus stepped forward. His anxious rat-face was more strained than ever, but he found an uncharacteristic courage from somewhere.

'Don't hurt him any more,' he begged. 'He

didn't kill anyone, not Luce . . .' His voice broke and he burst into sobs. For two *quadrans*, I realised, he would have flung himself to the floor beside the Phrygian and bathed him in tears.

But he had started to say 'Luce . . .' and I was staring like a fool. The scattered pattern settled into place, and I saw what I should have seen hours before. The slave that Hirsus loved and hoped to 'set up a household with'— why had I assumed that it was a woman? Hirsus, who visited Optimus's house when its owner wasn't there. I'd seen him walking from there in a cloak, and taken him for a female myself!

I turned to face the pontifex.

'I called the prisoner Lithputh, Mightiness,' I said. 'But that is not rightfully his name— merely a nickname I gave him with my slave. I think his slave name is Lucianus. "Lucianus the wretched" as he calls himself.'

CHAPTER TWENTY-FOUR

I was rather pleased with my deduction and expected my statement to cause a little stir, but I had forgotten that the steward's identity was no surprise to anyone but me.

Hirsus nodded tearfully, and Meritus said, 'Indeed, Sacredness, it's true. Lucianus was a penitent of mine. His master would not release him, and he felt that he had mortally offended the Imperial gods. He has made handsome offerings to the shrine.'

'I have seen some of them,' I said. 'Gold, silver, jewellery . . . all kinds of things. That's why I was so slow to recognise his identity. How could a mere slave afford such offerings?'

Marcus was tapping his baton on his hand. 'Stealing from his master, doubtless? Sevir, you are an expert in the metal trade. You must have known the value of such things? Did you not ask where he obtained them from?'

The sevir said coldly, 'It is not my place to ask him, Excellence. If a man comes to the temple, and offers repeated sacrifices in good faith, it does not occur to me that he may be a thief. That is a crime with heavy penalties. If that were proved . . .'

'There is no need to look for explanations, Excellence. I helped him,' Hirsus said, with unexpected dignity. 'He had no need to steal from Optimus. I am a wealthy man.'

Marcus looked at me, with an expression which said that he believed none of it.

'Excellence, I think he's telling you the truth,' I said. 'When we were working at the house one of the slaves told us that he'd seen Lithputh—Lucianius—secretly receiving money from a priest.' For services rendered, presumably, I thought to myself, although I didn't say the words aloud. In fact, I was careful not to say too much. Hirsus was already in danger from the law.

For a man to love another man is not unknown, and there is no legal barrier to having intercourse with a slave of either sex: many citizens keep pretty boys or youths precisely to gratify their procilivities. The danger for Hirsus—and a serious one—lay in the fact that this was not *his* slave. Using another man's slave, for anything, without the permission of his owner is legally a form of theft, and there are nasty punishments for that—though only, of course, if an accuser can be found. I didn't want to take that role—I was concerned with murder, not with lust.

The prisoner on the floor moaned softly and stirred, and I seized the interruption eagerly. 'In any case,' I said, 'it seems the Phrygian is regaining consciousness. You'll have an opportunity to ask him for yourself.'

'That is the least of what he has to answer for!' the high priest said, echoing my thoughts. 'If he has desecrated the Imperial shrine— committed murder in the precinct of the gods—and killed a Priest of Jupiter no less . . .!' He quavered into silence as if his voice had failed him.

Marcus nodded. 'The punishment will be terrible indeed.' He'd adopted his magisterial tone again. 'My judgement is that this has endangered the safety of the town, and would call for the severest penalties. The hook,

279

perhaps, even for a man with personal rights. For a slave like this . . .'

There was an uncomfortable silence. The hook is an appalling death—being whipped half dead, then dragged around the town behind a chariot by an iron hook thrust through the flesh. And when Marcus talked of 'his judgement' these were more than idle words: he was the highest magistrate in this part of the province. A freeman is entitled to a trial before the courts, and a citizen can even appeal to the Emperor, but for a mere slave Marcus's word was law. If Marcus had uttered the same words in the *curia*, the sentence would have been instantly imposed.

Hirsus had beads of nervous perspiration on his brow. 'How can you say so, with him lying there like that? He's hurt. He has been beaten. He's not even had an opportunity to defend himself—and you are already planning horrors for his death!'

Sevir Meritus looked at his assistant priest. 'It's hard to see how he *can* defend himself— discovered at the scene, where he'd no right to be, with bloodstains on his clothes. But perhaps we should have him locked up and brought to trial—it will satisfy the mob. They have been looking for a sacrifice. There will be no difficulty—there are accusers enough against him. And then we shall see what he has to say about his crimes.'

Hirsus blanched at this, and looked as if he

might faint. The outcome of a public trial might be crueller still. But he said nothing.

Marcus, however, was enthusiastic. 'A good thought, sevir. It will appease the crowd, and make it seem that justice has been done. And if we lock him up, he can't escape.' That was an important consideration—under the laws of Rome a man cannot be formally tried unless both an accuser and the defendant himself can be produced. 'Very well, take him away.'

The slaves half lifted the unconscious man. He moaned and for a moment his eyelids fluttered, but a swift kick from one of his captors quieted him again.

Marcus turned to me. 'He needs a proper guard. Where is the armed contingent that I sent?'

'Most of them are in the temple precinct, Excellence,' I said. 'Some are on guard, others are disposing of the bones, and the rest are dealing with Trinunculus.'

'And where is he?' Marcus looked avuncular.

'We have used the bed that's in the robing room. The sevir said . . .' But I didn't finish.

The pontifex had raised his head and begun to howl. 'The grove, the altar and the robing room. This is intolerable! This is the most holy place in Glevum, and you're turning it into a storehouse for the dead!'

'The centurion wanted to bring Trinunculus back here,' I pointed out. 'Custom demands that he should be anointed on his bed. But I did not wish to do so, without informing you. I know your vows do not permit—'

The pontifex, who had been in a state of agitation all along, suddenly seemed to give way to frustration, like a child. 'Great gods!' he whinnied, throwing up his withered hands. 'Don't ask me what I think. Do as you please. Bring them all in—soldiers, corpses, thieves, bones, murderers! What does it matter now? Why not hold a market in the temple court? I've spent long enough chasing them away— sellers of birds, charms, amulets—invite them all! I'm sure there are a hundred slaves and women who'd like to pay a visit to the sanctuary—as the Christians do—or have a hand in sacrificing bulls. Why not? Why not? Nothing is sacred any more.'

Everyone was staring at him in astonishment. Even the two slaves who were dragging Lithputh from the room paused for a moment in their efforts to look back at the priest. His usually ashen face was scarlet now, and he was trembling with emotion.

'Pontifex . . .' Marcus murmured, but it did no good.

'Pontifex!' the old man stormed, shrill with ineffectual rage. 'What kind of Priest of Jupiter am I? All these years of ritual, fulfilling every item of the law, and more! And look what it has brought me to! The legate coming, and my temple the centre of bloodshed and riot! Even Jupiter has turned against me. I thought I read his hand in these events—but what were they? The actions and machinations of a slave! The body of a beggar from the pit! He thundered earlier, and I hoped to learn his will—to what effect? Even my pathetic effort to placate the gods tonight is doomed! This will teach me to have inflated dreams of being Flamen Dialis. Go, slaves, tell the city the procession's cancelled and your foolish pontifex is duly punished for his presumption.'

There was an astonished pause. You could have heard a feather drop: no sound except the drumming of the rain. The two house slaves who were standing by the wall looked uncertainly at Marcus, as if appealing for his authority.

He gave it. 'Tell them it has been postponed. Until the legate's visit. Jove has delivered the culprit to us now. In the meantime, there will be perpetual vigil in the court. I think that's best.'

The slaves looked grateful, and slipped silently away.

'You see?' the pontifex said bitterly. 'My orders countermanded in my own house.' He turned and blundered wildly from the room, brushing past Aurelia who was coming in, accompanied by her page.

'Husband?' she called after him, but he disappeared without a backward glance.

She came into the room. 'Citizen, there

have been people asking . . .' she began, and stopped, aware of the startled atmosphere. 'Why, what has happened? Why is my husband so disturbed?' She looked at the two men dragging Lithputh out, and her face turned whiter than the lupin powder with which it was dusted. 'What are they doing to that man?'

Not 'who is this man and what's he doing here?' I noticed. It was his arrest which caused this alarm. Another little piece of pattern fitted into place. 'This is Lucianus, lady, steward to Optimus,' I said. 'As I believe you know.'

She did not deny it. She was still staring as they dragged him senseless from the room. 'But why . . .?'

'Because he was found lurking in the temple court,' I said. I was aware of the eyes of everyone in the room, watching me intently. 'He came through here earlier, I think?'

She looked at me then, her pale cheeks turning red. 'He did indeed. Is there some reason he should not have done? He had my permission—though I don't know how you knew.'

'You told me earlier, in this very room, that Optimus was pleased with the repairs to his pavement. I wondered about that at the time. How could you possibly have known that— unless you had some contact with someone from the house? When I saw the steward in the court, I understood.' She looked so taken aback that I took pity on her, and added, 'In any case he could hardly have gone in through the other gate—the slaves had closed it to keep out the mob.'

'So,' Marcus said, frowning at her, 'Lucianus chose tonight to ask if he could enter the temple by the inner door? After all that had been happening at the shrine! You didn't think that it was rather odd?'

Aurelia looked as if she was about to speak, but changed her mind. She stared down at her hands and said nothing.

'But it was not the first time, was it?' I was reasoning aloud. 'The Phrygian had often come this way before. It was some arrangement that he had with you—is that not so, lady?'

She nodded, but she did not raise her eyes. 'He sometimes carried things for me, that's all. Nothing of importance, to anyone but me.'

I thought of the time I'd glimpsed her in the garden, and the piece of folded bark she'd tried to hide. 'Letters, perhaps?' I hazarded, and saw by the scarlet in her cheeks that I was right. 'Letters you did not want your husband's slaves to see?' It was not a difficult deduction. Why else would a woman avoid using her own servants for the task?

She started as though I'd stung her with a lash. 'Well, citizen, and if it was? There is no infidelity in a piece of bark. I wanted news of someone, that's all, simply to know that he was safe—but my husband would not countenance even the mention of his name.'

'But surely, Optimus . . .?' I began. I was not making sense of this.

She interrupted before I could show my ignorance. 'Optimus knew nothing, citizen. He was in touch with his old cohort, that was all. He mentioned it one evening when he called on us. I knew that Tertius had been posted to the same legion. Of course I couldn't ask Optimus directly—he would have told my husband instantly—but I made a friend of him and enlisted his steward when I could. Whenever Optimus sent missives to the legion, Lucianus ensured that mine went too, with the messenger—and if there was a reply, he intercepted it and brought it here.' She seemed to realise the impropriety of this, and added quickly, 'It did not happen often, citizen. I am a married woman, and Tertius cannot take a wife until his service ends.'

'Tertius is the young cavalry officer you left behind in Rome?' I said.

She was quite feminine when she blushed so charmingly. 'He is in Britannia now, attached to one of the legions here. I did not wish the pontifex to know. Not for my own sake, but for Tertius. Marcellus Fabius is my uncle—as perhaps you are aware since it seems you know all my business, citizen—and my family always disapproved of Tertius. They would have posted him away, put him in the front line

286

somewhere where he would be killed. Tertius is a *contarius*,' she added with pride, naming the rarest and newest of the degrees of cavalry, 'and though he's a skilled horseman, that is dangerous. He writes that he has fallen several times—it's hard to balance that long lance while you're holding yourself on a galloping horse with nothing but your knees.'

Meritus was looking impatient at all this. 'So,' he thundered, 'not only do you deceive your husband by receiving letters from this man, but you encourage Optimus's slave to creep into the temple court at night—again without your husband's knowledge—to murder and desecrate the shrine. Are you attempting to make fools of us?'

'I'm not attempting to make fools of anyone, sevir,' she retorted with some spirit. 'Lucianus was unhappy and so was I. We tried to help each other, that is all. At first I paid him, or gave him trinkets and ornaments to sell—he was trying to acquire his slave-price and buy himself free—but he soon told me it was hopeless, and asked for my help in this instead. He often went this way to the temple secretly, sometimes quite late at night. It wasn't difficult. Even if my husband was in the house he wouldn't hear.'

'But what about your slaves?' I asked, aware of her page gazing up at her in disbelief. 'Surely they must have been aware of it?'

She smiled grimly. 'Lucianus always went

287

directly to the temple, sometimes with offerings in his hands. Often he didn't even speak to me. I told the slaves it was a sort of ritual—making secret offerings for me before the shrine—in case I should become the flamen's wife. They are accustomed to strange doings in this house. It's no odder than insisting a plate of new-baked cakes be left untouched on a table by your bed each night—just so that you have an instant sacrifice to hand, in case you're called on to officiate!'

Marcus got up from his chair to come and clap me on the back. 'Well done, Libertus. You have solved the mystery, as usual. That wretched steward came in here, and crept into the temple secretly. Presumably to meet his friend . . .' He emphasised the word derisively and glanced at Hirsus who was cowering by the door. 'I still think he was stealing from his master, too—those gifts we saw were too rich for a slave. Someone must have known of that, and threatened to expose him as a thief, so Lucianus murdered him and then exchanged the body for the bones.' He looked at Hirsus again, and this time his glance was much less friendly. 'No doubt with help, as Libertus suggested earlier.'

Servir Meritus nodded. He seemed deep in thought. 'That would make sense, Excellence. Perhaps Trinunculus disturbed him in the act and had to be silenced too, before he talked. Trinunculus was a pleasant fellow but he

288

always had a tendency to say too much. And—
I regret to say this—but Hirsus could have
been in the grove at the important time. I sent
him there myself.'

Hirsus had turned the colour of curdled
milk. 'Excellences, by all the gods I swear—I
was not part of this. I did not touch
Trinunculus—or the bones. And if Lucianus
came to the temple court by night, it wasn't to
see me. That would have been a sacrilege, and
besides there are always temple slaves about. I
wouldn't dare!'

But Marcus wasn't listening. He wore a look
of great complacency. 'Seize him, Libertus!' he
said, and there was little I could do except
obey.

CHAPTER TWENTY-FIVE

I seized Hirsus firmly from behind and
pinioned him. 'Well reasoned, Excellence! Of
course it had to be a priest!' I said, struggling
to hold my prisoner as he tried to wriggle free.
'You might send for the centurion and guard,
perhaps?'

Marcus nodded and gestured to Aurelia's
page, who was by now the only servant in the
room.

'Where shall I find them, Excellence? In the
temple court?' He sounded frightened, and I

could hardly blame him. I remembered how eerie I'd found it myself, crossing the courtyard earlier, and I'd had a companion and a torch. This lad would have neither of those things. But I needed him to go. Hirsus was still protesting violently.

'Look in the robing room,' I said. 'And when you've done that—with your permission, lady? —go to the slaves' waiting room and send my slave to me.'

Aurelia gestured her assent and the boy disappeared. We saw him open the door and disappear into the night, the rain still dancing in the peristyle.

'By all the gods . . .' Hirsus was struggling in my grasp.

'Secure him, Meritus,' I panted. 'I am an old man and I can't hold him long.'

The sevir whipped off his embroidered scarf, and made to tie my prisoner up, but Aurelia prevented him.

'Don't bind him! Not in my husband's house!' she cried.

I nodded. 'You are quite right, lady. I had forgotten that. Stop struggling, Hirsus.' I jammed my right arm firmly round his throat. 'It will do you no good, in any case. There are three of us—four if you count the lady here— and only one of you. The front door is guarded, and there are soldiers in the court. You would not get far, if you escaped.'

He quieted at this, and I relaxed my grip a

little, but he had closed his eyes in terror and I could feel him trembling—so much so that I thought he might collapse.

'It's time to tell His Excellence the truth,' I said. 'There is more behind this than your amorous affairs. The things that Lucianus brought to the shrine—you knew that they were stolen, didn't you?'

He gulped and nodded. 'It was not really theft. More like immortal providence. The very day that Optimus had raised the purchase price.'

'I wondered about that,' I said, not releasing his arms. 'You wanted Lucianus. You are a wealthy man. Why didn't you simply purchase him?'

He twisted round to look at me. 'I tried. As soon as I'd been elected sub-sevir and found Lucianus again, I went to Optimus and offered for his slave. That was the start of all our troubles. Lucianus had been saving for his price, and had saved up more than half the sum agreed, though Optimus had set it absurdly high.'

'Face this way, prisoner! You are answering to me!' Marcus rapped out sharply.

Hirsus did as he was bid, and said no more. He looked thoroughly defeated now.

'But Optimus saw a chance of making money?' I suggested.

Hirsus looked at me gratefully. 'The price went up like a ballista ball, and when I protested he made it clear that if I did not accept his price, he would change his mind and refuse to sell Lucianus at all. I had to agree to his terms eventually, but the cost of being sevir is so high, I knew I couldn't do it till my term came to an end. I was already facing ruin, with the cost of nomination, and if I didn't make sufficient contributions to the shrine, I wouldn't even receive the usual honours when I left.'

Marcus was unsympathetic. 'That is your own fault entirely. A man should not accept nomination to a post he can't afford. If you hope to enjoy the homage of the town, the gift of lucrative contracts and the friendship of the great, you must expect to pay for it. Some seviri have even found sponsors and become *equites*, in time. Naturally the authorities want something in return. That's why the wealth of offerings in a sevir's year of tenure directly affects his standing afterwards. What else do you expect? But you seem to show a lack of business sense. If you—a wealthy man— showed interest in buying Optimus's slave, naturally Optimus increased the price. I would have done the same myself.'

'So,' I persisted, 'the fates took a hand. What was it, Hirsus? An unlooked-for chance that came his way and tempted Lucianus into theft? It must have been something of the kind, to demand such costly acts of penitence. A man in need of money does not repeatedly make gifts unless there is some pressing reason for it—a threat of crucifixion as a highway thief, or worse.'

'He found a bag, citizen, inside these very temple grounds,' Hirsus confessed. Meritus gave a derisive snort, but Hirsus protested. 'He told me so himself, and I believe him. All sorts of goods and jewellery—silver plates, bells, drinking vessels, even coins! Just lying in the grove, he said—as if it had been waiting to be found.' He gulped. 'It would have paid the purchase price twice over. We thought it was the hand of fate. If only we had known!'

Marcus was looking thunderous. 'You knew that was theft, dishonest wretch, even if he found them as he said he did. If a slave discovers something in the street, it becomes his master's property, not his.'

'But this was not found on the street. It was found within the temple grounds,' Meritus put in. 'Clearly it was intended for the shrine. Those things were costly, highest quality. They would have meant a great deal to my sevirship. That's why I set him penance as I did.'

Marcus looked at him in astonishment. 'You knew?'

'Of course he knew, Excellence,' I said. 'Lucianus was his suppliant all along.'

The sevir threw me a furious glance, but his voice was calm. 'I have been selfish, Excellence, I confess. He came here offering a cup, and I saw at once that he could not have acquired it honestly. I should have denounced him to the authorities then. It was a weakness, but I reasoned that if he gave the items to the temple—where they should have been—that was sufficient punishment. I knew that he was saving for his price.'

'So you permitted him to pay his debt before the gods by offering these stolen goods before the shrine?' Marcus sounded reluctantly impressed. 'Weren't you afraid the owners would appear and lay claim to their former property? It is customary, after all, for people to nail up curse plates and petitions to the gods, especially when they have mislaid their possessions. And do you believe this story of the bag? More likely he was robbing Optimus.'

I shook my head. 'He was not robbing his master. Optimus would be the first to miss an *as*—if anything of value had disappeared he would have had the torturers in and the whole household flogged until the missing items were accounted for.'

'Exactly, citizen.' Meritus was looking pale and grim. 'The steward must have got them from elsewhere. In fact, I was convinced—the auguries convinced me—that he had not just stolen them, but killed the owner too. Though of course I could not go to the authorities with that. I had no proof of it.'

Hirsus let out a despondent wail. 'Lucianus swears he didn't, Excellence. I told him to say

I'd given him the jewels, but Meritus knew straight away that they were stolen. And when he spoke of murder—I don't know! I want to believe Lucianus, but—now that he's been found with blood all over him—perhaps the sevir was right after all.'

'Oh, I'm sure he is,' I said. 'I'm fairly sure the man who brought them here is dead. Remember, we found a body yesterday. The slaves assumed he was a beggar who had crawled in here to die, because they found him hidden in a ditch with no purse or possessions. Suppose he was not a beggar but a thief? Suppose the goods were his? The temple grove would be a splendid place to hide—no dogs or watch to worry you, and close to the wall it is particularly dark and unfrequented, as I suspect that he discovered to his cost! He tried to scale the wall, perhaps, and fell? He was peculiarly unlucky to land down in the ditch, where no one who was not searching would ever look for him. I think, if we examine those bones more carefully, we shall find that he has a broken back or neck. I noticed there was a strange angle to his spine.'

'So it was an accident?' the sevir said softly. 'Then I was wrong. And the bag? Why was it not found beside the corpse?'

'No doubt he threw it over as he came, well out of the way so that he didn't land on it. And it was Lucianus's good—or bad—fortune to discover it, while he was taking a short cut to the shrine.'

Aurelia had been listening to all this with a frown. She shuddered. 'What a fearful death. Pray Jupiter the end was quick. Imagine, lying helpless in a ditch, dying by inches . . .'

'He would not have fared much better if he had been found.' Marcus was matter-of-fact. 'If he was a thief, and on that scale, that would have meant a penalty of death. At least it proves that I was right to send the body to the pit—that is for paupers and for criminals.' He frowned. 'I wonder how Lucianus contrived to bring back the corpse? Do you know, Hirsus?'

'Excellence, on the Emperor's life, I swear—'

That was a mistake. Marcus was not an admirer of Commodus, but he had a position to maintain. He stepped forward and struck Hirsus with his baton, across the face, savagely enough to leave a red weal on the cheek. I felt Hirsus convulse with silent sobs.

'I have been thinking about that, Excellence,' I said quickly, before Marcus had time to strike him again. 'The bones may not have reached the pit at all. You told me that you'd given orders yesterday, and earlier the sevir said the same. You are people in authority, and you assume that when you give commands, they are as good as carried out. But did anyone actually see the body go? You, patron, you instructed Meritus . . .' my patron confirmed this with a nod, 'and you, sevir, passed on the command? To whom?'

He frowned. 'To Hirsus or Scribonius, I suppose. Or possibly directly to the slaves. I don't recall.' He shook his head. 'You mean, perhaps the body never left the premises? It went on lying out there in the ditch? I suppose it would make sense,' he went on slowly. 'If someone wanted to put it at the shrine, it would be much simpler to move it in from there. But who would dare . . . ?'

'Scribonius!' Hirsus twisted unexpectedly and wrenched himself free. (My fault, entirely; I had relaxed my grasp.) 'Scribonius! It must have been Scribonius. It wasn't me.' He was standing by the inner door by now, almost shouting at us in his desperation. 'Ask Lucianus when he comes round. Ask any of the temple slaves. Ask anyone.'

He made as if to flee, but in two paces Meritus was beside him, holding him helpless in one gigantic arm. 'What shall I do with him, Excellence? Take him to the guard?'

'One moment! Hirsus has a point,' I said. 'Scribonius was an Icenian after all. And he identified the legate's ring.'

'The one you discovered in the sanctuary?' Meritus did not relax his hold, though Hirsus was wriggling like a fish. 'I thought you had decided that was not a legate's ring but a messenger's?'

'Scribonius had seen it on the former legate's hand. He told me so. He was quite

297

positive. Something distinctive in the angle of the seal.'

'The legate who was murdered, years ago?' Marcus looked horrified. 'How could Scribonius have noticed that? The legate never got to Glevum then. He was attacked and killed a long way south.'

'Scribonius served a provisions officer.' Hirsus clawed at the arm around his neck and freed himself enough to speak. 'In Aquae Sulis, Excellence, among other towns. That would be directly on the route!'

Meritus nodded. 'I've heard him speak of it. We were discussing Aquae Sulis once.'

Marcus interrupted. 'Perhaps we should have Scribonius detained as well? What do you think, Libertus?'

'I think we should have him brought to us,' I said and then at last the tramp of military feet was heard, and barked orders rang out in the peristyle.

Marcus smiled. 'Ah! here's the guard! You'd better give the orders here, Libertus. Remember, I put them under your command.'

Thank all the gods for that, I thought. I did not know how much longer I could have kept it up. Even then there was a moment's horrible confusion before I could persuade the soldiers to let Hirsus go, and take charge of Meritus instead.

CHAPTER TWENTY-SIX

It was no easy matter. Once Meritus understood what was afoot, he did everything he could to save himself. He knocked down Hirsus, kicked a guard away, and picked up the pontifex's chair, laying about him like a club-man in the ring. Perhaps it was just as well he did. I believe Marcus might yet have countermanded me if the sevir had not aimed a blow at him!

It took four soldiers to overpower him, and by the time they had dragged him out into the peristyle to tie him up—they still could not bind a prisoner in the house—one man was lying gasping on the ground and the centurion himself was nursing a black eye, his transverse crest distinctly battered and askew.

When they were gone I glanced around the room. Aurelia was sitting on the bench, both hands pressed in horror to her mouth; Hirsus was still cowering on the floor, but the soldier had clambered to his feet and taken up a post beside the door. He was white-faced and shaken, and there was a darkening bruise beneath his eye, but his presence was reassuring all the same. Marcus gave a deep, heartfelt sight and began dusting down his toga folds.

'So Meritus was guilty all along?' He came

back, breathing heavily, and sat down on his chair. 'You might have given us some warning, my old friend.'

I shook my head. 'How could I, Excellence? I only worked it out tonight myself. Besides, he is a big man. If I had alarmed him—with respect—I don't think you and Hirsus could have captured him. And he was getting desperate—the murder of Trinunculus shows us that. I frightened him earlier when I let him see that I doubted his account of events, and he discreetly pointed out that he'd declared me cursed, and if I was killed it would be seen as divine vengeance! I had to work hard to make him feel secure again. Our best hope was that, in accusing Hirsus, he would say something to confirm my guess and give himself away. Which, fortunately, I think he did. Enough, at any rate, to teach the interrogators what lines to follow when they question him.'

Marcus was still looking shaken. 'And you are quite sure . . . ?'

'Completely, Excellence. If I had any doubts, his performance here a minute ago dispelled them. It had to be Meritus. I should have seen that from the start, when he told us he'd seen a body at the shrine but when we got there it had disappeared.'

'What happened to that body?' Marcus said. 'You think it was the robber with the bag, again, and afterwards Meritus put it back into the ditch?'

'There never was a body,' I explained. 'Who saw it? Only Meritus. None of the others did. He told us he locked the door on it before he called the priests, and had them light the purifying fires outside—which proved that no one could have come or gone. I made it clear I suspected human agencies, so the next day he went back to spread the 'reappearing blood'— and put back the ring which he'd taken from the water butt. But he used the inner door that time—presumably so that he would not be seen—and could not fasten up the bolt again. It was a very clever move, as it turned out. I must confess it misled me for a time.'

'And tonight?' Hirsus had managed to sit up, although his voice was still no more than a croak. 'There was a body then. I saw it myself.'

'But not a dead one. That was Lucianus, I believe,' I said. I added, as Hirsus gasped in disbelief, 'Probably Meritus demanded it. A last penance, no doubt he would say. Poor Lucianus. I wonder how he felt, lying there in darkness in the shrine, too afraid to move, with that blood-soaked cloak draped over him. He must have been in terror for his life ever to have agreed to such a thing.'

Hirsus shuddered. 'He didn't tell me. He told me less and less. Only that Meritus had read the auguries and knew that he had stolen everything, and was compelling him to pay it back. And when I saw him earlier tonight . . .'

'You did see him?' I said. 'This evening in the court? After the bones had been revealed?'

Hirsus slumped back on his heels and buried his head miserably in his hands. 'I thought—Mercury forgive me—I thought Meritus was right and that Lucianus *had* killed someone for the bag, and that now the sevir had compelled him to reveal the corpse.'

'That's why you said "he cannot have come to this"? And why you were so nervous in the court?'

He nodded. 'I glimpsed him when I came to fetch you here. I don't think he saw me. He was hiding in the grove, or trying to. But I would know him anywhere. And then, when they found Trinunculus, I thought—well, you know what I thought.'

Marcus brushed this impatiently aside. 'So, Meritus killed Trinunculus as well? But why, for Olympus's sake?'

'Because Trinunculus saw him move the bones. That is the only reason I can see—especially with the body where it was. The sevir would have doused the cloak with blood—easy enough to collect a bowl of that, with all the sacrifice going on—but I'm sure he would have done that nearer to the sacrificial shrine. A little extra blood would not be noticed there, and I know he washed the vessel in the water bowl. But the bones were out there in the ditch—of course, he never moved them to the pit at all. They must have been an afterthought—they were not found till yesterday—but once he knew about them he could not resist a chance to cause an even more dramatic stir. Those bones were his mistake. Without them he might have got away with it.'

Marcus was shaking his head. 'So there never was a murder at the shrine? At all?'

'Not until Trinunculus,' I said. 'That's the ironic thing.'

Aurelia had been listening intently. 'He strangled Trinunculus with that stole of his,' she said suddenly. 'Just took it off, like he did in here, and pulled it tight around his neck.' Her voice quivered. 'Poor little Trinunculus. He never did anyone any harm.'

'He simply talked too much,' I said. 'The sevir told us that himself. He relied on that, in fact, to spread the stories that I was to blame. But once Trinunculus had seen him with the bones the whole town would know. Meritus had to silence him, that's all. He could not be frightened into secrecy, like Lucianus, or dazzled by talk of auguries like Hirsus here.'

Hirsus looked hurt, and scrambled to his feet. 'But Meritus read the omens wonderfully.'

'He was no more skilled in augury than you or I. He knew how to convince you, that was all.'

'Then how did he know that those were

303

stolen goods, and I hadn't given them to Lucianus?'

'Because he was expecting them, that's why. Consider this. A thief comes to the temple grounds at night, carrying a load of precious goods. That's possible, I grant you, but what if the priest on duty is a dealer in metal artefacts? And is prepared to bend the law, as we now know. Does that suggest anything to you?'

Hirsus nodded gloomily. 'I suppose you're right. Certainly he dealt in metal goods—that's why Lucianus went to him in the first place. Meritus had already given him a price for Aurelia's gifts.'

'Of course!' I said. 'I hadn't thought of that. The things he found were not originally offered as a sacrifice at all. Why should they be? Lucianus was saving to be free. I'd wondered why he'd produced them at the shrine.'

'He did make one voluntary offering, the night he found the bag,' Hirsus said quickly. 'At the altar of Jupiter, that was, as a sort of thank you to the gods. A brooch that Aurelia'd given him—for bringing her a letter, I believe.'

Aurelia looked uncomfortable, and changed the subject instantly. 'Citizen, do you think the sevir killed the thief as well?'

I shook my head. 'I doubt it, lady, or he would have had the goods—and moved the body from the temple long ago. All these magician's tricks with bones came to him quite suddenly, I'm sure—when the body was discovered yesterday. He made sure he had the Imperial temple to himself—he told us he sent the sub-sevirs into town to buy some sacrificial doves. I think he forced Lucianus to play his part, and then, when the body was "discovered", he safely locked the door to "contain the evil". Lucianus crept out of the back, and Meritus smuggled in the bones while Scribonius stood guard at the front door and Hirsus was sent over here to ask for help.'

Marcus looked grave. 'I see. That meant that he had witnesses when the skeleton was revealed. You think he used the same technique to organise the boodstain this morning?'

'I'm sure of it. Not hard to find blood, after all the rituals. I'm sure he spread it there while the others were asleep, expecting that Hirsus would open up the shrine: but when that failed he insisted that they should all three go together, so that he had witnesses when it was found.'

Marcus said suddenly, 'Why was he doing it at all? All these false bloodstains and disappearing bodies? Simply to terrify the populace? If it brought people to the temple, I could understand—the gifts and sacrifice would be credited to him—but it seems designed to frighten them away!' Now that the immediate danger was over, he was beginning to sound irritated again.

I looked at him steadily. 'Ask yourself, Excellence, where he got that ring.'

He stared at me. 'More stolen goods? Surely he can't have staged all this simply to distract attention from his trade in dubious goods! It would be more likely to do the opposite.'

I said nothing.

He frowned. 'Pavement-maker, what are you telling me?'

'Forgive me, Excellence, but who owned the ring?'

'The legate who was mur—' He stopped. 'Great Mercury! Surely you're not suggesting . . .? But of course! The bodyguards. Chopped into pieces. Some of them were never recovered. Didn't you say the sevir didn't have a slave-brand?'

'And he could ride a horse,' I said. 'And play the temple instruments. And fight—we saw him demonstrate that tonight. And he knew Aquae Sulis too—and that the legate had been there on his route. He let that slip as well.'

'In fact, he knew too much about that dead legate altogether.' Marcus was smiling now. 'Why should an ex-slave from the borderlands have heard the details of that affair? By Jupiter, Greatest and Best, Libertus—I see. All these signs and corpses at the shrine, the bloodstained cloaks—and the reappearing legate's ring. That's what it was all about. He

306

had been part of that bodyguard. He wanted to stop the legate coming here.'

I nodded. 'It looks almost certain, Excellence. When the first attempt didn't work, he tried the blood, but Fabius wouldn't be deterred. Meritus must have been aware of that; he told me himself he knew the legate's messenger had called. So tonight he staged this desperate last attempt.'

'It must have been important to him.'

'A matter, literally, of life and death. Of course Fabius Marcellus served the previous emperor, too. I've no doubt he knew the earlier ambassador, and his personal bodyguard. And Meritus—with his height—is memorable. The legate would have recognised him at once.'

Marcus nodded. 'A legate's personal bodyguards are specially chosen for their strength. Meritus would have been particularly admired. And if it was discovered that he abandoned his post . . .'

'Or worse,' I said. 'He may have killed the ambassador himself. Remember that he had the ring. At the very least he stole that from the corpse, and chopped his companions into little bits. In either case, he could not face discovery. So as soon as Fabius's messenger arrived, and Meritus learned that the ambassador was coming and who he was, the incidents began. I think he meant you to see the connection. It was intended to make you conclude that the gods were warning you—and it almost succeeded, too. You yourself wrote suggesting that the visit should be cancelled.'

Marcus said, 'So did the pontifex!'

'And if you hadn't, I'm sure Meritus would have suggested it himself. In fact, if Fabius Marcellus was not such a stubborn man, with a wayward niece to visit in the town,' I glanced at Aurelia, who blushed, 'I've no doubt the sevir's plan would have succeeded splendidly. I am ashamed to say, I almost aided him. I found that ring that he put there for me to find—not once but twice—and thought that I was clever, doing so.'

'He will regret his scheming soon enough,' Marcus retorted. He turned to the soldier. 'Is the centurion there?'

The soldier opened the door and made a brief inspection of the court. 'Waiting in the peristyle, Excellence.'

'Have him come in and offer his report.'

The officer was still in disarray. His eye had turned a dreadful shade of blue, and although he had attempted to re-dress his plume, it still sagged deplorably. He had taken off his cloak, but the leather of his armour was stained with damp (just as Lucianus's tunic had been smudged with blood) and his polished greaves were dull with mud and rain. All the same he bowed to us in turn, with as much dignity as his appearance permitted. 'In the name of the Divine Commodus, Emperor of this province and of all of Rome, Centurion Gaius at your service, Excellence. We have secured the prisoner, and now hold him bound. What shall we do with him?'

Marcus rose to his feet with conscious authority. 'Have him taken to the garrison, and lock him up there. I do not trust him in the common jail. The Phrygian is safely in the cells?'

He nodded. 'Gaining consciousness, when I saw him last.'

'Don't have him tortured. We want him capable. He is an important witness here. I will wish to question him myself. But see what you can get out of the priest. If he confesses it will go easier at his death. Tell him that. Have him brought before me first thing in the morning. Now it is very late. Provide me with lamps and escort, and see me home.' He nodded to me. 'I will see you in the morning at my house, old friend. My thanks, as usual, for all your help.' And, accompanied by the soldiers, he was gone.

Hirsus stared after him. 'It's all over, then. Meritus is disgraced, and so am I. And yet he promised me the signs were good.' He sighed. 'But he couldn't really read the auguries?'

'You can hardly expect me to believe he could,' I said. 'He told the crowds that he had read the signs, and I had brought all this trouble on the town.'

'He told Trinunculus,' Hirsus agreed. 'And I believed, for one. But this was supposed to be the anger of the gods. Why should he want to put the blame on you?'

'Because I asked too many questions, and he feared that I would find him out, I suppose. He almost had me murdered by the mob.'

Hirsus nodded sadly, but Aurelia leapt to her feet. 'The crowds!' she said. 'Oh, Mercury! I had forgotten, with all that's happened here. Forgive me, citizen. The people who came here looking for you, earlier! They're here. That's what I came to tell you. Where's my page?'

'Here, mistress.' The lad stepped through the door, as though he had been waiting for her summons—as, by his next remark, it seemed he had. 'You told us never to interrupt when you were speaking to a visitor.' (I thought of those letters, and saw Aurelia blush.) 'But if you are ready to receive us now?' He turned to me. 'Citizen, I have done as you instructed. I fetched your slave boys for you, and they are here.'

'Slave boys?' I said stupidly. 'There is only Junio.'

Then I saw who was coming in, and stopped. There was Junio, of course, but behind him was Gwellia and last of all came Kurso, the little kitchen boy.

'Gwellia! Thank the gods you're safe!' I murmured, and then added in surprise, 'What are you doing here?'

She stepped forward humbly, and knelt

310

down at my feet. 'Master,' she said, 'I am sorry to disturb you here, and sorrier still to be the bearer of bad news. But I did not know what else to do. This boy,' she indicated Kurso, 'has come to you, appealing from his master.'

'All right, Gwellia, my dear. Get up.' I hated to see her kneel to me like this. Kurso was an unlooked-for complication, too, although the boy was perfectly within his rights—indeed it was almost the only right he had—to apply to another citizen for sanctuary. A man can no longer simply beat his slaves to death. By publicly appealing to me like this the boy was not legally a runaway, nor—mercifully—could I be held in any way to blame. It did, however, make me liable. Either I had to return him to his master, or the matter must be settled by a magistrate on the first possible day, and—naturally—at my expense.

'Master?' Gwellia said, and I was lost.

'Very well,' I said resignedly, seeing my commission for the pavement disappearing before I'd even seen the coins. 'I award him sanctuary. But why bring him here? Couldn't it have waited till I got home?'

She looked up at me, and I saw tears of weariness glistening in her eyes. 'That's the problem, master. There is no home to go to. When you had gone the mob came back, and when they couldn't find you they threw me and Kurso out into the street, and set the place ablaze.'

CHAPTER TWENTY-SEVEN

Strange, until that moment I had never felt much affection for the rented, tumble-down, rat-infested workshop that was my home, but suddenly it felt very dear to me—especially since I now had Gwellia to share it with. Also, it was extremely late, and we had nowhere that night to lay our heads.

Aurelia was very kind. She braved her husband's anger by rousing him (he had betaken himself to his room in pique) and asking if we might be offered hospitality. It is not customary for the pontifex to entertain, but the old man was so delighted to learn that the mystery was solved, and that he was unlikely to suffer the anger of gods or emperors—since the sacrilege was committed by another priest, and not even at his shrine— that I believe he would have turned out of his own bed for me, if I had demanded it.

However, with Trinunculus lying dead I was uncomfortable about sleeping in his room, or in the sleeping quarters at the temple, where they would be preparing his body and beginning the lament by this time. So when Hirsus offered the use of the guest room in his apartment, I accepted with alacrity.

It could only be a temporary solution, as I knew. Hirsus had been guilty of a crime—the technical theft of Optimus's slave—and had colluded in dishonesty. He was likely to be fined, at best, and stripped of his office. From what I now knew of his finances, Hirsus would soon be lucky to have a home himself. But it was late, and wet, and I was tired. I had enough worries to keep me tossing half the night, but as soon as we arrived at Hirsus's house I was overcome by weariness. I took off my toga and stretched out on the couch, without even a pretence at courtesies, and the next moment I was sound asleep, with Gwellia on a blanket at my feet. I didn't so much as stop to see where my slave boys were to be installed, but it must have been satisfactory because the next morning they were washed and fed and standing at my bedside when I awoke, all of them looking unreasonably refreshed and cheerful.

'Why are you grinning like a newly elected senator, you young idiot?' I grumbled, as Junio helped me from the couch, and I submitted to the unusual luxury of having three people compete to assist me with my ablutions and my clothes. 'There isn't much to smile about that I can see.'

Junio's grin widened. 'There is some good news, master. I went back to the workshop earlier, to see if anything could be salvaged there. It's not as badly damaged as we feared, and it didn't start a fire in the street.'

I nodded. That was a relief. Conflagration is

313

a constant hazard in a place like that, and contributions to the firewatch are a continuous but necessary drain on the purse. If my shop had been the centre of a fire, it might have been a very costly business, especially if neighbouring businesses had turned on me.

But Junio hadn't finished. 'The rain extinguished it, it seems,' he said. 'You have been very lucky. Upstairs is blackened, and the stairs have gone, and so has a portion of the roof, but most of your stone is still intact, and Gwellia had the wit to save the tools. There is a dreadful mess, of course, and smell—but it should be possible to save the shop.'

A great weight rolled off my spirit. I had not permitted myself to think about the future, how I would live without my craft, but suddenly I had a vision of how it might have been. I got to my feet shakily. 'I must see Marcus.'

'He is in high good humour, master, presiding in the court. He sent word to find you earlier, but when he heard that you were still asleep he ordered that you should not be disturbed. But we had to rouse you in the end. He has agreed to hear Kurso's case himself, and if you do not hurry you will miss the court. It is almost midday already.'

'Midday!' I could hardly believe my ears. And Junio was right. A trumpet is sounded on the steps of the *curia* each day at noon, as an official sign that the business of the court is

314

closed. If a man misses it, his chance has gone—and if I did not present Kurso before a magistrate today, I would be liable to a fine. I looked about desperately for my sandals, but Kurso was already holding them, and I was obliged to sit down again while he laced them on. 'I must explain to Hirsus,' I exclaimed.

'Hirsus is already at the court.' Gwellia took up the tale as she came behind me and rubbed a scented oil into my hair. A gift from Hirsus, obviously, I thought—such luxuries are not usual with me. 'Lucianus was a witness at the trial.' She caught my glance. 'Oh, of course you won't have heard. The whole town is buzzing with the news. Meritus was brought to trial at dawn. He has confessed to everything, and more, and this afternoon will be a public holiday. Marcus had thought of calling you to be accuser for the court, but the pontifex wanted to do it, and that was certainly effective. The crowds were ecstatic—they stretched right out of the forum, apparently—and the whole thing was over in a hour. Marcus commuted the sentence from the hook, since Meritus admitted everything, so he is to be given to the beasts instead.'

Kurso had finished with my footwear now, and I stood up again. 'Did he,' I said, choosing my words carefully, 'say anything about that *noise*? It is the one thing that has defeated me. I simply can't think of any explanation, although I'm sure that Meritus was contriving it.'

Junio grinned until I thought his face would split. 'He did! Marcus told me to tell you about that. That statue that Meritus commissioned had been specially designed. That's what those holes in it were for. If you blew into it, you could make it sound, it seems—if you could play a trumpet and had lungs like his, that is. He was going to use it, on the Emperor's feast, as a way of inspiring public awe and so attracting offerings to the shrine. He confessed all this, under torture, and they sent the slaves to try to make it work, but they didn't have the breath to do it properly. Just a faint muffled sort of groan, apparently.' He winked. 'But none of this was mentioned at the trial, at the high priest's request. He wants to keep it secret so that the gods aren't mocked, he says, but privately I think he hopes that someone can be found with enough technique to play it, in case he wants to use the thing again. But Marcus thought that you would like to know.'

I smiled. 'I should have thought of it, perhaps. But something so devious never occurred to me.'

Junio laughed. 'That's exactly what your patron said you'd say! But here's Kurso with your breakfast for you, master. We have already eaten. Choose quickly; there is not a lot of time.'

I gaped. Kurso was struggling with a basket heaped high with fruits of all descriptions, including some I'd never seen before. Hirsus might be anxious about money, but he certainly appeared to live in style. I selected a modest apple, and, when I had eaten it, prepared to go.

'What shall we do with your possessions, master?' Kurso said, backing nervously against the wall.

'Possessions?' I said bitterly. 'I have no possessions now. Oh, except my tools, I think. Thank you for that, Gwellia, at least.'

'Master,' Gwellia said patiently, 'the passageway outside is full of offerings. That oil, those fruits—all kinds of things. You have become a hero in the town.'

I stared at her. 'All this because I solved the mystery?'

She shook her head, and smiled. 'Not exactly, master. I gather Marcus took the praise for that. But the mob set fire to your house, and now they know it was a horrible mistake. A crime, of course, if we could find the perpetrators, but that would be very difficult to prove. And people have been bringing gifts in sympathy—and to assuage their consciences, no doubt. And it is not just the common populace. There have been messages from wealthy citizens offering you commissions at their homes—although that may be because the legate's coming. Optimus was very pleased with what you did.'

'He'll be even more pleased if you don't

turn up at court,' Junio urged. 'You would be fined, and he'd get Kurso back. It's just as well he doesn't know how much you helped in this; you've cost him a steward as it is. Marcus is trying the case against Lithputh now, for theft. The pontifex is accusing there, as well— though Optimus may join him, Marcus says, since both might have had a claim against the find. And then it will be Hirsus, I suppose. After the evidence from Meritus, none of it will take very long since none of them are Roman citizens.'

I allowed myself to be hustled out of the house. Hirsus's apartment was a fair walk from the forum, but we had not gone very far before we met the crowds, and it was quite difficult to force a path through them. I was worried that I would be delayed, but Junio murmured to the nearest man, and soon there were whispers running through the crowd—'That's him! That's the pavement-maker that the lying priest accused!'—and people began standing back to let me pass. There was even a ripple of applause.

It was embarrassing, but it was just as well. I made it to the court with only minutes to spare, and just in time to hear the judgement passed. Lithputh had been found guilty, I discovered, but the court had ruled that the temple, not Optimus, was entitled to the goods and that, in offering them to the shrine, sufficient reparation had been made. Lithputh was to be flogged and banished, since Optimus refused to have him back.

I was rather surprised at this, knowing what price had been agreed for him, but the judgement on Hirsus soon explained it all. Optimus was claiming 'usurpation' of his slave which meant that, instead of a fine, the 'usurper' could be required to pay the full purchase price and keep the goods—since they were now considered to be spoiled. The price for Lucianus had been agreed, he claimed.

That would cost Hirsus everything he had, but the ex-sevir looked almost as happy at the judgement as his accuser did. (Hirsus had become ex-sevir on the spot, because as a convicted criminal he was automatically disqualified from the office.)

He saw me and came over. 'I shall sell up and go with Lucianus, just as soon as he's recovered from the lash,' he said, with more cheerfulness than I would have believed. 'I have relatives outside the western borders, among the Silurians.' I nodded. That explained the redness of the hair. 'We shall be welcome there. And we have the money that Lucianus saved. We shall not be entirely penniless.'

He might have said more, but I was being called. The case concerning Kurso had begun.

It was odd, standing before Marcus, arguing a case as though we'd never met before, but that was what I did. Kurso told his story, and won the right to be sold on, as the law demanded, since his life was deemed to be threatened where he was, even with Lithputh banished from the house. So far, it had gone splendidly. It was, however, expected that I would purchase him—though it was not compulsory. Of course, after the events of yesterday, I had no money and—despite the generous gifts—no home to take a servant to. I explained the problem to the court, and proposed a compromise. I would purchase Kurso theoretically, as part of what Optimus owed to me, and find a buyer for him when I could.

Then Optimus sprang a surprising counter-claim. The bill I had was signed by Lucianus. (Of course it was, when I looked at it more closely—I could have solved that riddle long before!) But Lucianus was in disgrace, and convicted of dishonesty. Optimus disputed the account. It was a ploy, and I knew it, but there was nothing I could do. In the end, Kurso cost me the whole balance of the hundred sesterces I was owed, and Optimus left court looking as satisfied as the lion who got the slave. Kurso, too, was grinning like a cat, and even Junio looked pleased.

It seemed that Marcus had succeeded in satisfying everyone but me.

As he rose to leave the court, however, he signalled me to come, and I elbowed my way obediently to his side.

'Well, my old friend,' he said. 'I trust you slept?' I felt my face burn, but Marcus merely laughed. 'A most satisfactory conclusion, thanks to you. In fact, I am not at all sure that I would have managed it without you.'

There was nothing I could say to that, beyond, 'You flatter me, Excellence.'

'Not at all,' he said expansively. 'Credit where credit's due. Which brings me to what I want to say. I was sorry to hear the news about your shop. What will you do now?'

I stammered something about hoping to repair the place when I had found enough commissions. It sounded feeble and I knew it, too.

'Of course,' he said, 'there's that commission that we spoke of in the baths. That should be worth something. And I should reward you for your help in this. You know my country house?'

I thought for a wild moment that he was about to offer me the freedom of his palatial villa. I said carefully, 'I do, Excellence, I have been there several times.'

Marcus nodded. 'It occurs to me there is a roundhouse in the grounds. You may remember it.'

I nodded. It had been the scene of a particularly brutal murder, which I'd uncovered once.

'Rather the sort of thing you Celts admire, though it's in need of some restoration and repair.'

That was an understatement. The place was ruinous. But behind me, Gwellia gave me a gentle push, and I turned, to see hope and excitement shining in her eyes.

I knew what she was thinking. A roundhouse is not a Roman building, demanding architects and hypocausts. Our own roundhouse had been a grand affair, built almost entirely of stone, but many are constructed of wood and osiers around a central post, and—given the materials—a skilled family can weave a small shelter in an afternoon. I sighed. It would be inconvenient —a long walk to my workshop every day—but there were advantages. There was a little area of land in the enclosure. Room for some chickens and a pig or two. My own woodstack, and a patch of vegetables. And now that I owned an extra pair of hands . . .

'I remember, Excellence,' I said.

Marcus nodded. 'Then that's agreed. It's yours. In payment for the mosaic in the town. Oh, and take this too.' He opened his purse and thrust a few *denarii* in my hand. 'That should assist to buy some pots and pans. And I'll send down a blanket and a stool or two: Meritus's property is forfeit to the state. I'm sure that something can be found.' He smiled, and closed his fingers over mine as they held the coins. 'And get that toga to the fuller's, my old friend. You'll have to be presented to the legate when he comes.'

I was presented, too. I even attended an official banquet, given in his honour, and was complimented on the mosaic I had made. On that same occasion the high priest was named as flamen-designate, and I thought that he would die of rapture on the spot. (In fact he did die, later, on the journey back to Rome. The strain of travel proved too much for his frail body, and the pleasure too much for his aged heart, so he never became flamen after all. I never heard what happened to his wife.)

But I missed the public spectacles that were held, at great expense, to celebrate the ambassador's presence in the town. I had a celebration of my own that day. Scribonius— who had risen to be sevir overnight—and Marcus acted as witnesses in a quiet ceremony where I freed my slave and legally took her for my wife. We did it properly, with vows and sacrifice.

'Ubi to Gaius, ego Gaia.' Where you are Gaius, I am Gaia.

She even wore the orange-coloured veil, and after exchanging rings before the altar I took her in a borrowed waggon, and carried her—for the first time—over the threshold of our little new-built home. It was no more than a single room by then, but Junio and Kurso had the central fire lit and rugs and clean straw bedding waiting on the floor. And we already had our plans.

So I was spared the spectacle of Meritus being thrown to the beasts, although I have heard it said that—being such a big man—he took a long time to die. Fabius Marcellus was impressed. He said afterwards that Glevum had turned on the best welcoming entertainments he had ever seen.

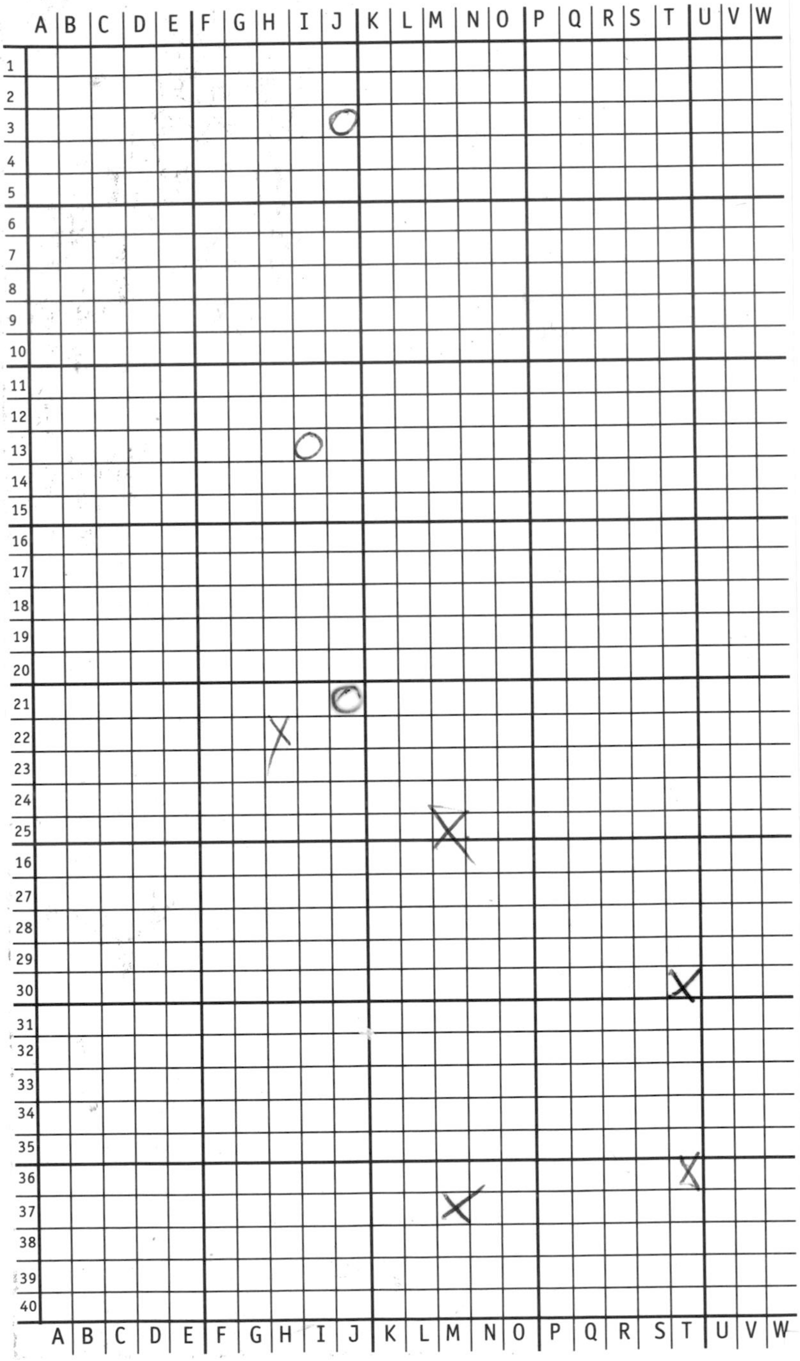
A B C D E F G H I J K L M N O P Q R S T U V W
1 2 3 4 5 6 7 8 9 10 11 12 13 14 15 16 17 18 19 20 21 22 23 24 25 16 27 28 29 30 31 32 33 34 35 36 37 38 39 40
O
O
O
X
X
X
X
X
A B C D E F G H I J K L M N O P Q R S T U V W